LET
THE
STORM
BREAK

Also by Shannon Messenger

Let the Sky Fall

Keeper of the Lost Cities

Keeper of the Lost Cities, Book 2:
Exile

LET
THE
STORM
BREAK

BOOK TWO IN THE SKY FALL SERIES

SHANNON MESSENGER

Simon Pulse
New York   London   Toronto   Sydney   New Delhi

SIMON PULSE

An imprint of Simon & Schuster Children's Publishing Division

1230 Avenue of the Americas, New York, NY 10020

First Simon Pulse hardcover edition March 2014

Text copyright © 2014 by Shannon Messenger

Jacket photograph copyright © 2014 by Brian Oldham Photography

Jacket design by Angela Goddard

All rights reserved, including the right of reproduction

in whole or in part in any form.

SIMON PULSE and colophon are registered trademarks

of Simon & Schuster, Inc.

For information about special discounts for bulk purchases, please contact

Simon & Schuster Special Sales at 1-866-506-1949 or business@simonandschuster.com.

The Simon & Schuster Speakers Bureau can bring authors to your live event.

For more information or to book an event contact the

Simon & Schuster Speakers Bureau at 1-866-248-3049

or visit our website at www.simonspeakers.com.

Interior design by Mike Rosamilia

The text of this book was set in Adobe Caslon Pro.

Manufactured in the United States of America

2 4 6 8 10 9 7 5 3 1

Library of Congress Cataloging-in-Publication Data

Messenger, Shannon.

Let the storm break / Shannon Messenger. — First Simon Pulse hardcover edition.

p. cm.

Sequel to: Let the sky fall.

Summary: While teenaged Vane discovers more of what it means to be a windwalker and his guardian sylph Audra struggles with her deepest desires, both must band together to face greater challenges than they have ever known.

[1. Supernatural—Fiction. 2. Spirits—Fiction. 3. Winds—Fiction. 4. Storms—Fiction. 5. Love—Fiction. 6. Orphans—Fiction.] I. Title.

PZ7.M5494Lf 2014   [Fic]—dc23   2013007403

ISBN 978-1-4424-5044-8

ISBN 978-1-4424-5046-2 (eBook)

For Laura Rennert,
maker of all things possible
and Keeper of my sanity

LET
THE
STORM
BREAK

CHAPTER 1

VANE

I t sucks to be king.

Maybe it wouldn't be so bad if I got a castle and servants and my face on a bunch of money.

But no, I get to be the king of a scattered race of mythical creatures that no one's ever heard of. And they expect me to swoop in and defeat the evil warlord who's been tormenting them for the last few decades. Oh, and hey, while I'm at it, I can marry their former princess and restore the royal line!

Yeah, thanks, I'll pass.

I already told the Gale Force—my "army" or whatever—what they can do with their "betrothal." And I've been tempted to tell them exactly where they can shove the rest of their little plans for my life.

But . . . it's hard to stay angry when they keep giving me this desperate *you're our only hope* look. And they're all so full of stories about the things Raiden's done to their friends and families, and the horrifying battles they've fought. Risking their lives to protect *me*.

The last Westerly.

The only one capable of harnessing the power of all four winds, twisting them into the ultimate weapon.

Well, they *think* I'm the only one.

Which is the other reason I'm playing along with the whole Your Highness thing.

I have someone to protect too. And I can do that much better as Vane Weston, king of the Windwalkers.

So I'll follow their rules and train for their battles. But as soon as Audra comes back . . .

She left twenty-three days, seven hours, and twenty-one minutes ago—and yes, I've totally been counting. I've felt every second, every mile she's put between us, like our bond has claws and teeth, tearing me apart inside.

And it's been *loads* of fun trying to explain to the Gales why my guardian left me unprotected. Every day that passes makes the excuses I've given seem weaker.

I thought she'd be home by now.

I thought . . .

But it doesn't matter.

Audra promised she'd come home—and I want to give her the time she needs.

So I'll wait for her as long as it takes.

It's the only choice I have.

CHAPTER 2

AUDRA

'm not running.

I'm *chasing*.

Racing the sun across the sky, carried by the whim of the wind.

I have no plan.

No path.

No guide along this journey.

Just the whispered songs floating on the breezes, promising that hope still lingers on the horizon.

The birds circle me as I fly, dipping and diving and begging me to join their game. But they're lost to me now, like everything else. Everything except the one person I *should* be trying to erase.

I can feel him in the air.

In my heart.

In the empty ache from the space between us, mixed with the delicious sparks that still burn in my lips from our kiss.

Our *bond*.

I will not regret forging it.

But I'm not ready to face it either.

Not until I've sorted through the tatters of my life. Swept away the lies and mistakes and found someone who's more than the guardian who broke her oath.

More than the traitor who stole the king.

More than the daughter of a murderer.

The last word turns my stomach, and I'm grateful I've gone back to denying myself food and drink.

I've paid for my mother's sins every day for the last ten years.

I won't pay for them anymore.

But is locking her away enough to erase her influence? Or does it sink deeper, like one of Raiden's wicked winds, breaking me down piece by piece?

I always thought she and I were sunrise and sunset—two opposites that could never meet.

But I have her dark hair and deep blue eyes. Her connection to the birds and her stubborn temper.

I'm more like her than I ever wanted to be.

Maybe I am running.

But not from Vane.

From *me*.

CHAPTER 3

VANE

I really miss sleep.

The clock by my bed says 3:23 a.m., and all I want to do is face-plant on my pillow and close my eyes for about a year.

I drop to the floor and do push-ups instead.

Exercise is the only way to stay awake. And hey, maybe Audra will appreciate how ripped I'm getting from these late-night work-outs. Though I'm not sure how much longer I can keep them up.

I haven't slept more than a few hours over the last two weeks—and it was hardly what I'd call restful.

Freaking Raiden and his freaking winds.

The Gales thought he'd wait to see how powerful I am before he made any sort of move—though they assigned me a new guardian and set up a base nearby, just in case. But after a few days Raiden found a better way to torture me.

Creepy, broken drafts keep slipping into the valley, drawn to me like heat-seeking missiles. And if they catch me when I'm asleep, they slip into my dreams and twist everything I care about into a Slideshow of Suck.

Walls and windows can't block them, and no one can find a command to keep them away. So it's either be a Vane-zombie all the time or suffer through the nightmares. I'll take zombie any day.

I've seen my friends and family tortured so brutally it's hard to look them in the eye. And Audra . . .

Watching someone hurt her is like drowning in boiling oil. I wake up screaming and soaked in sweat and it takes forever to convince myself it wasn't real. Especially since I can't hold her or see her to know she's really okay. The pull of our bond tells me she's alive, but it can't tell me if she's safe. For that I have to feel her trace. And that's not easy to do, considering my uptight new guardian, Feng—I call him Fang to annoy him—thinks the only way to protect me is to never let me out of his sight.

He's seriously insane—and I'd probably be going insane too if it weren't for Gus.

I glance at the clock, grinning when I see it's 3:32.

Gus is supposed to take over Fang's stand-outside-Vane's-window-like-a-stalker shift every night at three thirty, but I swear he shows up late just to drive Fang crazy.

Tonight he waits until 3:37.

Fang screams at him so loud it scares Gavin—Audra's stupid

pet hawk—out of his tree. But when I glance out my window, Gus is totally unfazed. He winks at me as Fang paces back and forth, waving his burly arms and shaking his head so hard, his dark, scraggly braid keeps whipping him in the cheek. The tirade goes on at least five minutes before Fang switches to the nightly update.

I stop listening.

It's always vague reports from other bases with weird names and weirder army terms, and the few times I've asked anyone to translate, it turned into yet another lecture on Why I Need to Teach Everyone Westerly. It's just not worth the fight.

I switch to sit-ups, trying to keep my energy up, and I've done 314 before Fang finally flies away. Physically, I'm rocking at my training. It's the memorizing a billion and a half wind commands that's killing me. That, and covering for Audra—though hopefully she'll be home soon and I won't have to worry about that part anymore.

If she—

I stop the thought before I can finish it.

She *is* coming back—and when she does, I can think of all kinds of awesome ways to celebrate. In the meantime I settle for making sure she's okay.

I stand and stretch, throw on the first T-shirt I find, and climb quietly out my window.

Well . . . I *try* to climb out quietly.

I can't help yelping when I scrape my arm against the pyracantha, and spend the rest of my sprint across the yard cursing my parents for planting thornbushes outside my bedroom.

"What are you laughing at, Legolas?" I ask when I make it to

Gus. He doesn't get that I'm teasing him about his blond, braided hair, and I've never explained the joke. Probably because he somehow makes the girlie hair work. That, and his biceps are bigger than my head.

"Just wondering when you're going to figure out how to jump *over* the plants, not into them."

"Hey, I'd like to see you do better—on zero sleep," I add when Gus raises an eyebrow.

Gus is, like, Captain Fitness, *and* he has a special Windwalker gift that lets him channel the power of the wind into his muscles. If he weren't such a nice guy, I'd probably hate him. A lot of the other guardians seem to, which is probably why he got stuck covering the late shift watching me. Rumor has it I'm *not* the most popular assignment. Apparently, I can be difficult.

"Maybe you should try wearing the Gale uniform," Gus tells me, pulling at the long, stiff sleeves of his black guardian jacket. "It would save you a lot of scrapes."

"Yeah, I'm good."

I'm not wearing thick pants and a coat in the *desert*. Even in the middle of the night, this place feels like living inside a blow-dryer.

Plus, I'm not a Gale.

I'll train with them and let them follow me around. But this isn't my life. This is just something I have to deal with.

"Off for another mystery flight?" he asks as I stretch out my hands to feel for nearby winds.

Gus never asks me where I'm going, and he's never tried to stop me.

"Make sure you stay north and west," he warns. "They're running heavy guard patrols in the south. Feng told me the Borderland Base had a disturbance yesterday."

I freeze.

"Disturbance" is the Gales' term for "attack."

"Everyone okay?"

"Three of them survived."

Which means two guardians didn't—unless Borderland is one of the bigger bases, where they keep a crew of seven.

"Don't worry—there's no sign of Stormers in the area. They're picking off all the fringes. Trying to leave us stranded out here."

Yeah, because *that* doesn't make me worry.

My voice shakes as I call three nearby Easterlies to my side, but I feel a little better when I hear their familiar songs. The east wind always sings of change and hope.

"Still don't trust me enough to use Westerly?" Gus asks. "You know I won't understand it."

I do know that.

And I trust Gus way more than I trust anyone else.

But I'm still not risking it.

My parents—and every other Westerly—gave up their lives to protect our secret language. And not just because they were brave enough to stand in the way of Raiden's quest for ultimate power.

Violence goes against our very being.

I'll never forget the agony that hit me when I ended the Stormer who'd been trying to kill Audra. Even though it was self-defense, it felt like my whole body shattered, and if Audra hadn't been there to help me through, I'm not sure I would've pulled myself back together. I can't risk letting the power of my heritage end up under the control of anyone who doesn't understand the *evil* of killing. Anyone who isn't as determined as I am to avoid it at any cost. Anyone who isn't willing to make the kind of sacrifice that might be necessary to prevent it from falling into the wrong hands.

Even the Gales—no matter how much they beg or threaten. And yeah, they've threatened. They've made it pretty dang clear that Audra's "desertion" is considered an especially serious offense right now, when they need her help so much more. But if they had the power of four on their side . . .

I still haven't figured out how to handle any of that—except to add it to my list of Things I Will Worry About Later.

"I'll be back before sunrise," I tell Gus as I wrap the winds around me and order them to *surge*. The cool drafts tangle tighter, stirring up the dusty ground as they launch me into the sky.

It takes me a second to get my bearings, and another after that to really get control. Audra hadn't been kidding when she told me windwalking's one of the hardest skills to master, and I definitely prefer letting her carry me. But it wasn't *quite* the same being carted around by Fang or Gus, and it's hard to sneak around in my noisy car. So I forced myself to learn how to get around on my own.

The first dozen times I tried, the drafts dropped me flat on my face. Then one night I had some sort of breakthrough. It wasn't like the times when Audra opened my mind to the languages of the wind—but I did hear something *new*. A voice *beneath* the voice of the wind, telling me what the gust is about to do so I can give a new command and keep control.

I asked Gus about it once and he looked at me like I was psycho, so I'm pretty sure it's something only *I* hear. Maybe something I picked up from Audra when we bonded, since I hear it best with Easterlies. Whatever it is, I'm grateful for it because it lets me fly faster and farther than even the most experienced Gales.

The lights of the desert cities blur below and I follow the streetlights lining the I-10 freeway, heading up into the mountains. It's a path I've flown dozens of times, but I still feel my insides get all bunched up as I soar over the San Gorgonio Pass Wind Farm. There are gaps in the rows of blinking red lights now. Places where windmills used to be—before Raiden's Stormers destroyed them in the fight.

Every time I relive the attack, I can't help thinking the same thing.

Soon we'll be fighting his whole army.

The air gets cooler as I fly, and as it sinks into my skin it feels like downing a shot of caffeine. Still, it barely makes a dent in my exhaustion, and my sleep-deprived body stumbles through the landing on San Gorgonio Peak. I sorta half sit, half collapse near the edge of the cliff.

I close my eyes, so tempted to curl up and grab even a few minutes of sleep. But it's not worth the risk. Besides, I came here for something much more important.

I reach out my hands, searching for Audra's trace.

I can't really describe the process. It's like some part of me connects to the wind, following an invisible trail through the sky that somehow always leads me to her. And I know it's *her*.

The rush of heat.

The electricity zinging under my skin.

No girl has ever made me feel like that.

It helps that she's the only connection I have to my past and that I've dreamed about her most of my life—and that she's ridiculously hot. But even if she weren't, Audra's *the one*.

Always has been.

Always will be.

I sink into the warmth, leaning back and letting the sparks shock me with tiny zings. It's almost like she's holding on to me across the sky, promising that she's still out there. Still safe.

Still mine.

And maybe I'm crazy, but the feeling seems stronger tonight.

Much stronger.

So intense it makes my heart race and my head spin. And the dizzier I get, the more I can't help but ask the one question I've been trying not to let myself ask since I found her dusty jacket and her hasty goodbye.

Is she finally on her way home?

I try not to get my hopes up in case I'm wrong. But it doesn't *feel* like I'm wrong. It feels like she's so close I could reach out and—

Vane.

The sound makes my heart freeze.

I hold my breath, starting to think I imagined it when she melts out of the shadows.

She stands over me, her dark hair blowing in the wind, her dark eyes boring into mine. I don't dare blink for fear she'll disappear.

She leans closer, giving me a peek down her tiny black tank top—but I'm more interested in her face. Her lips are twisted into an expression I can't read. Half smile, half—

She tackles me.

I know I should say something—do something—as she wraps her arms around me, but I'm still trying to process the fact that she's actually here, nuzzling her head into the nook between my neck and shoulder. Her hair tickles my cheek and her lips graze my jaw. I tilt her chin up, bringing her mouth up to mine.

She stops me before the kiss but stays close enough that I can feel her smile.

She's teasing me.

She knows it too, because she giggles against my cheek.

Giggles?

Since when does Audra giggle?

Before I can ask, she leans in and kisses me. Everything else drops away.

I've been waiting for this moment for weeks, but it's different than I pictured, and not just because she's lying on top of me—though that is a *welcome* addition.

Everything about her feels cold.

Her hands.

Her breath.

I feel myself shiver as her lips trail down my neck, and even when her skin touches mine, the rush between us feels more like pricks of ice.

I pull her closer, trying to warm her up—but why is she so cold?

I want to make sure she's okay, but she kisses me harder—almost desperate—and I lose myself again, until I'm covered in head-to-toe goose bumps.

Since when does Audra kiss first and talk later?

And since when does she climb on top of me like she's here to fulfill all my fantasies?

The last word feels like a slap to the face.

This is a dream.

But why aren't I waking up? Why is she still pulling me against her, running her hands down my back—

No.

It's not her.

As much as I want it to be, there are no sparks, no heat.

With Audra there's *always* heat.

This is a lie.

A trick.

Another evil trap Raiden's using to punish me.

I try to pull my mind free, but Audra fights back, locking her arms around me and kissing me again and again.

"No!" I shout, pushing her away.

She starts crying then. Telling me she loves me. Needs me. Can't face another second without me. Everything I always wanted Audra to say.

"Not like this," I whisper.

I want my strong, stubborn dream girl back, even if she'd attack me with questions—and probably a few wind tricks—long before she'd ever seduce me.

But that girl suddenly feels very far away.

Too far away. Like my consciousness has been dragged under by whatever wind Raiden sent, and no matter how much I beg my mind to wake up from this sick, twisted nightmare, I can't find the way out.

I can't move.

Can't breathe.

Audra crawls back to me, whispering that everything will be okay. She kisses my neck, my chin, my lips.

I want it to be real so badly.

Maybe if I just pretend . . .

A wicked pain rips through my finger and yanks me back to reality.

I peel open my eyes and find a panicked Gus leaning over me, my pinkie smashed between his teeth.

"You bit me?"

He unclenches his jaw and I stare at the jagged line of punctures in my skin.

"I tried everything else. I even punched you in the stomach. Biting was all I had left."

I'm betting there was still a better option than chewing on my hand, but who knows? I can feel the sore spot on my stomach where he must've hit me—and I didn't feel a thing. Raiden had me pretty good that time.

"How did you know where to find me?"

Gus rolls his eyes. "You really didn't know I followed you? What kind of guardian do you think I am?"

I sigh, trying to figure out how I'm going to explain this mess to the Gales. But I guess it's a good thing Gus isn't as crappy at his job as I thought.

CHAPTER 4

AUDRA

Panic stabs my heart, so sharp it knocks me out of the sky.
Red and black rims my vision, making it impossible to
see which way is up or down. I call the nearest draft to catch
me, shivering as the warm Southerly stops my fall.

I've never experienced this kind of pain before. A tempest deep
in my core, growing stronger with every breath. It only rages harder
when I realize what it means.

Vane's in danger.

Mortal danger.

The word makes me tremble, and I order the wind to change
direction, letting our bond point the way. The path to Vane is laced
through my heart—but the connection feels so faint.

Too faint.

Getting weaker every second.

If something happens while I'm gone I'll never forgive myself—I'll never recover—I'll never ...

The thought has no end.

There will be nothing without Vane.

I call every nearby draft, commanding them to swell into a torrent. But I know it won't be enough.

I close my eyes and search for a Westerly.

There are none within my reach, so I shout the call, not caring if it gives away my location. Still, it feels wrong branding the wind so boldly.

A tranquil breeze sweeps in from the west and I coil it around the others, struggling to decide which command to use. Combining drafts is a game of words—coaxing them to cooperate or daring them to rebel. I've practiced with the other winds for most of my life, but the Westerly tongue is new. A secret power I stole from Vane with our kiss. One I've barely begun to master.

"Come on," I whisper, sending the plea to the sky. "Tell me what to do."

All I hear is the pulse in my veins.

Tears streak down my cheeks and Vane's face fills my mind. I can picture every curve, every line. The perfect blue of his eyes and the dark brown of his warm, earthy hair.

But it's a thin shadow of the reality.

I can't let this memory be all I have left.

"Please," I whisper, feeling the word sweep off my lips in the Westerly language. *"Please help me."*

The words are a breathy sigh mixed with a soft hiss, and the harder I concentrate on them, the more a cool rush builds in my mind, twisting and spinning until it shapes into a word.

"Unite," I whisper, and all the winds tangle into a bubble around me. *"Soar."*

The stars blur to streaks as I rush forward, and I tell myself that the power of four will help me reach him in time. But his trace still feels so distant.

Why did I run so far away?

I'm not sure where I am, but I know I've been flying north for weeks. Even with my frenzied speed, it'll be hours before I reach him.

All I can do is hope and fly.

But after a few minutes the pain in my heart drains, leaving me cold and empty. The shock breaks my concentration and the winds carrying me unravel.

Vane's not . . .

I can't even think the word.

The searing pull of our bond returns, jolting my heart back to a rhythm and helping me regain enough control to grab an Easterly. But I've fallen too far and there isn't enough time to stop myself from crashing into cold, churning water.

Dark waves swell around me, nearly splattering me against four columns of rock that jut from the ocean near the shore. I steer myself away, struggling to keep my head above the water as the next wave washes me to the rocky sand. My body shivers as I gasp for breath, but I can't feel the cold.

I'm numb.

Empty.

But my mind echoes with the only thought that matters.

He's alive.

Is he safe, though?

I can't tell.

His trace feels steady but weak.

I try to get up, but my insides writhe and I roll to my knees, choking and gagging up the water I swallowed in the ocean. Sour bile coats my tongue and I spit it into the retreating waves until there's nothing left. Still, I continue to heave, like my body is trying to purge all the dark, sickening truths I've been trying to deny.

I swore an oath to protect Vane.

Swore to train him and fight with him and ready him to be our king.

Bonding myself to him should've made me *more* willing to uphold that promise.

And yet, here I am, alone on a cold, empty beach, far away from him when he needed me most.

I'm shaking so hard I barely manage to crawl out of the waves before my knees give out, leaving me facedown in the smooth, round rocks covering the beach.

The sharp ocean breezes nip at my tear-stained cheeks and I open my mind to their songs.

One is an Easterly—the winds of my heritage—singing the melody I used to search for, beg for, cling to with everything I had. A gentle song about carrying on despite the turbulence all around.

For years I've wondered if the draft is some small part of my father. A hint of his presence that stayed behind to guide me, keep me fighting his battles for him. But since I learned my mother's secrets, I've been hoping he's really gone.

He loved my mother more than life. More than air. If he knew the truth—knew she sold our lives and the Westons' for a wasted chance at freedom—it would destroy him.

"Go," I whisper as the breeze dries my tears. "Don't waste your time on me."

The wind tangles tighter, lifting my head and forcing me to open my eyes and see that I'm not alone.

A white dove watches me from her roost on a piece of driftwood, her black eyes glittering in the moonlight. She coos as I sit up, begging me to reach for her. And for the first time in weeks, I do.

She hops onto my finger and nuzzles her beak against my thumb and I realize that I know this dove. She's one of my mother's messengers—the loyal birds who perched on her roof, waiting to carry her updates to the Gales.

She's been following me since I left, and as I stroke her silky feathers, I feel her *need*—her craving for shelter now that my mother left her alone. It's one of my gifts. Part of what I've been fighting, trying to resist the talent my mother and I shared.

But as I stare at this fragile creature, I realize how precious that connection is. How much I've missed it.

She flutters to my shoulder, bending her slender neck to peck at my necklace.

I left behind the jacket from my uniform, but I never removed the guardian pendant the Gales gave me. The cord is vivid blue, flowing with the life I breathed into it when it became *mine.*

My hand clutches the silver feather pendant, and somehow touching the cool, smooth metal gives me the courage to accept the truth.

"It's time to go home," I whisper, hoping I haven't destroyed everything that matters by leaving.

The pull of my bond feels sharper than ever, so I have to believe Vane's still safe. And soon enough I'll be back to do my job.

The dove flaps her wings and takes to the sky, circling above me as I stand and dust off my sandy clothes. I reach for my hair and smooth it back, hesitating only a second before I divide it into five equal sections and weave them into a tight, intricate braid.

The style of a guardian.

I am a guardian.

And I'll never let myself forget it again.

CHAPTER 5

VANE

I must've looked pretty bad when Gus brought me home, because my mom *flipped*.

I barely had a chance to explain what happened—minus all the ultra-embarrassing stuff, of course—before she ordered me to my room and spent the next hour bandaging my Gus-bite and forcing me to choke down giant glasses of blended vegetables.

My mom's been on a juice kick ever since she found out I'm a sylph, like she's convinced she can turn me human again if she just gives me enough liquefied celery. It sorta makes me wish I had to give up eating and drinking, but the Gales think I'm too weak to handle that kind of sacrifice right now. Plus, now that we know Raiden can destroy the wind with only a few words, shifting into our wind form is really not the best battle strategy. So brownish-green sludge every morning it is!

Honestly, though, my mom's been strangely cool about the whole my-adopted-son-is-an-air-elemental thing. She didn't scream or run away when I told her—even when I showed her how the wind obeys all my weird, hissy words. And my dad just clapped me on the back and told me to remember that this kind of power comes with extra responsibility, like he expected me to put on spandex and start calling myself *Windman*!

I'm surprised he didn't buy me a cape.

Fang was the one who freaked out about them knowing. But I don't care if the Gales have a code of secrecy. They're my *family*. I may not look like them—and I may not even be the same species. But they're the only parents I've ever really known, and I wasn't going to lie to them.

Besides, *how* was I supposed to explain why I was suddenly surrounded by a bunch of guys with long, braided hair and black soldier uniforms? And no way was I moving to the Gales' new base a couple of miles away. Raiden knows where I live. My family needs just as much protection as I do. Maybe more, since they can't exactly defend themselves against wind warriors.

A cool breeze slips through my window and I know it's a Westerly before I even listen to its song. I swear they come to find me, and I always keep my window open for them—even if it lets out all the AC and makes my bedroom feel like an oven. I need to have the wind around. It makes my heritage feel *real*, and like maybe the tangled-up, scattered memories of my past will unravel someday and actually make sense.

Plus, I always want Audra to have a way to reach me.

I close my eyes and let the soft whispers float around me, promising myself I will *not* fall asleep. But it's hard. I've reached that point of exhaustion where everything actually aches. If I could just nap for ten minutes—even five—I would take it.

"You up for a visitor, Vane?" my mom asks.

I yank my eyes open as she leans through my doorway. "Uh, sure."

I'm assuming it must be Fang, come to rip me a new one. But when my mom steps aside, a Gale I've never seen before strides into my room.

On the left side of his face, part of his long, dark hair is twisted into a braid that's tucked behind his ear. The rest hangs loose—a style worn only by Gale Force leaders.

Ruh-roh.

He clears his throat and stares at my mom, waiting for her to leave. I watch her jaw lock, and I know she's about to remind him that this is *her* house. But I give her my best *please don't embarrass me in front of my army* look and she caves, promising to be back in a few minutes with my breakfast.

When her footsteps have retreated down the hall, the Gale leader steps forward. He has two red scars on his cheek that cross like a T, and they stretch as he gives me a thin smile. "It's nice to finally meet the king."

I fidget when he bows. "Um, you can just call me Vane."

"As you wish."

He stares at my wrinkled Batman T-shirt, looking less than

impressed. But he can glare all he wants, I'm not wearing their stupid uniform.

"And you are . . . ?" I ask when he doesn't say anything.

"Captain Osmund—though you can call me Os. I'm the captain of the Gales."

Double ruh-roh.

"I've been away at our Riverspan Base for the last few weeks, trying to help them hold off a band of Stormers who've been especially aggressive. But when I got wind of last night's incident, well . . ." He shakes his head. "Guardian Gusty already—"

"Wait—hang on. Gus is short for *Gusty*?"

I laugh when he nods.

"Anyway," Os says, clearly not as amused by this as I am. "Guardian Gusty already briefed me on what he witnessed. But I'm hoping you can shed some further light on the attack."

It's strange to think of it as an attack, but I guess that's what it was.

"There's not really much to tell," I mumble. "I went to the mountains to get some fresh air and I've been so tired from not sleeping that I guess I dozed off and Raiden's creepy wind found me."

"Gusty told me you go up there a few times a week. He assumed you were searching for someone." He raises the brow on the scarred side of his face.

I shrug, trying to stay calm as I search for a believable lie. "Fine. If you really want to know, I go up there to check on my friend. I like to make sure he's still safe, and I didn't want the Gales to know because they've asked me to stay away from him."

Told me is more like it, but I'm trying not to sound bitter.

I know they're right that being around me puts Isaac in danger—but it hasn't been fun cutting off my best friend. He bought my excuses for a few days, but eventually he figured out something was up. And when I wouldn't—couldn't—tell him the truth, he stopped calling.

I haven't talked to him in almost two weeks.

Os doesn't look as satisfied with my explanation as I'd like. But all he says is "What did Raiden's wind do to you?"

I *really* don't want to relive any of it, but Os insists. So I rush through a few details.

"A girl," he interrupts. "You didn't know who she was?"

"No."

It's not even a lie. That girl was *not* Audra.

"And what did the girl do?"

I feel my face get hot as my mind fills with the memory of *not*-Audra lying on top of me.

Os must notice my blush because he says, "Oh." Several seconds of awkward silence pass before he quietly asks, "Is this why you canceled your betroth—"

"No."

I give him my *I don't want to talk about this* glare and he falls silent. But just when I think he's dropped it he adds, "If you're experiencing urges—"

"Dude—we are so not doing this."

I barely survived my parents' you're-becoming-a-man-and-your-body-is-changing talk when I was a kid. I'm *not* going through it again—especially with someone named Os.

He clears his throat. "Fine. But it sounds like Raiden has found a way to lure you deep into your consciousness with your desires. That will be a much harder trick to resist."

He doesn't have to tell me. I know better than anyone how close it came to working. "But why would he want to do that? Doesn't he need me conscious if I'm going to teach him what he wants?"

"I'm sure he has a way to release you. But you'll be much easier to catch if you can't use the power of four to defend yourself. And there's no telling if we'll be able to pull you back if this happens again."

I stare at my bandaged pinkie, trying not to think about how desperate Gus must've been to *bite* me. "So, what's the plan?"

As soon as the words leave my mouth I realize what I just walked into.

"I'm not teaching anyone Westerly," I jump in before Os can ask. "And it won't help anyway. I've already tried every command I can think of."

"Yes, but those of us with more knowledge of the other winds will be able to think of things that you can't."

"Not an option."

And somehow I doubt that. I've been practicing with Westerlies *a lot*, and it's amazing the things they'll let me do. But this trick is beyond them. They're too trusting and agreeable to block another wind—which I know sounds crazy, but it's true. Westerlies like to get along with the other drafts, and that makes it kind of hard when the other drafts are evil.

Os puts a hand on my shoulder. "Listen, Vane, I know you want to protect your heritage, but if you would just listen to reason—"

"No, if you guys would just listen to *me*. Aren't people supposed to listen to their king?" I ask, shaking his hand away. "Do I need to start threatening beheadings or something?"

It feels weird playing the royalty card, but I'm *so tired* of this fight. I'm tired of everything.

I'm just *tired*.

Os sighs. "If that is truly your decision, then I can only think of one other option."

"Okay . . . ?" I prompt when he doesn't say anything.

He sighs again, this time letting it rock his shoulders as he reaches up and plays with the ends of his braid. "It's something I'd prefer to keep secret. But it's the only place the wind can't reach and the only place I can think of where you might be able to sleep."

I yawn so wide it feels like my face is stretching. "Sleep sounds good—I vote for that."

"You might not be so eager if you knew where you'll be going. It's a place I created for a much darker purpose."

His voice has turned to the kind of hollow whisper you hear in horror movies when a character's just seen a ghost.

"Uh, then thanks. I'll pass. I'll just do some more push-ups."

"You can't stay awake by sheer force of will, Vane—look what happened last night. You *have* to sleep. If you won't give us the language we need to protect you, you will have to come with me. The choice is yours."

Doesn't sound like there's much of a choice—but that's probably the point. This is just another dare to try and force me into giving them what they want. And I'm not caving.

"Fine," I tell him, throwing off my covers. "Take me wherever you want—but there better be a soft bed."

Os shakes his head. "I wish you would change your mind."

"Yeah, well, I'm not going to."

He closes his eyes, and his voice has that ghostly tone again when he says, "So be it. But you'll need your walking shoes. We have a long journey ahead."

CHAPTER 6

AUDRA

I should be home by now.

I can't tell where I am. Flying with the power of four turned the journey into a blur of color and light. But I can feel the sun directly above me, telling me it's midday, and I see no bright yellow desert on the horizon. Only the dark blue of the sea.

I command the drafts to slow so I can get my bearings, but they ignore me—and when I shout at them, they rush faster, spinning into a squall. The more I resist the more they tighten their grip, crushing me in their cyclone and dragging me far too fast toward the ground.

I have no idea what's happening, but I curl into a ball and focus on the air brushing my skin. It's not the same as wind, but it fuels my strength and steadies my nerves. I let the energy build inside me until I feel ready to burst. Then I shove myself forward and launch out of the vortex, squinting in the bright sunlight.

A quick glance down tells me I'm high above the shore, but when I call a draft to catch me, they rebel and whisk away. Leaving me alone in my free fall.

I force myself to stay calm.

I cannot fly without wind, but I'm still a part of the sky. I can float like a feather on a breeze—I just have to hold still and trust that the air will carry me.

I stretch out flat, trying to keep my body flexible as I take slow, deep breaths and concentrate on the white puffy clouds. I wish I could sink into their softness, bury my face in their cool mist. Instead I drift with the currents, dipping and diving and swooping so much I can't tell whether I'm falling or flying until I collide with the rocky sand.

It's not a soft landing, and I can feel my cheek sting from where my skin met a splinter of driftwood.

But I'm safe.

For now.

Something is wrong.

The wind always has a mind of its own, and sometimes it refuses to obey—but I've never seen *every* draft rebel. Some other force is at work. Something dark and powerful, if it could spook the winds that way.

I pull myself up and scan the shore, wincing as my muscles complain. The dark gray sand and white pieces of driftwood remind me of the beach I left hours ago.

In fact . . .

I turn to the ocean, feeling my heart jump into my throat when I see the stacks of stone standing tall among the waves. The glaring sun shows a fifth peak that I couldn't see under the moonlight. But the twisted shapes are unmistakable.

I never left.

I never *moved*.

All that time I thought I was flying, I was really just hovering in the sky, spinning like a windmill rooted to the ground.

I have no idea what kind of command could bind me that way, but whoever gave it has to be *here*.

The beach is too empty.

No seals sunning themselves on the rocks.

No dolphins splashing in the waves.

Not even a single bird in the sky.

I reach for my windslicer, cursing myself for leaving it back at my old shelter. I was so focused on escaping my problems that I never considered that Raiden might come after me.

I should've known better.

He's always trying to capture Gales to interrogate. And I'm Vane's former guardian. He'd expect me to know all kinds of secrets about . . .

I sink to my knees as a horrifying thought hits me.

I know Westerly.

But no one knows that except Vane and—

No.

A few hours ago I shouted a Westerly call. If someone was watching . . .

My chest starts to burn and I realize I've stopped breathing—but how can I breathe?

I have the prize Raiden's after, and I've basically hand delivered it to him, coming here with no weapons, no backup, no one even knowing where I am.

Bile rises in my throat, as bitter as my regrets. I choke it down and stand.

I'm a trained guardian.

I harness the power of four.

No Stormer is going to defeat me.

I turn toward the cliffs lining the beach, trying to guess which dark hole my attacker hides in.

It's impossible to tell—but I *know* they're watching me.

I call the nearest Westerly and coil it around my wrist.

Let them see how powerful I am.

Let them know that they don't scare me.

"Show yourself!" I shout.

My words echo off the rocks before they're swallowed by the waves.

I march toward the cliffs, but I've barely gone two steps before the winds vanish, turning the air quiet and still.

The calm before the storm.

CHAPTER 7

VANE

You're leaving?" my mom asks as I drag myself down the hallway, following Os to the front door. "I made you a torpedo."

She points to the table, where one of her life-changingly good breakfast burritos is waiting for me. My dad's there too, working on the crossword and trying to choke down a glass of questionable-looking grayish-green juice. The table is set for three.

I can see the hope in my mom's eyes.

I haven't had time for a family meal in weeks.

Os clears his throat. "We need to get going, Vane."

My mom frowns, and my appetite vanishes. I know that protective *you're not taking my son anywhere without my permission* look. She's been using it a lot lately. And I'm not sure I have the energy for another fight.

"Where are they making you go *now*?" she asks me.

"I—"

"That's an official Gale Force matter," Os interrupts.

"You can call things *official* all you want," my mom snaps back, "but it doesn't change the fact that Vane is my *son* and—"

"Actually, he's your *adopted* son—and the only reason we allowed you to raise him was—"

"I'm sorry, did you just say that you *allowed* me to raise him?"

"Ooooooooooooookay," I say, stepping between them before my mom goes into full-fledged Mominator mode. "We can fight over who gets to control my life when I get back. I'm sorry about breakfast, Mom. But right now I'm *really* tired, and apparently I have a long journey ahead of me, so . . . I'm pretty much maxed out in the things-that-I-can-handle-without-my-head-exploding category."

I can tell by my mom's glare that this is definitely not over. But she stands aside to let us pass, and I promise my parents I'll see them tomorrow as Os follows me outside.

"Your mother is much more attached to you than I realized," he says after the front door slams shut.

"Yeah, that tends to happen with *family*."

I'm so sick of the Gales acting like nothing about my human life matters.

This is my real life—sylph or not. The sooner they get that through their windblown heads, the better.

"Yes, well, I guess we'll have to discuss this later," Os tells me as he wraps himself in Northerlies. "For now just try to keep up."

He blasts off into the sky, and I'm tempted to run back inside and lock him out of my room. But I really do need to sleep.

I grab a pair of Easterlies and follow, spinning the winds fast enough to obscure my form in the sky—not that anyone's around to see me. Os is leading me east, to the part of the desert where no one actually wants to go. Cactus-and-tumbleweed land, with no sign of life in any direction for miles and miles and miles.

The sun beats down, and I'm starting to feel like a Vane-crisp when thin, dark shapes appear on the horizon. They look like crooked poles, but as we fly closer I realize they're trees.

Dead trees.

Palms with nothing left but twisted trunks and crumbling bark. There are dozens of them, arranged in random circles, like they were once supposed to *be* something. But now they've been abandoned, like some sort of palm-tree graveyard.

I move to Os's side as he starts to descend. "Ugh, please tell me we're not going to Desert Center."

It's the kind of town you go to only if you *have* to, and the deserted gas station by the freeway does not look promising.

"We won't be there long," Os promises. "It's just the starting point I use to guide me from the sky."

I'm not loving the whole starting-point thing. Especially since I can see pretty far in every direction, and other than some old, crumbling buildings, there's basically nothing, nothing, and more nothing no matter which way you go. But Os sweeps low, landing in the center of the most isolated circle of trees. I have no choice but to follow him.

It smells like something died here.

Actually, it smells like lots of things died, and given the graffiti and the scary-looking shacks nearby, I wouldn't be surprised.

"So now what?" I ask as I move to one of the crooked shadows, taking what little escape from the heat I can get. I'm still soaked in sweat in about thirty seconds.

"Now, we walk," Os says, turning toward the foothills.

"Whoa, wait—you mean *wind*walk, right?"

"No, we dare not take the winds any closer. We would only get sucked in."

"Sucked into what?"

"You'll see."

I'm about to press for an actual answer when I realize where Os is heading.

"Uh, hang on—that's the *freeway*. You don't *walk* across the freeway—not unless you want to get splattered against a few windshields."

"We can weave our way through tornadoes, Vane. You need to learn to trust your instincts."

"I've only known I'm a sylph for a month—I don't have any instincts!"

But as the words leave my mouth, I realize I do.

I remember running through the tornado that killed my family, easily avoiding the drafts and debris and keeping my feet on steady ground. I never thought about how weird that was until now.

Still, as I watch the cars and semis whip by at seventy-plus miles per hour, I'm glad I didn't eat my torpedo. Pretty sure I'd be spewing it all over the ground.

"Just watch for the breaks in the air," Os shouts, crouching on the side of the road like a runner before a race.

"You realize that makes no freaking sense, right?"

He rolls his eyes and reaches for me. "If you need me to hold your hand . . ."

I know this is my chance to prove that I'm a big, brave Windwalker king and can do this all by myself. But three more semis whizz by and I grab Os's hand and hold on as tight as I can.

He sighs. "Let's go."

And then we're running. Darting forward and sideways through the lanes like a terrifyingly real game of Frogger. I can see the breaks Os means—wide distortions in the air in front of each car that tell where it's safe to step—but I don't dare let go of his hand. And when we finally make it across both sides of the freeway, my legs are so wobbly I can barely stay standing.

I wrap my arms around myself, trying to steady my shaking.

"I'm surprised how disorienting this is for you," Os says quietly. "Some things come so effortlessly, like your windwalking and your mastery of Easterly."

Both of those came from my bond to Audra—but I can't exactly say that. So I shrug and say, "I'm learning as fast as I can."

He frowns, like he's not convinced that's true. "Come on—still a ways to go."

"Seriously?" I'm not sure how much longer I can last. The sun is sucking up what little energy I have.

But Os starts walking away, so unless I want to stay here alone, I have to follow.

We hike across the desert toward some weird piles of rocks that look like giant anthills. My shoes fill with sand and I keep scraping my shins on the cacti—but none of that is as uncomfortable as the *stillness*.

The air doesn't move. It presses down on my shoulders like the sky has turned heavy.

"That's the pull of the Maelstrom," Os explains as I rub my arms, "a name that is not to be shared—with anyone. Do you understand?"

"Why?" That's the second time he's talked about how secret this place is, and it's starting to creep me out.

Os looks up at the sky, his fingers tracing the lines of his scar. "The Maelstrom is a place that shouldn't have to exist. It emerged from a necessity the average citizen cannot comprehend, and should they learn of its existence, it would shake them to their very core. As king, it is your job to protect them from the shadows and secrets that would rob them of what little security they have."

Okay . . .

I would ask for an answer that doesn't make Os sound like he's one Froot Loop shy of a box—but honestly? I'm too tired to care. If this Maelstrom has a place to sit and some shade, I'm game.

The closer we get to the weird clumps of stones, the more my head rattles from some sort of high-pitched scraping sound, like a million angry math teachers dragging their chalk across the blackboard at the same time. I thought it was coming from the wind or the giant black birds lining all the rocks, which—by the way—do *not* make this place more inviting. But when we reach the base of one of the hills, there's a narrow opening in the ground, and I realize the sand around the hole is *moving*. It swirls slowly downward, like a tornado has been sucked into the earth and keeps right on spinning, and in the center is a walkway leading into the darkness.

"Have I mentioned I'm not a fan of small spaces?" I shout over the noise as Os starts to descend.

"It's not too late to decide to teach us Westerly instead," he calls over his shoulder.

I gotta admit, as I follow him underground I'm tempted to give in.

Fresh air doesn't exist down here. Only a hot, sticky mist that feels too thick to swallow, like I'm trying to breathe inside someone else's mouth. And even though the screeching sound dulls, it's replaced by a low rumble that makes my teeth chatter.

But the scariest part is feeling my connection to Audra fade. The pain and pull of our bond lessens with every step and I have to remind myself that she's not actually slipping away. *I'm* the one cutting myself off from the winds.

I wonder if she can feel the change.

"So what exactly is the Maelstrom?" I ask, brushing my hand along the slowly spinning wall. My fingers sink into the sand, leaving tiny trails. I'd be tempted to write "Vane was here," but I'm not sure I want to leave my mark on this place.

"It's a special vortex that can only be woven from hungry winds. They consume any normal drafts that dare to come close, swallowing them into the earth and keeping this place completely sealed off from the sky."

"How do you make the wind hungry? Wave a cheeseburger in front of it?"

Os spins around, his face all tight and twisted. "You dare to disrespect their sacrifice?"

"Whoa, easy, it was just a joke."

"Altering the essence of the wind is *not* a joke, Vane. The wind is our kin. It deserves respect and dignity. Exerting our dominance over it is a last resort—a reluctant choice I made because there was no other option."

"Hey, relax, okay? I get it—it's a big deal. I never meant that it wasn't."

He bites his lip, like there's something else he wants to say. But he turns around without another word.

We walk in uncomfortable silence for a few steps. Then he mumbles, "I know you grew up without your heritage, and that you still have much to learn. But you are our *king*, Vane. People will look to you for guidance." He turns to face me, grabbing my arm like my dad does when he wants to make sure I'm listening. "You have to understand, our world has been ruined by Raiden—scattered and broken by a tyrant who cares only for power. He'll break and destroy anything to serve his own agendas. And in this case, I've had no choice but to do the same. But I—we—*all* of us—have chosen to put our faith in *you* because we're hoping that you're going to be different."

Funny, I thought they'd put their faith in me because I'm the only Westerly left.

I'm about to say that when my eyes find the scar on his cheek.

"What happened?" I ask, pointing to the deep red marks.

He traces a finger over the lines again.

"A gift from Raiden. He branded me a traitor when I refused to be his second in command." He smiles sadly when my eyes widen. "Raiden used to be my friend, Vane—as he was for many of us in his generation. We worked in the Gales together. Fought together. Trained in the might and majesty of the storms, pushing ourselves to master their power. I thought we were doing it to be better guardians. To better control the forces that were wreaking havoc on the earth and spare the innocents who weren't strong enough to fight them. But it was different for Raiden. The more powerful he grew, the hungrier he was for more, pushing the lengths and limits beyond any reason. Beyond what was *natural*. When I saw what he was doing, I tried to pull away, but I now wish I hadn't. Maybe I would've uncovered his mutiny before it was too late."

He looks away, and I take the chance to study his face, trying to guess how old he is. It's hard to tell in the dim light, but he can't be *that* much older than my parents—which feels wrong to me. I mean, I know the rebellion went down within the last few decades. But I guess somehow it felt further away than that.

Could an entire world really crumble in *one* lifetime? Isn't that supposed to take, like . . . generations?

"I organized an early counterattack, trying to stop Raiden before it went too far," Os says through a sigh. "But we weren't prepared for his unfathomable brutality. He overran us without a single loss on his side. Bound us all in strange winds that dragged us back to him if we tried to run and made me watch as one by one he murdered my guardians. But he didn't kill me. He told me I should have to watch the rest of our world fall to him and know that I was too weak to stop it. And he's right—I am too weak. I've had to make compromises that shouldn't have had to be made." He runs his hand along the wall, whispering something I can't make out before he turns back to look at me. "But now I have you. *You* have the power to fix things, bring them back to their natural order. Erase the black marks Raiden has carved into our history and usher in a new period of peace."

I swallow the lump in my throat.

I have no idea how I'm supposed to be the savior he expects me to be. But I'm surprised to realize that I *want* to.

Someone needs to stop Raiden. And if that someone has to be me, well, then . . . I guess I'll find a way.

I wonder if my resolve shows on my face, because Os nods, like he's pleased with what he sees. Then he squeezes my shoulder and turns to head down the dark hallway.

I follow him until the ground levels off and we reach a round cavern about the size of my bedroom. A pale, tired-looking Gale stands between two curtains made of some sort of metal mesh. They look as flimsy as my mother's flowery drapes, but when I touch one it's solid like a wall. Os hisses a word I can't understand and the curtain on the right sweeps to the side.

"You should be able to rest in there for the night," he tells me. "I'll be back to get you in the morning."

The Gloomy Cell of Doom hardly looks inviting. But hours of nightmare-free sleep sounds pretty dang good to me.

I head inside, relieved to find a pile of soft, feathery things in the otherwise-empty half circle of space. But an all-too-familiar voice stops me before I collapse.

"Hello, Vane," Audra's mother says, watching me through the gaps in a wall that looks like it's made of chains separating our cells. "It's about time you came to see me."

CHAPTER 8

AUDRA

can handle this.

I have to.

It's not just about staying alive. It's about protecting the fourth language. Keeping it from falling into Raiden's hands.

I run and squat by the largest piece of driftwood, keeping my back to it as I try to pick up my attacker's trace. But the air is empty. Stripped of any winds. Severing the pull of my bond and leaving me clueless.

Defenseless.

But not completely without hope.

Whoever my attacker is, they couldn't take away the Westerly I'd coiled around my wrist, and I concentrate on the cool draft, wishing there were some secret code word I could say to twist it into the ultimate weapon. Though, at this point I'd almost prefer a shield.

"Shield."

The word slips off my lips without my meaning to, like my inherited Westerly instincts have taken over. And the wind obeys, stretching thin and wide before blanketing me like a second skin of breezes. I have no idea how much protection it will really provide, but I'll take any help I can get.

Without the crisp ocean winds, the beach has turned sweltering. I suspect my attacker is trying to sweat me out. Hide in the shadows of their cave while I bake out here in the sun. But I've braved ten years in the desert.

I can handle a little heat.

I duck into what little shade the driftwood log provides and scour the beach for sharp rocks. The sea has smoothed most of the stones, but I find one with a deep crack, and when I slam it against the side of the driftwood, it splits, leaving me two halves with rough, jagged edges. I shove them in my pockets.

A draft springs to life behind me, whipping my hair with such a frenzy it unravels my braid. I shake the dark waves out of my face as another wind rips away my guardian pendant and sends it rolling across the beach, burying the blue cord in the sand. I move to chase it and a new wind whips me backward, sending me somersaulting so many times I lose track of where I am. But when I pull myself up I have no cuts or scrapes.

My shield is living up to its name—though I wonder how much abuse it can really take.

I stand again, facing the caves.

"Your tricks do not impress me," I shout, earning myself another faceful of sand. I spit out the grit and clear my throat. "They're not going to frighten me either."

The winds swell again, shoving my feet out from under me and sending me sprawling into the rocks.

I pull myself back up, tired of getting tossed around and humiliated. Plus, those tricks have given me an idea.

"Is that really all you can do?" I call, letting my voice crack this time, like I'm starting to break.

Two drafts surge in response, but before they can attack, I command the winds to obey *me*, and mercifully they listen. I coil them into a wind spike, wishing I had a third wind to make it stronger. But the two winds still form a cold spear of air, and I hold it in front of me like a sword as I scan the beach, pointing the sharpest end at every shadowed area.

A strange hiss slices through the air and a new gust appears, weaving itself into my wind spike and spinning so fast the weapon turns hot. I try to bear the pain, but when my skin starts to blister I'm forced to drop it, and it explodes in an enormous blast of scorching air. My shield spares me the cuts and bruises as I tumble across the beach like a fallen leaf. But when I try to run forward, another draft knocks me back.

Then another.

And another.

They shove me into the ocean, and I scream as a giant wave washes me away.

Salt seeps into my blisters as I fight to keep my head above the freezing water, but more waves wash over me, dragging me away from the air. My lungs burn and my head spins as I crash on the sand, gasping for breath.

I crawl toward the beach, but another wave sucks me back, spinning me around before slamming me onto the shore.

Then again.

And again.

It's a never-ending cycle of pain, and my poor Westerly shield starts to unravel. I could command it to re-form, but I know it's not going to save me.

My attacker is too strong—too full of tricks and traps and schemes. I'll never get out of this free, and I won't let them take me. I've seen the horrors Raiden's subjected the other Westerlies to, and I can't let that happen to me. I'm not sure I'm strong enough to resist, and I *won't* be the one to let the fourth language fall into Raiden's hands.

Ending things now is the only way to protect the Westerly language, and what better chance will I have than in the cold, churning ocean?

Lost to the sea.

It's one of the worst deaths a sylph can face.

Away from the sky.

Away from the air.

But the Westerly tongue will stay safe.

And at least I have a chance to say goodbye.

I rally my strength, and when the next wave slams me into the shore, I use the last of my energy to crawl forward a few extra feet. It won't spare me for long, but it gives me the seconds I need to send one final message to Vane.

I uncoil my Westerly shield, wishing the draft felt faster and stronger. The sluggish wind won't reach him for days, and in its weakened state it will only be able to hold two short words.

The last two words I'll ever say.

"Love you" is on the tip of my tongue, but at the last second I change my mind.

Vane knows that.

I think he knew it before I did.

Besides, there's only one thing I really want him to know.

One thing that might help him to hold it together when my echo—the part of me that will float on the breeze, telling him the story of what happened—reaches him.

Telling him I'm gone forever.

I add my words to the wind's song and send the gust to the sky.

Then I close my eyes and wait for the water to wash me away.

CHAPTER 9

VANE

I should be angry.

The woman who murdered my family and ruined Audra's life is standing ten feet away, separated by only a thin wall of chains.

But when I look closer at her, all I feel is pity.

Arella used to be this gifted, powerful beauty.

Now she looks pale and greasy, her pants and tank top filthy and ripped, like the crazy homeless lady who hangs outside the grocery store muttering about people stealing her socks.

Still, I don't like the way she's pressed up against the chains, like she's trying to get as close to me as she can. Whatever she thinks, she's not going to be able to manipulate me. I won't even give her the chance to try.

"I changed my mind," I say, spinning around to find Os blocking the exit. "I can't stay here."

Os shakes his head. "You need to rest."

"Then move Arella—"

"I can't, Vane. I built the Maelstrom for her. It was the only way I could keep her contained."

"They're afraid of me," Arella chimes in, laughing when I turn to glare at her. "But don't worry, down here I'm completely useless." She rattles the chains, her skinny arms flexing and straining. The metal barely wiggles. "See?"

Os marches toward her, stepping right in her face. "If you do *anything* to bother Vane, I will have the guard silence you. I'm sure you remember how unpleasant that was."

"I do." She says it with a slight smile, but her voice cracks and what little color she had seems to drain from her skin.

"Good." Os gives me what I'm assuming is meant to be a reassuring smile as he says, "Rest well, Your Highness."

Oh yeah, because nothing says "rest" like being locked up with a psychopath in a place too creepy to let normal people know about.

I try to look confident as he leaves, but everything inside me shudders when the weird mesh curtain latches closed, leaving me trapped underground with the devil woman.

I turn my back on her and study my tiny cell.

Stubby candles are set into the spinning walls to provide faint light, though their glow seems strange. It takes me a second to realize it's because they don't flicker. Their flames are solid and steady, and even when I blow on them nothing happens, like the air is swallowed as soon as it leaves my lips.

"Feels wrong, doesn't it?" Arella whispers.

I ignore her, making my way to the pile of fluffy things and collapsing on my back.

I close my eyes, and they burn behind my eyelids, like they're screaming at me for keeping them open too long.

I let out a slow breath, trying to relax.

"So it's Your Highness now," Arella says, refusing to be ignored. "Does that mean I should congratulate my daughter on being queen?"

Faster that I thought possible, I'm on my feet and across the room, slamming my fist against the chains. "There is nothing between me and Au—"

"Relax, Vane," she whispers, leaning closer instead of backing away. Her breath smells like a rat crawled into her mouth and died as she tells me, "I haven't told them about you two and I don't intend to."

"There's nothing to tell."

"Of course there isn't."

She winks.

I back away. "Whatever you think you know—you're wrong. And if you don't shut up right now, I'll call the guard and have him silence you."

"Oh, fine, have it your way. But if there *were* something to tell, your secret would be safe with me."

"Right. Like I'd ever trust you."

"Look at me, Vane."

She waits for me to meet her eyes and I'm struck by how much they remind me of Audra's. The same dark blue that almost looks black. The same intense stare.

"In a strange way, I should be thanking you," she whispers. "I never realized how much the winds affected me—how much the pain fueled my life. Not until you had them suck all the winds away. It was like I could finally *think* again, after living in a fog for so long."

She steps back, rubbing the skin on her arms.

Audra never told me much about her mother, but I know she feels things on the wind that no one else can. A rare gift that gives her crucial insights. And causes her incredible pain.

"I won't waste my time apologizing for what I've done," she says after a moment. "But I do want you to know that it wasn't *me*. Not really. My gift is very . . . confusing."

"Hey—you know what else is confusing? Growing up an orphan with no memories of my past. And I'm betting Audra thought it was pretty confusing growing up without a father—especially since you let her believe she killed him."

I'm done with this conversation.

I stalk back to my pillows, lying on my side with my back to her.

"How is she?"

There's an ache in Arella's voice that I'm not used to hearing. It *almost* sounds like she cares. And even though I'm sure it's all part of her game, I decide to answer her question.

"She's free."

"Good."

I glance over my shoulder, stunned by the peaceful smile spread across her lips.

This woman is a murderer, I remind myself.

"You're wasting your time with this *I'm a changed woma*
I don't buy it—and Audra won't either. You're lucky I stoppe
from killing you that day in the desert."

"You mean when she was attacking me with Westerlies?"

She drags out the last word as she raises one eyebrow.

I sit up, trying to stay calm. "I taught her a few command

"I'm sure you did. But you haven't taught anyone else, ha
I wonder why that is." Arella presses her face against the
smashing her pale skin through the gaps. "There's no point
it, Vane. I can see it in your eyes. But I'm not going to tell th
if you're wondering. I see no point in being on the bad sid
only person who can release me. Or his future wife."

The word "wife" throws me. I guess Audra *will* be
someday, given that we're already bonded.

But that's still a weird thought.

I try to picture Audra and me living in a house some
normal people—though *is* that how normal sylphs live? A
seen are the Gales, and my only childhood memories are fro
were on the run. I have no idea how it works for regular W

Of course, if I'm king, wouldn't we be living in some s
wind palace?

Focus, Vane.

Psycho woman threatening you right now.

"If you think you can force me to let you out of h
bigger idiot than I thought. So why don't you skip the
mailing thing and let me get some sleep?"

55

"You do look exhausted, Vane. When was the last time you slept?"

"I don't remember," I admit, lying back down and rolling away.

She's quiet for so long I start to drift off—or I must have because when she finally speaks it makes me jump.

"Is it nightmares or fantasies?"

The question is so spot-on I can't help turning back to face her. "How did you know?"

"The winds told me many things about Raiden's tricks. I've just never seen their effect." She squints at me, and it's like she's staring into my brain. "It's been nightmares mostly, hasn't it? Though I'm sure the fantasies linger? And I bet I know what they were about."

Okay, that's just creepy.

"Stop acting like you know me."

"But I do know you, Vane. We're not as different as you'd like to believe. We both know how to break the rules and take risks when it comes to something we really want."

"You realize you're talking about *murdering my parents*, right?"

Does she really not get that I could order her execution if I wanted to?

Well, I think I could.

I could certainly try.

"I'm just trying to show you that I can help you. Whatever games Raiden's playing. Whatever brought you down here, pale and weak and willing to be locked underground in this miserable place just so you can finally sleep. I can stop it. It's my gift."

I watch her rub the skin on her arms and hate myself for being a tiny bit curious.

If anyone could figure out how to block Raiden's winds, it's Arella. But she's forgetting one key detail.

"So let's say I actually believe that you've changed and are no longer the heartless, murdering psychopath we all know and hate. If I ship you back up to fresh air and put you to work protecting me, how long before the madness takes over again? How long before you're back to scheming and betraying and not caring who gets hurt—or killed—in the process?"

"It wouldn't be—"

"Yes, it would."

I turn my back again—for real this time.

Still, I can't quite tune her out as she tells me, "I can help you, Vane. I might be the only one who can."

CHAPTER 10

AUDRA

'm not dead.

The water crashed over me, swallowing my air. And as I drifted with the waves, I felt my consciousness slip away.

But here I am.

Still breathing.

Facedown on the soggy sand of an eerily silent cave.

Thick cords bind my arms to my sides, telling me I'm a hostage. But I feel no hint of my captor's presence. Only a suffocating stillness in the air.

The entrance to the cave is unguarded—but I dare not try and run. My enemy has always been five steps ahead of me. This is just another part of their game.

I pull myself up, wincing as my bonds twist tighter. I can feel the sharp rocks still in my pockets, but given my attacker's ghostly methods, I doubt they'll ever get close enough for me to use them. Still, I twist and squirm as much as I can to bring one closer to my reach.

The cave is empty and unremarkable. Rough gray walls and dripping stalactites. No signs of life except the tiny green crabs skittering across the sand. No breeze except the rush of my own breath.

My only clue to what I'm facing is the broad piece of seaweed coiled around my palm. Cool tingles sink into the blisters underneath, easing the pain of my burn.

An unnecessary mercy, probably meant to soften me. See if they can coax my secrets instead of beating and breaking.

I shudder.

I've worked my whole life to protect the Westerly language, but I've never been so directly responsible for its safekeeping. I want to believe that I'm strong enough to stay silent. Willing to lay down my life like I was on the beach.

But Raiden's a master interrogator.

Four years ago, he captured two of the Gales' best guardians and tortured them for days, weeks—no one knows how long. All we know is that he broke them, finally learning that Vane is still alive.

Am I really stronger than them?

The Westerlies resisted, I remind myself.

But then I think of Vane's face, pale and tinged with green, ready to vomit or faint or worse. All because I'd told him that he *might* have to kill. The longing for peace flows so strongly through the Westerlies, it's involuntary. Giving them an unending supply of courage. Unlimited strength to resist.

I'm an Easterly.

The swift, tricky winds.

Easterlies do whatever it takes to survive. . . .

But I have my bond, I tell myself, wishing I could feel the pull in my chest. Without the wind, the pain has faded. And even though Vane's still a part of me, I can't help worrying that our connection won't be enough. That Raiden will find some weakness and push until I break.

I'll know soon enough.

The damp air makes me shiver as I watch the sun melt into the ocean. But the hollowness inside me feels far colder. The silence starts to smother me, so I hum one of my father's favorite songs, letting the low, deep melody fill the air. It's a sad tale of loss and longing. Chasing things that can never be caught.

I've always wondered why my father loved it so much, but sitting here, waiting for my enemy to return, I think I finally see the appeal.

Success isn't always about triumph.

It's about carrying on, continuing the battle. Even if the fight can't be won.

"You didn't scream," a raspy, male voice says, making me jump. He has an accent I can't place—clean and precise. Like each word has sharp edges. "Didn't you want to call for help?"

His words echo off every inch of the cave, making it impossible to tell where he hides.

I clear my throat. "I'd rather save my voice."

"It *is* a lovely voice," he agrees. "I've been very much enjoying it. But do you really think so little of yourself that you believe no one would come to your rescue?"

Yes.

Instead I say, "You left me ungagged for a reason. I decided not to find out what it was."

He laughs. A creaky, hollow sound that gives me chills. "You are a clever girl, aren't you? I must admit, I find you incredibly fascinating."

"Glad to entertain you."

"Oh, it's far more than entertainment. Far more." He falls silent, and I can tell he's studying me, even though I can't see him. "So tell me, clever girl. What should I call you?"

"Audra." I see no point in lying. Plus there's genuine curiosity in his tone. Maybe even a trace of sincerity. I decide to test my boundaries. "What should I call you?"

"Let's stick with *you* for now, shall we?"

"But I've answered all your questions. Shouldn't you have to answer at least one of mine? It's only fair."

"Ah, so you still foolishly believe that the world we live in is fair?"

"No. But you eased my pain." I nod toward my seaweed-wrapped wrist. "So I'm assuming you have some sort of moral compass."

He's quiet for so long that I worry I've crossed a line. But when he speaks again he says, "Pick a different question and I'll answer it."

Hundreds of options swarm my mind, but I pick something easy. Something that might earn me another.

"Where am I?"

"A cave."

He laughs when I scowl.

"Fine. Fine. Apparently you want questions *and* quality answers. Such a demanding prisoner. I believe the precise name is the Lost Coast. The groundlings decided it was too difficult for their clunky, land-bound bodies to get to, so they all but abandoned it years ago. Which makes it an excellent place to hide."

So he's hiding from someone.

Working alone.

That doesn't sound like a Stormer.

But he fights like one. . . .

"Your turn," he says, interrupting my musings. "And since these questions are costing me now, I'm skipping to the more interesting ones. How did the Gales convince you to join the guardians?"

"I volunteered." At the time I thought I was making amends for causing my father's death. Plus he'd begged me with his final breaths to take care of Vane.

If I'd kept that promise and stayed to do my job, I wouldn't be here.

"You volunteered?" he repeats, stepping from the shadows near the entrance. Even though a dark cloak completely covers his face, I can feel his eyes boring into mine. "I thought your kind were supposed to be peaceful. And how did you keep yourself hidden all these years? Last I heard, all we had left was a boy."

I bite my lip.

He must think I really *am* a Westerly—which may actually work in my favor. Better that he doesn't know how much easier I might break.

"It's supposed to be my turn to ask a question," I remind him, avoiding all of his.

He grins. "There's fire in you. *Fight.* You would've run me through on the beach with that pathetic little wind spike if you could have, wouldn't you?"

I'm still trying to figure out how to respond when a cold wind whips my cheek, stinging like the edge of a blade. I choke down the pain, refusing to let him see that he can hurt me.

"See? *Fire.*" He moves closer, his steps so light they don't leave impressions in the sand. It's unnatural the way he moves—almost a slither—and when he calls a draft to his side, I can't understand the words. "You're different from the others," he whispers.

I stare at the wind coiled around his wrist. It's turned sallow and dull. Sickly.

"The others," I whisper. "You mean the other Westerlies you killed?"

"No—I mean the Westerlies who *chose* to die. The Westerlies who lay down and let the life be stripped out of them instead of standing up and fighting back."

His anger makes no sense.

Raiden was furious when the Westerlies wouldn't share their language—and he killed them in retribution. But he never wanted them to fight back. That's what the Gales wanted—what they're still hoping for with Vane.

"Who are you?" I ask, wishing my hands were free so I could throw back his hood and see his face.

"I told you I'm not going to answer that question!"

He holds up the sickly draft to threaten me, but if he's who I think he is, I don't believe he'll hurt me.

Everyone assumed the two guardians Raiden captured were killed when he was done with them. But what if they survived?

I search my brain, trying to find their names—but the memory is buried too deep, filed away with all the other bits of our brutal history that I didn't want to remember.

A haunting melody snaps me back to the present. Whispered words with a series of dark hisses that slice through the heavy air.

I can't understand what he's saying, but the song crawls beneath my skin, sinking into the deepest parts of me and humming with a new sort of energy.

The shift starts in my gut. A brewing storm that surges with every sound, like the words have brought some unknown part of me to life. And now that it's been activated, it wants *control*.

Pain laces through my body, a ripping, tugging sensation that makes me feel like I'm being pulled apart—and I'm horrified to realize that I am. I know this feeling—I've lived it twice now. Both times I've shifted to my wind form.

"Stop!" I scream, shaking my head to try to break free of the melody's hold. But the song is inside me now, raging and roaring and building to a crescendo.

If it triggers the shift, it will end me.

Our wind form cannot be merged with anything that's tied to the earth, and I haven't deprived myself of food for long enough to truly be able to separate. Parts of me will crumble and scatter to dust. The rest will float away.

The singing continues and I close my eyes, bracing for the coming breakdown. But just before the pain boils over, he falls silent and the breaking urge recedes, leaving me cold and trembling on the sand.

"You're an Easterly!" he practically growls. "Your essence never would've responded to that call if you weren't."

He grabs my shoulders, squeezing so tight it feels like he'll crush me. "Who taught you the fourth language? Was it the boy? Has he had the Westerly breakthrough?"

Vane's face fills my mind, and I feel my panic calm as I stare into his imaginary eyes.

"So it *was* the boy." He laughs darkly, shaking his head. "Apparently, all Raiden needed was a pretty face and the right curves. Someone will have to tell him."

He releases his hold and I collapse, earning yet another mouthful of sand. I spit out the grains and pull myself back up. "Why don't you tell him yourself? You could send him a message right now."

He doesn't accept my dare.

"You can't get anywhere near Raiden, can you?" I ask quietly.

"I can if I hand-deliver you."

"Could you? Or would he take me and still kill you, to punish you for escaping?"

His grabs my shoulders again. "Whatever you think you know—"

"I *do* know. I know everything. Everything except why you never came back. The Gales would've understood—"

"Would they?" He drops me again and stalks away, staring at the sky. "You really think the Gales would've accepted the traitor who gave away their most protected secret?"

"You were tortured—"

"You know the oath we swore. 'Sacrifice before compromise.'"

I find myself repeating the words.

I remember swearing them four years ago, crouched in the shade of the lone oak outside my mother's shack, when I became the youngest guardian in Gale history. They'd been reluctant to appoint me before, but after the betrayal of—

"You're Aston, aren't you?" I whisper.

Aston and Normand—those were their names. But Aston was younger and stronger, and famous for his skill in a fight.

"That name belongs to another life," he whispers. "A life that ended the moment Raiden ripped Normand apart piece by piece until I told him what he wanted to know. I thought he would finish us both, but he kept me alive. Told me he 'saw potential' in me."

My mind flashes back to the assault on the beach—the way Aston dominated every move I made—and I know what Raiden saw.

"He kept me for two years after that. Taunting me with freedom and then punishing me to make sure I knew my place." He shudders. "I obeyed just enough to earn a window to escape. Then I ran. Holed up here in this forgotten place, trying to finish my days. But then I heard *you*." He reels around. "I heard you shout at the west wind and watched it obey. I thought you were a long-lost Westerly, a valuable tool to trade with the Gales. But you're more of a traitor than I am."

"How do you figure that?"

I can't see him smile, but I can hear it in his voice when he asks, "So you're not bonded to the betrothed king?"

The question hits harder than anything he's thrown at me.

And my reaction gives me away.

"How did you know?" I whisper.

He shakes his head, turning away and moving toward the cave's exit. "You still haven't figured out Raiden's secret, have you? How he dominates the winds?"

I rack my brain, trying to guess what clue I could have missed—but nothing he's said has made sense.

Not until he unfastens his cloak, letting the silky fabric slide to the ground.

Pants cover his legs, but the rest of his body is exposed.

What's left of him, anyway.

He steps into the moonlight, giving me the full effect, and I can't stop myself from gasping.

Pricks of light leak through his skin—a million tiny holes that make him more empty space than person.

I want to gag, cry, run away from the horror.

But his eyes hold mine—sad and vulnerable as he whispers, "There's much more power in pain."

CHAPTER 11

VANE

This place is messing with my head.

I'm so fre'aking tired, but every time I close my eyes, my mind floods with all the doubts I've been trying to deny. All the questions I've been trying not to ask.

I never realized how much the pain of my bond calmed me. Gave me something to hold on to—something to prove that my connection to Audra is *real*. Now that it's gone, it's like all my pathetic insecurities are feeding off one another, leaving me needy and desperate and tempted to do something really stupid, like wake Arella up and ask her if she thinks her daughter loves me.

I know I'm being crazy. Audra told me she loved me before we kissed—and I made *sure* the whole thing was her choice.

But she's been gone so long.

Twenty-four days may not sound like a lot. But considering we were only together for five days—and most of the time she spent fighting with me or accidentally almost killing me—it's a *long* time. Enough to make me seriously wonder if she's really coming back.

I hold my right arm up to the dim candlelight and focus on the braided copper bracelet Audra gave me.

I can almost feel the sparks of her touch from when she latched the band around my wrist. She found it in the ruins of the storm that killed my parents and held on to it for ten years so that I'd have something that belonged to them.

She wouldn't do something like that if she didn't care about me, would she?

Then again, she did give it to me after she told me that loving me would be a *permanent mistake* . . .

She changed her mind after that, though.

But . . . couldn't she change her mind again?

Stop it!

I'm tempted to say the words out loud so that maybe I'll actually listen to them. It's just this place making me crazy.

When I get back to the winds and find Audra's trace, the rushing heat will blast away these stupid worries—though I have no idea how I'm going to pull that off. I'm sure the Gales will be watching me even closer now, which makes me want to bury my face in these pillowy things and scream until I have no voice left.

Instead I stare at the silver compass set into the center of my bracelet. It usually channels my heritage somehow and points to the west.

Right now it's just spinning and spinning. Like it's feeling as lost as me.

"I wish Liam were here," Arella whispers, making me jump. I didn't realize she was awake.

I roll over and find her sitting in the center of her floor, staring at the ceiling.

"Liam?"

"Audra's father. He knew how to weave the winds into lullabies, and they always gave me the sweetest dreams."

I really shouldn't be encouraging her, but I can't stop myself from saying, "He sounds like his daughter."

Audra used to send winds to my room every night. It's how I dreamed about her for ten years, watching her grow up along with me. How I fell in love with her before I even knew if she was real.

"He was," Arella agrees. "That was the hardest part, after . . ."

Her voice cracks and she turns away, but through the chains I can still see the tears that streak down her cheeks, leaving shiny trails on her gray, dirty skin. It almost makes me feel sorry for her.

Almost.

"You get that it's your fault, right?"

She opens her mouth and I expect her to blame Audra, me, anyone she can think of—like she did the first time I confronted her about this.

All she says is "I know."

She walks to the farthest part of her cell, keeping her back to me. I watch her shoulders shake with quiet sobs, trying to understand how the frail, broken woman I'm looking at could be the same person who murdered my parents and tried to kill Audra right in front of me.

She really does seem different now.

Which is the most dangerous thought I can have.

Arella's smart—and patient. Odds are this is just another part of her game.

"How are your memories, by the way?" she asks, smearing away her tears with shaky hands.

"Why? Did you commit any other murders you don't want me to remember?"

"Of course not, Vane." She rubs the skin on her wrist, which I notice is bare now. The gold cuff that she used to wear is gone. "I only ask because I've been worried things might be a bit . . . jumbled."

I glare at her, hating that she's right.

She knows it too.

"That's what I was afraid of. Releasing memories is a very tricky thing. I had a feeling Audra didn't do it properly."

"She did it just fine."

But she didn't—and the chaos is almost more frustrating than the blank slate I used to deal with. It's like my past is a jigsaw puzzle where all the pieces look the same, and no matter how much I try to sort through them, I can never figure out how any of them fit back together. Not without a bigger picture to guide me.

"Well, if there *were* a problem," Arella says quietly. "I do know how to fix it."

And there it is. Right there. The play she's been building toward.

SHANNON MESSENGER

"Let me guess, you need me to take you aboveground, to the winds?"

"I would need a few Southerlies, yes."

"Wow, do you really think I'm that stupid?"

"Of course not. Have as many guards with us as you want. Have the whole Gale Force. Do you honestly think I'd be able to overpower them all?"

I want to believe that she couldn't, especially with how scrawny she looks now. But I've seen her in action. She moves like a blur— and she's ruthless. She didn't even blink before launching deadly attacks at her own daughter.

Plus, she wouldn't have to take out the whole force. Just a few key people so she could get away.

"Thanks, I'll figure it out on my own."

"You won't though, Vane. That's what I'm trying to tell you."

I ignore her, flopping back on my pillows.

They're *my* memories. If anyone can sort them back into place it's *me*.

"Well, if you change your mind, you know where to find me. For a little while longer at least."

I hate myself for letting her suck me back in. But I *have* to ask. "Why only for a little longer?"

"You really can't guess?" She runs her hands over the walls, letting the grains of sand shower her feet. "There's a reason this place is so secret, Vane. Os crossed a line that shouldn't be crossed. But I guess he figures one crime deserves another. I did do . . . terrible things."

"You did," I agree, trying to snuff out the sympathy I'm starting to feel for her.

It's not easy.

Especially when she wraps her arms around herself, looking like a small, frightened bird as she whispers, "But this place, this Maelstrom, as he calls it. It doesn't just contain me. It *consumes* me."

CHAPTER 12

AUDRA

This is why the Gales will never win," Aston murmurs as he steps closer, giving me a clearer view of his scars.

There's something sickeningly beautiful about the way the moon's glow seeps through the holes speckling his skin. Almost like Raiden created tattoos of light, carved out piece by piece.

"What did he do to you?" I whisper, not sure if I really want to know. I can see other changes too. A blue tinge to his lips. Wavy lines running along the sides of his torso. He's probably only ten years older than me, but his eyes look a hundred years old.

"Oh, this?" He waves his hands, making a disturbing whistle as the air squeals through the gaps. "This was simply the product. The power comes from the process."

The *power in pain.*

I can't help shivering as I ask, "How does it work?"

"You don't want to know."

"I don't," I agree. "But maybe if we knew more about what we're facing we could—"

"You could what? Do this to others?" He steps so close that I can see straight through his wounds to the rocky cave behind. "Watch them writhe and scream as you make their bodies crumble? Is that the future of the Gales?"

"No. But what about the tricks you used to capture me? If the Gales had those in their arsenal maybe they could stand a better chance."

"You don't understand what you're requesting."

"Then explain it to me."

He laughs.

A sad laugh.

A broken laugh.

Then he throws his cloak back on, scoops me up, and carries me through the cave. His strength is remarkable given his hollowed-out form. I can't even twist in his grasp.

"Now, I'm going to need you to be a very good girl and not get any ideas about escaping," he tells me as we step through whatever barrier he's built to keep out the winds. "I'd really rather not have to hurt you again, but we both know that I will."

I nod, even though I'm not sure I believe him.

He's crazy and erratic and his mind is just as ruined as his body.

But he's *a Gale.*

Then again, so was Raiden . . .

Cold Northerlies blast my skin, and I close my eyes, fighting back tears when I realize I can't feel the pull of my bond.

I don't know if it's some trick of Aston's or a sign or something more, but I need to find a way back to Vane.

"A throne for Her Majesty," Aston says, setting me down on a flat-faced rock just outside the cave's entrance. "Or do you prefer Her Highness?"

"I prefer Audra."

He shakes his head. "You're going to make an interesting queen."

It's hard not to cringe at the word.

I may be bonded to the king, but I doubt the Gales will ever do more than *tolerate* our connection. There's still a chance I could be charged with treason.

The thought makes me want to squirm, but the rope around my waist is too restricting, cutting into my skin with every breath.

I resist the urge to call a Northerly to sever it.

"I knew you were a clever girl," Aston says, hissing a word that makes a draft slice through my restraints. "And yet you still foolishly believe your worthless army can stand against Raiden."

"The Gales aren't worthless."

"Oh, but they are. Let me show you the many ways."

He calls an Easterly, using the command I've said thousands of times over the years.

"You've been taught to give the wind a choice," he says as a swift draft streaks between us and coils into a small funnel. "You tell it to come to you swiftly and you expect that it will. And most of the time it does. But the wind still has a *say*. Which is why you will never truly be in control."

"I don't need to be."

"Really? It looked to me like you nearly died several times this afternoon when the winds abandoned you."

"But I'm still alive. And they only did that because you made them."

"Which is why the Gales will never win. You can't beat someone who doesn't play fair, and they aren't willing to cross the line between request and demand—most of them, at least. And if they did, it would only destroy them."

He points to the Easterly in front of me and I have a horrible feeling I know what he's going to do. I want to send the wind away—save it before it's too late. But I have to know Raiden's secret.

Aston snarls a harsh word I can't understand, and the draft howls. A deep, primal wail that shreds every part of me as I watch the wind of my heritage—my kin—stripped bare.

Everything good and pure crumbles away.

Its energy.

Its drive.

All that's left is a pale, sickly gust that hovers lifelessly between us.

Still.

Silent.

I feel a tear streak down my cheek.

Aston crouches in front of me and wipes it away.

"I wanted to strangle Raiden the first time I saw him do that," he whispers. "Wanted to beat him bloody until he understood the kind of pain he just caused. And when he ordered me to learn the skill, I refused, not caring that he would punish me. I wasn't going to turn into a monster."

"What changed?" I ask, unable to hide the anger in my voice.

He laughs and slips his cloak off his left shoulder, running his hand along a line of holes that trace his collarbone. They're different from the small, jagged holes covering the rest of him. Perfectly round—and twice as big. And they go through skin *and* bone.

"He gave me one for each day I resisted. Twenty-nine in all. I almost made it to thirty, but then he found a better way to break me."

He doesn't explain further, and I decide not to push him. I already know where the story ends.

"So why keep ruining the winds?" I ask, watching the sickly draft groan and hover. "Why not—"

"Because breaking the winds breaks *you*. The power becomes a craving, like . . . part of you dies and the only way to fill the emptiness is to spoil everything around you. And you can't fight it because you don't *want* to fight it, because then you'd never be able to experience the rush again. It's why the Gales can't win, Audra. They can't compete with this kind of ultimate control. And if they tried to embrace it, they'd just be consumed by it."

I stare at the sallow wind swirling between us, hating that he's right.

It would explain how Raiden commands such loyalty from his Stormers. I'd always assumed they were fueled by fear or greed. But maybe they're also slaves to their bad choices.

"That's why you never came back, isn't it?" I whisper. "Why you hid in a cave, let us all think you died?"

"Aston *did* die. This thing I've become"—he stares at his ruined hands—"I'm not going to let anyone know it exists."

There's a darkness in his final words.

A warning.

I know what he's going to tell me, but I still have to ask the question anyway.

"What about me?"

His lips curl into a smile, but it's the coldest smile I've ever seen. "We both know I enjoy your company. And if you ever try to leave, I'll kill you."

CHAPTER 13

VANE

A rella's lying.

She has to be. There's no way Os would . . .

The thought stops me cold as I remember what Os told me about *hungry* winds. And as I watch Arella rub her pale, sickly arms, I realize there's a thin dust sweeping off her skin that I hadn't noticed.

It floats toward the walls like a sheer mist and disappears into the swirling sand.

"Relax," Arella tells me as I run for the metal curtain blocking my exit and try to pry it open.

Stupid thing won't budge—and when I pound on it, it swallows the sound.

I can't breathe.

"Calm down!" Arella shouts as I wobble on my feet. "The

Maelstrom only affects *me*. I'm the one it was built for. Do you really think Os would bring his *king* here otherwise?"

I guess that wouldn't make sense.

I may be driving the Gales crazy, but they definitely need me alive.

But still, if it's affecting Arella, then she's . . .

I drop to the ground and put my head between my knees, trying to keep myself together.

"So you're . . ."

"Dying?" Arella asks when I can't finish.

I force myself to nod.

She holds out her hands, staring at her fingers. They're practically skin and bone, so it shouldn't surprise me when she says, "Yes." But I still have to fight off another dizzy fit.

Arella is *dying*.

Audra's *mom* is dying.

"How long do you have?" I whisper.

"It's hard to say. I've never experienced anything like this before. But if I had to guess, I'd say probably a few more weeks."

"Weeks?" That's a lot less time than I was expecting. I don't know what to say except, "I'm sorry."

"No, you're not."

No . . . I guess she's right.

I have to remember—Arella's not just a murderer. She's a *serial killer*. Humans have the death penalty for crimes like that. Why should sylphs be any different?

But I hate it.

I hate knowing about it, and I hate that I'm wondering if I have the power to stop it, and I especially hate that I'm sort of responsible for it.

If I hadn't turned her in and made sure the Gales knew what she'd done, she'd . . .

Still be crazy and killing people.

This is her fault—not mine.

She stays quiet after that, and I close my eyes, trying to make this awful night worth it. If I don't get some sleep, Os might make me stay here again, and I'm pretty sure I will lose it if that happens.

But every passing minute makes the ground harder and the air thicker and my skin itchier. So I'm ready to cry with relief when the mesh curtain to my cell finally opens and Os walks in.

He frowns as he looks at me. "You don't look rested."

"This isn't exactly the most relaxing place."

"No. But I'd hoped you'd find a way."

"I can think of one," Arella offers.

Os glares at her until she backs away from the chains. "Are you up for the journey back?" he asks me.

I'm wiped, and the freeway part's going to *suck*, but I am *so* ready to get out of here.

"Vane," Arella calls as I make my way to the exit. "I know I have no right to ask this, but I'm hoping you'll tell Audra to come see me. I would love to say goodbye."

The plea in her eyes is hard to ignore. It looks too much like a last request. "When she comes home, I'll try."

Arella straightens. "Audra's gone?"

"Yes," Os says, and I want to kick myself for being so stupid. "She's been gone for weeks. Searching for the mysterious *third* Stormer."

Arella glances at me and I shake my head, begging her to drop it.

I've never been a very good liar, and when the Gales demanded to know where Audra was, the best story I could come up with was that she was out hunting down the Stormer I'd knocked out of the sky when I escaped. It seemed like a believable enough excuse. Until they found his body. Then Fang cornered me about it and the only thing I could think of was to say that I'd meant a third Stormer who'd been part of the attack.

"We never found any trace of a third Stormer," Os says, looking at me the same way they *all* look at me when they point that out.

"Well, you wouldn't have," Arella jumps in, tossing her greasy hair. "I was the only one who could detect him."

"You?" Os repeats.

She flashes her most dazzling smile and for a second she looks more like the old Arella I remember. "You know I have a *gift*."

Os nods, actually believing her.

"Can we go now?" I ask, needing to get of this place before I go crazy and start trusting Arella.

She did just help me, though.

Big-time.

We make the long walk back to the surface, and it's twice as miserable the second time—and not because I'm more exhausted than ever.

Everything I've just seen and learned feels like it's dragging me down, and I can still hear Arella's words in my mind, echoing with every step:

Os crossed a line that shouldn't be crossed.

Is she right?

This place is *beyond* horrible. But . . . I can also remember how pained Os looked as he described the hungry winds to me.

And the scar carved into his face is a mark Raiden gave him to punish him for choosing the *good* side.

Plus, it's not like he locked an innocent person in his Maelstrom. He locked *Arella*—and I have to believe she deserves to be there, no matter how different she might seem.

Still, it feels especially eerie when we reach the open air and I notice all the giant black birds lining the rocks all around us. I remember seeing them on my way in, and I remember Audra telling me that birds are drawn to her mother—one of the few things the two of them have in common.

But I can see now that these are *vultures.*

I don't want to think about what they're waiting around for.

We race even harder on the way home—like both of us can't get away from the Maelstrom fast enough—and I draw what energy I can from the wind. But I wish I could feel Audra's trace.

The pull of our bond is so weak it's almost like it's not there, and that's *not* what I needed after all my crazy doubts.

"I have something special planned for you today," Os tells me as the Coachella Valley comes into view—stretches of green and color that seem totally out of place surrounded by so much barren desert. "A new trainer."

"Really? I'm done with Fang?"

I can't say I'm sad. The guy blasts the crap out of me every session.

But Os shakes his head. "Feng and Gus are still your guardians, and you will continue to train with Feng for the Northerlies. But it's time you start practicing with Southerlies."

He smiles as he says it, and it reminds me of my dad when he's about to make me do something I'm definitely going to hate but that he thinks will be "good for me."

But when I ask Os about it, he just steers toward the Gales' base—an empty field of sand with a row of scraggly pine trees shielding it from the freeway. Giant holes in the dunes are the only things that set it apart from the billion other desert fields around here, and it still bums me out that the headquarters for my sylph army looks more like the home of mutant gophers. But the Gales try to stay underground as much as possible, away from Raiden's searchwinds. And it's not like they need a lot of fancy equipment. All they need is *wind.*

"What's with the crowd?" I ask as I spot at least a dozen Gales gathered in the wash that cuts down the center of the field. It's more guardians than I've ever seen aboveground at once.

"You'll see."

My suspicions grow when we land in the wash and I see the way all the Gales are grinning. Even Fang looks ready to crack a smile, and Gus gives me a cocky nod.

"Vane," Os says before I can ask Gus what the hell is going on. "I'd like you to meet your Southerly trainer."

They all move aside, revealing a seriously gorgeous girl with blond wavy hair rustling in the warm breeze. She stares at me with shy, clear blue eyes, and her peachy cheeks flush pink.

I can guess who she is before Os introduces her.

Solana.

The one they all want me to marry.

CHAPTER 14

AUDRA

I need a plan.

The second Aston finished his warning, he snuffed out all the winds and dragged me back to the cave.

I should've seen it coming.

Should've fought harder.

Should've . . .

There's an endless list of things I should've done. It's too late for any of them.

"And how's my new roomie doing?" Aston asks, reappearing in the cave's entrance.

He used sickly green drafts to tie me to a sharp-edged boulder and told me to get all my crying out of my system while he went to patrol his perimeter. But I haven't shed a single tear.

If I learned one thing from growing up with my mother, it's how to survive with a selfish, psychotic killer. I just have to stay calm and keep him distracted until I figure out a way to escape.

"Still sulking, I see," he says when I don't respond. "It's really not a good look for you. Almost as unpleasant as this."

He slips out of his cloak and I have to look away. The midday sunlight makes his wounds even more disturbing.

He laughs. "Don't worry, you'll get used to it. I certainly have."

He waves his hands around, making the gaps in his arms whistle before he utters a string of unintelligible commands and the cave fills with salty ocean breezes.

"I figured you could use some fresh air," he tells me as he plops down across from me, "but don't do anything foolish. Then I'll have to hurt you—and contrary to what you may be thinking, I'm really not interested in torturing you. I never developed a stomach for that sort of thing. Especially with pretty girls."

"I'm not going to try anything," I tell him, ignoring his flirtatious smile.

Not yet.

Not until I'm sure I'll succeed.

Cool drafts whisk around me, filling the air with soft songs that promise a calmer time ahead. But I'm more relieved to feel the scorching pull of my bond again.

Vane's still safe—and still far away.

I'm not sure how much longer that will last.

Between the message I sent him and the way Aston keeps cutting off my trace from the sky, it's only a matter of time before Vane realizes I'm in trouble. And he would be no match against Aston if he came after me.

Sharp hisses bring me back to the present, and my heart aches as three of the drafts turn dull gray and coil around Aston's waist.

"It's the only way to keep myself together," he explains as the winds vanish into the holes in his skin. "Another way Raiden tried to secure my loyalty. He wanted to be sure I could never escape, even if I wanted to."

"But you *did* escape," I remind him.

"Only from his fortress. Never from his influence."

He traces his fingers along the twenty-nine holes in his shoulder, making me wonder again what Raiden did before number thirty.

I ask a more important question instead. "How did you get away?"

A smug smile twists his lips. "Raiden's greatest weakness is that he *has* no weakness."

"What does that mean?"

"Exactly what it sounds like. His fortress has more security than anyone could ever need and none all at the same time. Once I figured that out, getting away was easy."

I try to make sense of his riddle, but it's far too vague to tell me anything useful.

"Why are you so interested?" he asks, narrowing his eyes. "Planning a friendly visit to Raiden?"

"I'm not *planning* anything. But there's always the possibility that he could find me."

"Not if you're with me. I know how to keep Raiden away—

something you can thank me for when you're done mooning over your lost beau. I must say, I'm rather surprised I felt no trace of him coming to rescue you. I figured he'd be racing here as fast as the winds can carry him, and I was looking forward to thwarting his daring rescue. Are you two having a lovers' quarrel?"

"He knows I can take care of myself."

"Yes, you're doing a smashing job." He hisses a command, and the greenish winds tighten around my chest. My lungs burn and my vision clouds, but just before I black out, Aston releases me. "That ought to get his attention. Unless an incomplete bond isn't strong enough to feel that kind of thing."

"What?" I ask when I've stopped hacking and coughing.

"Please, I've felt your essence. I know you held part of yourself back."

"I have no idea what you mean."

"Don't you?" He grabs my chin, twisting my face from side to side. I try to hold his gaze, but my eyes keep going back to his scars.

Without them he would probably be handsome.

"Interesting," he whispers.

"What?"

"I can see why he wanted you."

His thumb brushes my lower lip and I jerk my head back.

"Oh, relax. I only meant it as a compliment."

Maybe he did. But the way he's staring at me makes my skin itch.

He whispers something that makes everything inside me stir, and I brace for whatever pain is coming. But it lasts only a second before he falls silent and the sensation fades.

"Feels like he didn't hold back with you. You were the only one who had doubts."

I don't know what he wants me to say.

"Wow, you really don't know, do you?"

I glare at him and he laughs, rubbing his chin like he's deep in thought. It makes a vile, hollow sound.

"Let me ask you this," he says after a second. "When you were"— he puckers his cracked lips—"was there a little voice in your mind telling you it was *wrong*?"

"Of course."

Mostly my head was a blur of burning heat and wanting more and trying to take in every single detail.

But I still knew that what we were doing was forbidden.

He taps my nose. "And that, right there, is why your bond isn't complete. It's *mostly* there," he adds as I clutch my chest, trying to feel what he feels. "But there's a slight separation. Perhaps because some deeper part of you knew you really wanted someone who makes up for what he lacks in flesh and blood with a charming smile and lightning-fast wit."

He winks at me and I swear my skin actually crawls.

"Oh, fine, you don't have to look so disgusted. But it seems like a rather telling thing, don't you think? Loverboy happily gave all of himself to you. And yet *you* couldn't fully surrender to *him*."

"That's not—I just . . ."

I don't know why I'm explaining this.

I'm not even sure if I believe him.

But if he's right, I never *wanted* to hold back. I love Vane more than I've ever loved anything, and if my guilty conscience affected something when we kissed, it was an accident. One I will be correcting when I finally get home.

My lips burn just thinking about it.

Though . . . that's assuming Vane will even want me.

I abandoned him.

Left him to deal with the Gales and my mother and the mess of problems we should've been facing together.

I wouldn't blame him if he hates me now.

I certainly hate myself.

"Can Vane tell that our bond isn't . . . ?" I can't seem to say it out loud.

Aston smiles and shakes his head. "You know, I've threatened your life multiple times and you barely batted an eye. But the slightest mention of boy troubles and you get all weepy?"

I want to tell him I'm not going to cry, but my eyes *are* burning. I do my best to blink back the tears.

"Oh, cheer up. Even if he *can* tell, I hardly doubt he's running off to break your bond." He laughs as I frown. "Don't tell me you still foolishly think that bonds can't be broken?"

His question swells inside my mind, refusing to sink in.

I can't believe it.

I *won't* believe it.

Aston sighs.

"Honestly, haven't I taught you anything?" He points to the row of twenty-nine symmetrical holes in his shoulder. "*Everything* can be broken, Audra."

CHAPTER 15

VANE

've been on some pretty awkward first dates in my life—most of which were epically ruined by Audra in her chaperone-from-hell days. But meeting The Girl I Canceled My Betrothal To with half the Gale Force watching definitely wins the prize for Most Ridiculously Uncomfortable Moment in the History of Uncomfortable Moments.

I mean, what do they think I'm going to do? See how hot Solana is and drop to one knee, begging her to marry me after all? Or maybe we're just supposed to make out right here.

Not gonna happen.

Though she *is* hotter than I expected, I'll give them that. And the tiny yellow dress she's wearing, hugging every curve—and there's quite a *lot* of curve on display—is a nice touch. But when I look at her, all I think is: *no*.

Just . . . *no*.

I take a deep breath to try to stay calm, but when I turn to Os and see his hopeful smile, I hit my breaking point. "I can't believe you did this."

"Vane, it's not what you thi—"

"Don't start," I warn him. "I'm not an idiot, okay? And *clearly* you think I am if you thought I'd fall for this."

I'm shaking now, but I can't help it.

Os puts a hand on my shoulder. "I promise, Vane. Solana is only here to train you."

"Oh, really? Funny, because Fang never wears a sexy dress for our training sessions—so is that the new Gale Force uniform? Will you all be wearing that from now on?"

"Well, I can if you want," Gus interrupts, "though yellow really isn't my color."

If I weren't so pissed I would probably laugh. Instead I just glare at him before jerking away from Os. "Find a new trainer."

"Vane—"

"Find a new trainer!"

A painful silence follows and I wonder if I'm really allowed to shout orders at the captain of the Gales. But I'm done being calm about this.

I do feel a little bad when I glance at Solana, though.

She's staring at the ground, her face all red and blotchy, like she's trying not to cry.

I hate that I've hurt her—and I hate the Gales even more for putting me in this situation.

I rub my temples, feeling a massive headache forming. "I can't deal with this today. Call me when you find a real trainer."

Then I wrap myself in the nearest Easterly and launch into the sky.

I'm sure someone will try to follow me, so I add extra winds to speed my flight. I have no idea where I'm going—I just need to get away. But somehow I end up at the last place I really want to be. The place I've been trying to avoid.

I shiver as I touch down in front of the crumbling, fire-scarred shack, even though it's easily the hottest day of the summer. I thought the place couldn't look any crappier, but the palm branches that used to line the scorched roof beams have all blown away, and there are date roaches everywhere. They crunch under my feet as I make my way inside and find more dirt and chaos. The leaves Audra used to sleep on are scattered on the floor and there's a pile of rotting animal carcasses, probably courtesy of her stupid hawk. I can see him watching me from a nearby tree.

I should try to clean things up, but I feel too sick.

Sick of not sleeping.

Sick of dealing with all the problems by myself.

Sick of waiting for her to "be home soon."

"This isn't soon!" I shout, picking up a rock and throwing it at the cracked window.

Of course I miss.

Audra's stupid hawk screeches at me as I reach for another.

"Don't tempt me!" I shout, aiming at his gray head.

Gavin's red-orange eyes glare at me for a second. Then he dive-bombs me.

I flail and duck, expecting him to rip out a chunk of my hair, like he always did when I was a kid. Instead he lands on my wrist.

I freeze.

I hate birds—especially *this* bird.

But as I stare into Gavin's eyes I realize he's the only one who understands what I'm feeling. The only one who misses her as much as I do.

"You must be really desperate," I whisper as I scrape together the courage to stroke his feathers. I'm half expecting him to snap off one of my fingers. But he leans into my hand, cocking his head so I can scratch his neck.

"Well, at least you made one friend today," Gus says from somewhere behind me, making Gavin screech again. "I can't say the same about the Gales."

I roll my eyes and stroke Gavin to calm him. "I guess I should've known you'd be the one to follow me. That's kind of your specialty, isn't it?"

"Yeah, and I saved your life because of it. You're welcome for that, by the way."

"Right. Thanks for chewing on me." I hold up my bandaged pinkie. "Let's hope I don't have rabies."

"Wow, are you always this pissy? Because I'm starting to get why Audra needed a break."

His words sting way more than he realizes, and I have to blink hard to force back any tears.

"Look," Gus says quietly, "I get that you're exhausted and the Gales are putting a lot of pressure on you. But if you would just give them a chance to—"

"If you're going to try to talk me into training with Solana, you can stop right there. It's not going to happen."

"I know. You made that pretty clear when you screamed at Os— and you're lucky he didn't launch you across the desert for disrespecting him like that. But I gotta say, I don't get what the big deal is."

I roll my eyes. "Maybe betrothals are normal for you—"

"They're not, actually. You and Solana are the first. *Were* the first. And that's the thing, Vane. You canceled it. It's over."

"Is it? Sure seemed like they were trying to change my mind today."

"So what if they were? What, are you afraid it's going to work?"

"Of course not!"

"Then why do you care?"

"You don't understand."

"You're right—I don't." He sighs, kicking the ground a few times before he mumbles, "Solana's a good girl. She doesn't deserve to be treated like that."

"You like her so much? Take her."

"I can get my own girls, thanks. But how nice of you to pass her around like that."

"I didn't mean it that way. I just meant . . ." Gavin flies off my arm, like even he's disgusted with me. "No, you're right, I'm being a jerk."

Gus doesn't argue.

I sink to the filthy ground, leaning against the scratchy stucco wall. "I just want to have control over *one* thing in my life."

"But you *do*. That's what I'm trying to tell you. I learned Southerly from this crazy, old Gale with no front teeth named Teman. Obviously, he was *way* hotter than Solana—and yet somehow I managed *not* to fall in love with him."

I can't help smiling. And I know he's right, but . . .

The idea of training with another girl besides Audra feels *wrong*. Especially training with my ex-fiancée.

God—I can't believe I have an ex-fiancée.

And everyone will be watching us, hoping that I'll change my mind. What if Solana thinks that?

"It wouldn't be fair to lead Solana on."

"Uh, after the way you treated her today, I'm pretty sure Solana wouldn't take you if you begged."

I feel my cheeks flame.

He's probably right.

She has to be just as relieved as I am that this betrothal is over.

"It's a shame, too," Gus adds quietly. "You guys could've been friends."

"Somehow I doubt that."

"No, I mean it. You have a lot in common. You both had to grow up without knowing your family. You both know how it feels to have Raiden kill the people you love."

Crap—I forgot about that.

Now I *really* feel like a jerk.

I sigh. "So . . . her dad used to be the king before Raiden . . . ?"

"Sort of." Gus kicks away a date roach and sits down beside me. "He was a prince. But he and his wife were the only ones who escaped the palace when Raiden attacked, so everyone in the resistance saw him as their king, even though he was in hiding, moving every few weeks."

I don't remember much about my life, but I do know I hated living on the run. Always leaving a place just when it started to feel like home. Always looking over my shoulder, wondering when they would find me.

"How old was Solana during all of that?"

"Actually, she hadn't been born. In fact, no one knew we had a new princess until after the royal massacre."

I have a feeling I can guess the rest of the story, but I let Gus tell it anyway.

"We still don't know how the Stormers found them. Even the Gales didn't know where they were until their echoes arrived. They followed the winds back to the battle site and it was . . . well, I've heard it's still the bloodiest mess anyone has ever seen. The only clue to what happened was a message left by the queen, branded to a Southerly with her final breath. It said to 'find the tree.' So they scoured the nearby forest, and deep in the heart, woven carefully into the branches of the sturdiest elm, was a small basket. Inside was Solana. Sleeping in a whirl of breezes, with no idea her whole world had just been torn apart."

The story is fairly similar to mine—though at least I was old enough to get to know my parents before they died.

Well . . . if I could get my memories pieced back together.

"How do you know all this? Are you and Solana friends?"

Gus looks away. "No. I've only met her twice—though our families have some . . . history. But *everyone* knows the story of our last princess. Just like everyone knows the story of the last Westerly."

"Seriously?"

"Uh, yeah. You're kind of a big deal, Vane."

I guess that shouldn't surprise me, given the whole Your Highness thing. But I can't seem to wrap my head around it.

I mean . . . I'm just *me*.

"You still don't get it, do you?" Gus asks, staring at me like my algebra teacher did when I would give the wrong answer *again*. "You're the guy every kid grows up wanting to be. The one everyone's hoping will make our world safe, so we don't have to wander and hide to avoid the Stormers—hey, relax," Gus says as I get up to pace.

But I have to move. I feel like I can't breathe.

I knew the Gales were counting on me and I knew there were a lot of people who needed my help. But I never really thought about an *entire world* looking to me as their hero.

That's a lot of pressure.

"I can't do this, Gus. I'm not . . ."

Not *what*?

Brave enough?

Strong enough?

"I'm not ready," I finally mumble.

"You think the Gales don't know that? Why do you think Feng pushes you so hard? And why do you think they picked Solana to train you—and don't say to fix you up. Yeah, I'm sure that was part of it. But they also know it's not going to be easy for you to adjust to your new role. And you know who understands the pressures and responsibilities better than anyone? *Solana.*"

I sulk at the ground.

"Just *talk* to her. You might be surprised at how much she can help you."

"But . . ."

I realize I'm out of excuses.

All I have left is that I don't want to—and I'm not even sure if that's true anymore.

"Fine," I mumble, refusing to look up and see Gus's smug grin. "Tell the Gales I'll *try* training with her. But not until tomorrow. Tonight, I need a break."

"Sounds fair," Gus agrees.

I have a feeling I'm going to regret this. But at least I'll get a chance to apologize to Solana for the way I acted.

Gus waits for me to head back toward my house, but I can't make my legs cooperate. My mom will be there, waiting to finish our fight—and I'm just not up for it today.

I lean against the crumbling wall, feeling the sharp stucco poke my skin. "I know it's your job to protect me, Gus, and I really appreciate what you do. But I'm going insane here. Is there *any* way you could give me a few hours alone?"

"I don't know, man, if you doze off and something happens—"

"I won't. I'll do jumping jacks the whole time if you need me to." I start jumping and waving my arms and manage to do about twenty before I get winded. "Okay, maybe I'll just pace or something."

Gus laughs as I bend to catch my breath. "It's always so inspiring to see our ultimate warrior in action."

"Hey, I'd like to see you—actually, never mind."

Gus could probably do jumping jacks all day—and then run thirty miles to cool down.

"My point was, I'll find a way to stay awake," I tell him. "Just, *please*. I need some space or I'm going to lose it."

Gus closes his eyes and stretches out his hands. "The winds do feel pretty calm right now, so I guess I can leave you here and keep Feng away. But you *owe* me."

I can't help smiling. "Sounds fair."

He waits for me to start pacing before he leaves, and every few steps he turns back to make sure I'm still moving. I keep it up until he's gone. Then I call a draft and float myself to the top of the nearest palm tree.

I know I'm not high enough to feel Audra's trace—but I have to try anyway. I have to find *some* way to reach her.

"Come on, Audra," I whisper, struggling to concentrate *and* keep my balance on the wobbly palm branches. "Give me something—I'm dying here."

I push my senses as far as they can go, and, almost like she hears me—or the universe decides to finally cut me a freaking break—I actually feel something. A hint of warmth carried on a breeze that's *barely* within my reach.

A Westerly.

It's not her trace. I don't actually know what it is.

But it's *there.*

My voice shakes as I call the draft to my side, ordering it to fly slow and steady so the Gales won't notice the movement. The warm tingling increases as the draft draws near—and when it finally sweeps to my side, I can feel it's a weary wind, singing of a long journey and the burden it carries.

A whispered message from Audra.

Tears prick my eyes.

She finally reached out to me.

Maybe she'll tell me where she is.

Maybe she's actually coming home.

I hold my breath as the breeze unravels, releasing the words Audra wove inside.

Only two of them—and not the ones I'd been hoping for.

Not ones I even know how to understand.

I listen to the message over and over but it still won't make any sense.

She could've told me anything in the world. And she chose to tell me: *I'm sorry.*

CHAPTER 16

AUDRA

You've been staring into space for a troubling amount of time now," Aston says, snapping his fingers in front of my eyes. The drafts in the cave disappear, leaving us in still silence.

Aston sighs when I don't say anything.

"I don't see why you're so upset. Just because a bond can be broken doesn't mean it *will* be—and given that your little boyfriend didn't hold any part of himself back, I don't think you have to worry about him choosing freedom. Unless this is the chance *you've* been hoping for."

"No!"

The word echoes off the cave walls, and I focus on the pull in my chest, hating to feel it fading now that Aston's cut me off from the wind again.

My bond is the *one* thing that I thought no one could take away.

The Gales may not like it.

Vane may decide I don't deserve it anymore.

But it's supposed to be *permanent.*

If it can be broken, then . . .

I don't even know how to finish that sentence.

"How?" I finally manage to ask. "How do you break a bond?"

"It depends. If you're doing it yourself, it's a bit like shifting. Your instincts guide you, and all you do is listen—and suffer through the pain. If someone *else* is doing it for you, well, I've never had the particular pleasure, but I've seen Raiden do it enough times to know that it's . . . unpleasant."

He gets up, barely leaving footprints in the sand as he moves to the cave's entrance and stares out at the sky. The afternoon sun seeps through his wounds and I can't help feeling sorry for him.

He's the victim, not the villain.

"Let me go," I whisper. "You know how it feels to be held against your will. Are you really going to do that to me?"

He stays quiet so long, the sun sinks beneath the ocean. It's a dull blue-gray sunset that paints the whole world in shadow.

"Nice try," Aston says when he finally turns back to me. "Appealing to my common decency is a clever play—I wasn't expecting it. But you're forgetting something."

He snarls a word and the winds binding me tighten, digging into my skin.

"I have no decency."

My bonds clamp even tighter, and I'm barely able to bite back my cry of pain. But I still don't believe him.

He's spared my life. Treated my wound.

There has to be a way to get through to him.

So I don't struggle, suffering in silence as he wanders around the cave, gathering the tiny green crabs skittering across the rocks. He bundles them up in his cloak and carries them toward the entrance, where he barks a sharp word and a small pile of dried seaweed erupts into flames.

He tosses a handful of crabs into the fire and they thrash and flail for a few seconds before lying down to die.

"I'm sorry for losing my temper," he says, reaching straight into the fire to snatch out the seared bodies. "Let's not let it spoil our lovely dinner, shall we?"

He hisses a command that relaxes the winds binding me.

I try to move to a more comfortable position, but all I really manage is to shift my weight onto the rocks in my pocket, making them cut into my leg.

He approaches with a handful of roasted crabs, dangling one under my nose. "They taste better than they look."

Somehow I doubt that. The tiny, scorched body looks like one of the spiders I used to find hiding in my bed of palm leaves.

But even if they taste like the cheeseburger Vane bought me on that crazy, indulgent day, I'd find a way to resist. I can't have more ties to the earth. Not when any second Aston could call for my essence and crumble me to dust.

"I don't eat," I tell him.

"Ah yes, the guardian's life of deprivation. How I do not miss those days." He shoves the crab in his mouth, crunching on the spindly, blackened legs. "Another advantage to Raiden's methods. No sacrifice required."

"Unless you count destroying the wind and taking the lives of innocent people and losing your sanity."

"Perhaps," he agrees, crunching on another crab. He sits down across from me. "But I wonder if you'd be able to hold to your principles when they cost you something you love. Not your own life— I've seen enough to know that you care nothing for that. But what about loverboy? If Raiden gave you a choice: *Ruin the wind or the king dies*, which would you choose?"

"There's always another option."

"Believe me, Raiden is a master at controlling all the variables." He points to the twenty-nine holes on his shoulder. "Pick!"

"But it's not a logical comparison. Of course I'd save Vane—he's the last Westerly. Keeping him alive saves everyone."

"Interesting."

He hisses something that snuffs out the fire, leaving us in the dark. My eyes slowly adjust to the dim light and I can see him watching me as he finishes his dinner. But he says nothing else.

Eventually I give in and ask, "Why is it interesting?"

"Many reasons. But mainly because you seem blindly ignorant to the fact that *you* know Westerly. So *you're* just as capable of saving everyone as he is."

"I . . ."

I can't believe he's right.

And I want to argue that Vane is still more powerful because Westerly is his biological heritage. But . . . he's also known about his heritage for only a few weeks. Meanwhile I have a lifetime of knowledge—plus a decade of training in the other winds.

"I can tell I just blew your mind," Aston says, laughing as he swallows the last crab whole. "Though what I find even more intriguing is that here you are—one of the only two people in the entire world who's capable of harnessing the power of four. And you're tied to a rock, completely at my mercy."

Shame makes my face burn.

"It's not your fault," he adds quietly. "No one could've beaten me. *That's* what I keep trying to tell you. The Gales can't win—even with the power of four. You're all forgetting that for six years Raiden believed Vane was dead and that the fourth language was lost. Do you think he just sat back on his laurels, pouting because he'd missed his chance? Or do you think he found a better way?"

He holds out his hand, letting the moonlight shine through his skin.

The power of pain.

"But . . . then why does Raiden want Vane so badly?"

He searched for him tirelessly for four years—sent two of his best Stormers to come get him.

"Because he always wants *more*, Audra. And if breaking down the three winds makes him this powerful, why not break down the fourth and have ultimate control? It's about *greed*, not fear."

I sigh.

Maybe he's right.

Maybe the fight *is* already lost.

But . . .

I stare outside the cave, at the stars slowly peeking out of the velvety black.

I'm not sure why I always turn to them. All they give are tiny pricks of twinkling light—barely enough to make a dent in the darkness.

But they're always *there*.

Holding their own.

Guiding everyone until sunrise.

And the sun *always* rises.

"You're better off here," Aston insists, like he knows what I'm thinking. "Better off not wasting your life for a hopeless cause. In a few months—years, however long it takes—the world *will* crumble to Raiden. And you'll be glad you're safe over here. Carrying on in the shadows."

"If that's true, then I would rather die with the rest of the good than live on in the emptiness without it."

I turn to study him. His face is a portrait of frustration and pity. But I swear there's a hint of respect, too.

It lasts only a second. Then he smirks and says, "Well, then I guess it's a good thing I'm not giving you a choice."

I don't bother replying.

He's never going to let me go.

Not when he's so convinced that he's right and I'm wrong and the whole rebellion is a wasted endeavor.

The only way I'll get my freedom is to fight for it—steal it back. And I might have a way—though it would be a huge risk. But if I—

"So how about another song?" Aston asks. "You know, to fill the awkward silence? I so enjoyed your fragile voice earlier."

"And what will I get in return?"

"Hm. Well, I *could* point out that as your captor I don't really *have* to give you anything. But I suppose if you want to turn this into a game, I'll bite. What would *you* accept as a fair trade for a song?"

I choose my answer carefully, though there's really only one thing I need. "Unbind me."

He clicks his tongue. "Sorry, darling, I'm not that easy. Well, not when it comes to *that* at least."

I roll my eyes. "If you're as powerful as you claim to be, you shouldn't need bonds to keep me here."

"And if you aren't planning to escape, you shouldn't have a problem with it."

"You're right, it couldn't have anything to do with the fact that I'm losing feeling in my legs."

I shift my weight and wince to sell my point.

"Nope. Pick something else."

"There's nothing else I want."

"Then I guess we don't have a deal."

"Then I hope you enjoy the silence."

I lean back and close my eyes.

Several minutes pass. So many I start to worry I pushed too hard.

Finally he sighs. "All right, *fine*—new offer. I will untie you—*after* you sing me a song. But I want a Westerly song."

My mouth goes dry.

"Oh, relax. If Raiden knew a way to absorb a language just by hearing it, he'd already know Westerly by now."

"Then why . . . ?"

"I just . . . want to hear it again."

I don't miss the word "again" in there. But I can tell by the warning in his eyes that it wouldn't be a good idea to ask about it.

I can barely find my voice to be able to whisper, "Deal."

"Excellent. And you'd better pick a good one."

I know exactly which song I'm going to sing. A song that's hung in the air for most of my journey these last few weeks, giving me hope and spurring me on. Filling me with the warm peace only Westerlies carry.

But I'm feeling suddenly shy. The only people I've ever sung in front of are my parents. Mostly my father, who was the real talent in the family. We always sang duets.

I close my eyes, picturing my father standing next to me, humming along as I sing the words in the Westerly tongue:

Whisking through the clouds as the birds pass by
Ignoring all the storms that try to ruin the sky
Chasing down the setting sun
Forever
And ever
Never let the day be done
No never
Never

Diving through the stars toward the earth far below
Rushing through the places no one else dares to go

Don't sink into the violent sea
No never
Never
Find the path that sets you free
Forever
And ever

The last note is still heavy in the air when I open my eyes and find Aston wiping away tears.

"I know you won't translate it for me," he says, clearing the thickness from his throat, "but can you tell me what the song's about?"

It's a difficult question.

The winds' songs are vague and relative. Everyone interprets them their own way.

"It's about finding peace. And not being afraid."

"Thank you," he whispers.

It takes him a few minutes to compose himself. Then he stands, dusting off his pants. "I guess I need to hold up my end of the deal, then."

He crouches in front of me, holding my gaze as he points to the greenish winds binding me. "You're going to be a good girl, right?"

I nod.

But I make sure my hands are as close to my pockets as I can. I'm only going to have one chance for this.

He orders the draft away.

"Thank you," I say, smiling to put him at ease as I start to stand—and in the same motion I grab a jagged rock from my pocket and knock him to the ground, pinning him with my legs as I press the sharp edge against his neck.

Do it! my head screams, knowing I have only a few seconds left. *Sever his vocal cords and run.*

But when I see the stream of blood trickling from where the rock digs in and imagine spilling more, stabbing and slicing and stealing his voice—and probably his life—my head spins and my body shakes and I want to throw up and pass out and scream and run and curl into a tiny ball and never get up again.

I start to sway and he shoves me backward, knocking away my only weapon. I should get up—keep fighting. But I'm too sick to move. I close my eyes, feeling sweat drip down my face as I wait for him to end me.

"I'm guessing that didn't go according to plan, now, did it?" he says as he picks me up and carries me across the cave.

I'm shivering too hard to speak—not that I have anything to say.

Vane's Westerly influence sinks far deeper than I realized. I hope that means it will give me the strength I'll need to protect the language. But how can I fight as a guardian if I can't do anything violent?

Aston hisses a word and the fire springs back to life near the entrance. I half expect him to burn me alive, but he sets me down next to it, draping his cloak over my shoulders before he goes to stand on the other side of the flames. Blocking the exit.

"I've got to admit—that was actually a fairly brilliant plan. It probably would have worked if you hadn't forgotten that *you're bonded to a Westerly!*" He holds up the jagged rock I used and I feel dizzy just seeing the bloody point. He shakes his head and flings it into the fire. "You almost killed me."

I force myself to meet his eyes. "I didn't want to hurt you. But I can't stay here. Vane needs me. The Gales—"

"The Gales are never going to win!"

"Then I'd rather die with them."

He mutters something I can't understand, and I tense, waiting for some ruined wind to attack. Instead, normal drafts rush in. He sends a swarm of Easterlies to me and they brush my skin, drying my sweat and sharing their energy.

"Go," Aston says quietly.

I turn to look at him and he rolls his eyes.

"If you're willing to slice my head off with a dull rock then it's best I not keep you around. I'm rather attached to my head. So go. Fight the pointless fight. Die with the others. But do yourself a favor. Take a detour through Death Valley. It's to the east of here, where Raiden has his—actually, I won't ruin the surprise. Just look for the sailing stones and you'll figure out what I mean. And maybe if you see what Raiden does to resisters, you'll finally grab your little boyfriend and head for the middle of nowhere and hope the Stormers never find you."

I can't believe he's letting me go. But I'm not going to give him a chance to change his mind. His cloak slips to the floor as I stand on shaky legs and stumble away.

"And if Raiden ever *does* catch you, look for the guide I carved into the wall. If you're as smart as I think you are, it'll tell you how to get out."

I stop at the mouth of the cave. "You could come with me. The Gales *would*—"

"It's too late to save me, darling," he interrupts. "Besides, how could I leave such *fine* accommodations?"

"If you change your mind ..."

"I won't. And I wouldn't go telling anyone where I am. Next time I find a stranger on my beach, you can bet I'll kill first and ask questions later."

"Your secret is safe with me," I promise.

Then I turn back and exit the cave.

Taking my first steps of freedom.

CHAPTER 17

VANE

Audra's apology has played in my head on autorepeat all night, and I still have no freaking idea what she means.

Sorry for *what?*

And why send a Westerly to tell me?

Why not just come home?

But there's a worse question festering in the back of my mind.

I'm trying to keep it there, trying to lock it away and pretend it doesn't exist so I won't have to answer it. But as I stare out my window at the empty sky, I have to whisper it to the passing breeze.

"Is she breaking up with me?"

The words should sound stupid. We're *bonded*. Of course she wants to be with me.

But . . . why isn't she here, then?

My room starts to spin and I have to get out.

I shred my shoulder on the thorns as I climb out my window, but I barely feel the pain. A terrifying numbness is swelling inside me, like my body is already accepting what my head is fighting to resist.

I have to fight harder.

"Where do you think you're going?" Fang calls as I race across the grass.

Honestly, I have no idea, but I shove past him and head into the date grove.

I guess I shouldn't be surprised when he follows me. Or when I end up back at the burned-down shack. But if I'd been hoping to find another message—one that magically explains everything—I'm completely disappointed.

There's nothing left.

No warmth on the wind. No wisps of the draft I felt earlier. I can't even feel the pull of our bond, but I can't tell if it's just because I'm freaking out or because she's finally run far enough away to break free.

I'm not letting her go that easily.

I reach for the winds and tangle them around me. I have to find her. Fix this.

My feet barely lift off the ground before someone tackles me.

"What are you thinking?" Fang shouts as I try to wrestle him away. "Have you lost your mind?"

Maybe I have.

Or maybe this is a dream—another trick from Raiden to trap me—and I just need to find a way to snap out of it.

I bite my thumb, waiting for the sharp pain to rip me away.

All it gives me is a bloody wound and an iron taste on my tongue.

"Hey," Fang says, yanking my hand away. "Tell me what's wrong. Let me help you."

The kindness in his voice is so un-Fang—it has to mean this isn't real.

But . . . it hurts too much to be fake.

I stop fighting and Fang loosens his grip and lets me crawl to the corner. I grab a few of the palm leaves Audra used to sleep on and curl up with them, not caring that they're covered with bugs. Even if I could get away from Fang, what am I going to do? Fly around the world hoping I can track her down?

And then what?

Beg her to take me back?

I would. She's worth begging for.

She's worth everything.

But I know it won't help. Once Audra makes up her mind . . .

Has she though?

I don't know.

I don't *want* to know.

I'm too tired to think anymore. Let Raiden's winds find me—the nightmares can't be worse than this. . . .

I can hear Fang shouting at me again, but his voice is too far away. I can't understand him. At some point I hear others around me too, but I don't have the energy to listen. I just want to sleep.

Maybe I get my wish, because I feel a strangely warm breeze sink into my mind, filling me with its sweet rush. And as it swirls around my head, I feel a memory untangle from the chaos.

A white, snowy forest. Cold and quiet and way more wet and slippery than I expected. I don't have boots or a coat, and my fingers and toes are freezing, but right now I just need to get away.

Snow soaks through my jeans, turning my skinny legs numb—but it feels good to be outside after so many days trapped indoors.

I'm never going back to that cabin again.

No more hiding from the wind.

No more listening to my parents fight through the walls, trying to guess why I keep hearing my name.

I run until my lungs feel ready to explode, and when I stop to catch my breath, I'm shivering so hard my teeth chatter. I hug myself, trying to keep warm, but I'm not used to this kind of weather. The worst I've had is a cloudy day.

Fresh snow begins to fall and I start moving again, trying to find some sort of shelter from the storm. But the trees are too thin—their branches too weak and scrawny to give me any protection. And the farther I run, the more tired I get, until I can barely lift my legs through the thick dredges of snow.

I have to go back—even if it makes me want to scream.

I turn to retrace my steps, but I can't find the trail. Everything is smooth and white and looks exactly the same, and the more I try to find my way, the more confused I get.

I call for help, but the snow muffles my words, and even when I shout at the top of my lungs I know they'll never hear me back at the house.

They probably haven't even realized I'm gone.

The snow falls harder, and I stumble in circles, looking for anything that might tell me where I am. It all looks the same—empty and scary, and I want to cry but my eyeballs are too frozen, so I run as fast as I can.

I don't remember tripping. I can't even feel my feet. But I remember the pain in my head as I fall and the way the light flashes behind my eyes. I try to move, but I can't—all I can do is watch the spots of red on the snow grow bigger as I count my heavy breaths.

I don't know how long I lie there, but I know the shivering stops. I feel my heartbeat slow, and I close my eyes and let my mind drift with the icy wind.

"Vane?"

The soft voice feels like a dream. I want to reply but my mouth won't work. The most I can do is open my eyes.

A dark-haired girl squats in front of me, watching me with dark, worried eyes.

I don't know her name, but I know her. She lives with the people who dragged us out of our house in the middle of the night. Who told us we had to trust them if we wanted to stay alive. Who ordered us to stay inside and who keep making us move to new houses every few weeks.

I hate that girl—and I hate her parents more.

But as she drapes her jacket over me and presses her warm hand against my cheek, I find the strength to whisper, "Don't leave me."

"I won't," she whispers back.

And she doesn't.

She stays by my side, holding my hand and calling for help until her dad finally finds us and carries me back to the cabin. And she keeps holding on as my mom cries and my dad screams at me for running away and everyone wraps me in blankets and bandages my head.

Even when they're done with me, and lay me down next to the fire, I can still feel her holding my hand.

"Stay," I whisper, afraid to be alone.

"I will," she promises, sitting down beside me.

I can still feel her warmth as I drift off to sleep.

CHAPTER 18

AUDRA

I shouldn't be doing this.

I should be racing back to the safety of the Gales.

To *Vane.*

I thought that's where I was headed. I even passed the first groundling road that could've guided me into the east.

But as soon as it was behind me, the fear Aston planted started to take root, making me wonder if I was turning my back on something crucial. And when a second gray, winding road appeared below, a swarm of Easterlies tangled around me, pulling me toward the unknown.

At first I tried to resist them, but then I heard the familiar melody of my father's song in the air. A lyric had been added, singing of bravery and searching for truth and carrying on the fight. But mostly it was about trusting the wind.

So I let the winds pull me east. Leading me to a valley of death.

I drift with the Easterlies for most of the journey, but when I pass a glowing tower in a small, sketchy town, I land and send the drafts away. The strange structure is apparently "The World's Largest Thermometer," and it has a round, red sign at the base that says THE GATEWAY TO DEATH VALLEY.

There's no turning back from here.

I call three Westerlies to carry me for the rest of my journey. If there *are* Stormers where I'm going, I'll need to sneak in undetected, and flying with Westerlies will hide my trace. No one can understand their words.

Their peaceful songs steady my nerves as I launch back into the sky, following an empty road into the mountains. The sun starts to rise as I crest the highest peak, painting the stark valley with orange and pink. It should be a breathtaking sight—and in many ways it is. But everything about this place screams Raiden's name.

The parched, empty dunes.

The erratic flurries in the sky.

There's no peace here. No calm.

Only an endless struggle to survive.

And it's *massive*. Stretching for miles in every direction until the desert meets the dark rocks of the mountains.

I ask the strongest of the Westerlies to blanket me in a shield as I steer toward the nearest peak and touch down by the ruins of a mine, trying to figure out where to start looking.

"Come on, Easterlies—you wanted me to come here. Any help?"

No answer.

A few footprints mark the white, chalky ground, and below me are a couple of crumbling buildings, but it's obvious no one has come up to this place in a very long while. In fact, I've seen none of the groundlings' disgusting smog machines along the road. No tents or settlements along the trails. It's like the entire valley has been abandoned—and I can't say I blame them. Even this early in the day, the heat is almost choking.

I close my eyes and listen to the winds, hoping to find a melody about the sailing stones Aston mentioned. But they sing only of the pounding sun and the quiet emptiness of flying alone. I'm about to move on when I find one draft singing of devils and games.

If there were a way to sum up Raiden, that would be it.

I call it to my side and ask it to take me where it's been.

The Northerly is weary and reluctant to obey. But I make my request again—firmer this time—and it carries me over stretches of cracked earth and rolling dunes until it sweeps down a row of mountains and sets me in a wide basin of flat white ground. The sharp smell of salt is laced through the air, and I realize I'm in a dried lake bed. A remnant from a time when this valley must've been lusher. Friendlier.

Before it all withered away.

It makes me uneasy being below sea level, like I've sunk too far from the purer air above. But I suppress an urge to run to higher ground, and make my way across the jagged, salty formations until I reach a sign that tells me where I am.

THE DEVIL'S GOLF COURSE.

This must be what the draft meant about devils and games—*not* the lead I'd been hoping for.

The winds are much more unhelpful here, whispering their songs so softly I have to strain to hear them. They scoot away from me before I can call them to my side. One gust mentions a place where the wind ends, but when I ask it to take me there, it zips into the cloudless sky before the command fully leaves my lips. So I backtrack through the basin, crossing ground that's crackled like a honeycomb as I try to find steadier drafts.

The sweltering heat leaves me soaked in sweat and crusted in salt and sand. I'm starting to worry I'm wasting my time when I catch the tail end of a Westerly breeze singing about stones that creep and crawl on their own. I call the draft to my side, relieved when it obeys. And when I listen to the uneven melody, I know I've found what I need.

The song starts as a ballad about boulders that etch their own trails in the earth. But it ends as a lament, mourning an indescribable loss in a valley of stillness and sadness. The Westerly feels especially reluctant to take me there, but when I add a plea to the end of my command it tightens its grip and lifts me into the sky.

The air turns heavier as we fly, like it's trying to force me back to the ground. And as I enter a flat basin, the sky turns achingly empty. The draft carrying me panics.

I keep control long enough to land on the pale, cracked ground, but as soon as the wind releases me, it streaks away in terror. My Westerly shield is just as uneasy, but I beg it not to leave me alone, and it chooses to stay, wrapping even tighter around me.

I don't blame the winds for their fears. The unnatural stillness is *eerie*.

It's not a calm. Those are always paired with silence—and the basin rings with a grating, nerve-shattering screeching. Like everything rough and horrible is being scraped together and ripped apart. I try to find the source of the chaos, but all I see are large boulders scattered randomly along the parched ground. Crooked lines are etched into the earth all around them, marking their wandering journey through the basin.

They have to be the sailing stones.

But where are the Stormers?

Large cracks cut deep into the mountain along the badlands, and I assume Raiden's soldiers must be lurking somewhere in those shadows. But I can't tell where, and until I'm sure, I have to stay hidden. I will not make any mistakes this time.

I find a narrow crevice in the nearest foothill and crawl inside, tucking myself out of sight. If the Stormers are here they'll reveal themselves eventually. I just have to be patient.

It's not easy. The searing afternoon sun makes the jagged stones I'm pressed against feel like burning coals. Even the shade provides no relief.

I distract myself by rebraiding my hair, surprised at how good it feels to wear the guardian style again. For years the braid had become almost painful. Pulling too tight and putting too much pressure on me. But now it feels natural.

It feels *right*.

I only wish I'd had a chance to retrieve my guardian pendant from where Aston tossed it along the beach. Hopefully, the Gales will give me another.

Assuming they let me continue my service . . .

Honestly, it's possible they'll assign a guardian to protect *me*—which is too bizarre of a thought for me to process.

My life has never been worth keeping safe. I lived simply to serve others.

But I'm a Westerly now—sort of. And I'm bonded to the king.

Everything is going to change.

My mind runs through a list of Gales I've met, trying to decide who I'd prefer—but a clap of thunder rips me back to reality.

I glance up, stunned to find heavy gray clouds blanketing the sky. A few minutes ago it was a clear stretch of blue.

Lightning flashes and I lean forward to get a better look at the valley, sucking in a breath when I see two Stormers suddenly stationed outside the widest crack in the badlands. Their gray uniforms have an even darker patch on their arms, marking them with Raiden's storm cloud.

Thunder claps again, and a blinding flash of lightning streaks down from the sky—right next to a man who seems to have appeared out of nowhere.

Dressed in a head-to-toe white cloak with his long blond hair swirling around his face, he looks like the gods in the groundlings' myths and legends.

I know who he is even before the Stormers drop to one knee.

Bowing to their leader.

CHAPTER 19

VANE

I wake up in my bed, not sure how I got there. My head is a blur and my memories are even blurrier. But I'm *very* aware that there's an arm wrapped around me.

I pull myself up and all I see is blond wavy hair.

"What the crap?" I shout, jumping to my feet.

I'm relieved when I see that I'm still wearing yesterday's clothes, but: *How the hell did Solana end up in my bed?*

And what happened while she was here???

"It's okay," she says, sitting up and brushing her hair out of her eyes, like it's totally normal that we just spent the night together. At least she's wearing clothes too—though I don't know if her itty-bitty dress really counts. I'm sure my mom would—

"Oh, God—you have to get out of here. My mom's going to freak."

I'll be grounded for the rest of eternity and she'll make me sit through every after-school special on teenage pregnancy and STDs and . . .

"Actually, your mom knows I'm here."

"What?"

"She insisted I stay on top of the covers, and we had to keep the door open—"

"Okay, *what?*"

I spin around, and sure enough, my door is open. And those definitely sound like my mom's kind of rules, but . . . she wouldn't even leave Audra and me alone for two seconds.

"She fought us at first," Solana admits. "But when I explained that I could help you sleep, she agreed."

Still. I can't even . . .

"Wait, I slept?"

"What else did you think you've been doing all night?"

My turn to blush. "I don't know. I was kind of a mess."

"Yeah, I noticed." She stands up, looking around like she's trying to decide whether or not to leave.

Part of me wants her to go. But I remember my promise to Gus.

Plus, she *did* help me sleep—for a really long time. According to my clock it's 12:24, which is later than my mom has ever let me sleep in. I'm still tired, but the worst of the exhaustion has faded.

I run my hands through my hair and sit on the edge of the bed. "Sorry. This is all just *really* weird."

"I know," Solana mumbles, smoothing the thin yellow fabric of her dress, making it hug her curves even more. "It is for me, too."

She says the last part so softly it's almost like she doesn't want me to hear her. But I do. And I feel even more like crap.

"Look, about yesterday . . ."

I don't even know where to start. I'm still trying to wrap my head around the fact that she's *here*. With creases from *my* pillow pressed into her cheek. Standing next to a pile of folded boxers I never bothered putting away.

So I go with the only thing I can think of. "I'm sorry for what I said."

She bites her lips and looks away. "It's fine."

Wow, she's an even worse liar than me.

But I don't know what else to say to make it better.

"So, um, how did you help me sleep?" I ask, deciding it's easier to change the subject. "I thought the Gales had already tried everything they could think of."

"They didn't know about *enticing*. It's a trick I came up with a few years ago, and I've only tried it on one other person." She walks to my window, which is closed tight for the first time since Audra left. "My former guardian used to have horrible flashbacks at night, and I knew Southerlies could draw memories, so I tried sending one into her mind to see if I could change her dreams. It took me a little while to find the right command, and it only works if I'm there to keep control. But she said it helped."

"It does."

Now that my head is clearing I can remember reliving a memory of Audra and me in the snow. I've never had any flashes of that moment before, but now that it's back, I'm going to hold on to it as tight as I can.

She stayed with me that cold, scary day, holding my hand.

She cared.

And if she wouldn't leave me when we were just stupid kids who didn't even like each other, how could she leave me now?

But she did leave, my brain reminds me, and I want to rip it out and stomp it into a pulp. *She's been gone twenty-five days.*

Yeah, but she *promised* she'd be back, and I have to believe that. I'm not giving up hope just because she sent two vague words across the sky.

Not yet, at least.

"Are you okay?" Solana asks as I get up and walk to my dresser, searching for gum or something to get rid of my toxic morning breath. I settle for a crushed Mento that's probably been in my pocket for at least a month, but hey, it's minty—not that I'm trying to impress Solana. Which is good because I also catch a glimpse of my hair in the mirror, and dang, I never realized it could be tall-and-bumpy *and* greasy-and-plastered-to-my-head all at the same time.

"Yeah, I'm fine. I'm just still tired."

"I know. The Gales said you hadn't slept in weeks." She drops her eyes to her hands, twisting a wide gold cuff on her wrist. "They asked if I'd be willing to stay with you at night to help you sleep. I told them I would, if you were okay with it."

I accidentally swallow my Mento.

I'm coughing so hard I can't speak, which is probably better because I don't know what to do with the idea of having a hot girl in my bed all night. I mean, that's kinda the ultimate fantasy, except . . .

Wrong girl.

And what if Audra came home and found us together?

"That sounds like a really bad idea," I tell her when my voice is finally working again.

"Why?"

"Because . . ." I can't believe I even have to explain this. She's my ex-fiancée—sorta—and I usually sleep in my boxers! "I don't know. You *really* don't think it would be weird?"

Solana shrugs and looks away, and I can see her cheeks turning pink. And that's when I realize . . .

When I woke up, *her arm was wrapped around me.*

All this time I've been assuming Solana's just as relieved about the no-more-betrothal as me. But maybe . . .

Solana pulls her hair around her face, hiding behind it as she picks up a framed photo from my desk. It's a picture of me with my parents on a hiking trip from a few years ago.

"I guess we come from two different worlds," she says quietly. "You grew up here, in a house with a family—not knowing anything about sylphs or Raiden or *me*. But I've spent my whole life on the run, never having a home or more possessions than what I could carry. Even my guardians were sometimes taken from me. . . ." Her voice cracks and she sets the picture down and turns to face me. "The only thing I ever had to hold on to was you."

It's hard to swallow again, but this time it's a lump in my throat, not a Mento.

I clear it away. "Solana—"

"Don't," she whispers. "I'm not saying I'm in love with you. I don't even know you. I just . . ." Her eyes well with tears and she blinks them back. "It's just hard getting used to the idea of a completely different life."

I can definitely understand *that* feeling.

"I'm sorry," I mumble, sitting back down on the bed. "This is all such a mess, isn't it?"

"It is," she agrees, sniffling.

It's so insane. Solana's standing here crying over me—meanwhile Audra may have already dumped me.

I sigh. "You're better off without me. Really. I'm a pain. And I'm horrible with girls. Just ask anyone I've ever dated."

"Oh. So . . . you've dated?"

My brain turns into a running stream of expletives.

Why? *Why* did I bring this up?

"Um . . . well . . . that's kinda what everyone does around here, so . . . yeah. But Audra always stepped in and broke things up before anything could happen so—"

"Audra went on your dates?"

I can't help smiling as I remember some of my most infamous dating disasters. "Let's just say she took her job very seriously."

"Oh." Solana sweeps back her hair and adjusts her dress, making her cleavage pop out even more. "That's good, I guess. I always thought it was strange that the Gales chose her as your guardian. I mean, isn't she our age?"

"She is."

I'm about to say more when I realize that the frown on Solana's face looks a lot like *jealousy*. And the last thing I need is any Audra-Solana drama.

A really really really really really really really really long, uncomfortable silence follows. I'm reaching the point of wanting to scream into a pillow when Solana finally says, "So . . ."

She hovers near the edge of the bed, like she's debating about whether she should sit next to me. I scoot over and she sits.

It's hard to ignore the part of my brain screaming, *PRETTY GIRL ON MY BED!!!!!!!* Especially when she turns to me and asks, "So, you really don't want to sleep with me?"

I can't help blushing. "I don't know."

"You need to sleep, right?"

I really do—and it's a pretty sweet bonus that her little dream trick also helps me bring back more memories.

I clear my throat. "I guess we could try it. But I'm not up for every night."

"Don't worry. I have to sleep sometimes too."

"Oh, right. Wait—were you awake last night?"

She nods and I can't decide if that's embarrassing or creepy—but I'm guessing it's both because I feel almost *violated.*

Especially when she adds, "You mumble sometimes."

My face seriously feels like it's going to burst into flames at this point. "Do I want to know what I said?"

"Probably not."

"Oh, God."

"Relax, I'm kidding. I honestly couldn't understand most of it. The only word I caught was 'stay.'"

"Stay," I repeat.

"Yeah. When we brought you home. Your mom was arguing

with the Gales and I wasn't sure if I should be here, since you'd been so angry earlier. But when I tried to pull my hand away your grip tightened and you mumbled, 'Stay.' So I did."

Her cheeks flush and she stares at her right wrist, twisting the golden cuff again.

She must've thought I meant that for her.

"Is that bracelet from your parents?" I ask, trying to change the subject.

"Actually the Gales gave it to me." Several seconds pass before she adds, "It's what we call a *link*. Most people wear them on their left wrist to symbolize their bond, but they gave me this to represent . . ."

She doesn't finish. But when she holds it out to me I can see the letters *S* and *V* etched into the center of a carving of the sun.

"Well," I say, trying to keep my tone light. "Guess you don't have to wear that anymore."

"Yeah. True."

And yet, she doesn't take it off.

I have a feeling I know what that means.

"Morning, sleepyhead," my mom calls from the doorway—because apparently the universe decided this moment needed to be even more awkward. "Did you have a good night?"

She grins at me and I'm pretty sure it's proof that my mom's been body snatched. Especially when she turns to Solana and says, "Thank you so much for doing this."

"Of course."

I'm relieved to hear the slight squeak in Solana's voice. At least *she* realizes how weird this is.

My mom hands her a pale yellow satchel. "I had the Gales bring over your things so you can shower and change. You'll want to use my bathroom. Vane hasn't cleaned his in so long it's probably a public health hazard."

"I've had a *few* things going on," I grumble.

"The bathroom's just through my bedroom," my mom tells Solana, pointing down the hallway. "Clean towels are on the counter and help yourself to anything else you want. You know how to work a shower, right?"

"She's a sylph, not an alien, Mom," I interrupt as Solana slips past my mom and disappears down the hall.

My mom blushes. "Right." She waits until Solana closes the bathroom door. Then she turns to me and says, "So, interesting night."

"Yeah, no kidding—and since when are you okay with letting a hot girl sleep in my room?"

I glance back at the bed, not sure how to get rid of the image of Solana stretched out there. I think I'll need to have Audra help me replace it . . .

"Oh, please, Vane. I knew you two were only sleeping—and I was happy to see you finally get some rest."

"Okay, who are you and what have you done with my mother?"

My mom laughs. "Stop being so weird and go get cleaned up. I'm making breakfast."

I'm being weird?

Me?

I stomp to the bathroom and jump in the shower. The water falls like a trickle and I realize Solana's stealing all the water pressure—

which is a bad thing to think about because suddenly I'm imagining her all wet and steamy and—

Why does she have to be *hot*?

Couldn't the Gales have betrothed me to some hook-nosed hunchback with warts and a snaggletooth?

Or couldn't she at least be as uninterested in me as I am in her?

I think about the sadness in her eyes when she told me I was all she's had to hold on to.

I know what she means. That's how it was for me, with Audra . . .

I rinse my hair and turn the water off, relieved when I hear Solana's shower still running. Let's hope she's one of those girls who takes forever in the bathroom because I need to have a talk with my mom. She's being a little *too* nice about this whole thing, and I have a horrible feeling I know why. My mom's never been the biggest Audra fan. She basically blames her for all the dangerous things that have happened lately—and the last thing I need is for her to play matchmaker.

The smell of bacon hits me as I make my way toward the kitchen, but my mom's not making torpedoes like I thought. The counter is covered with her waffle iron and bowls of strawberries and candied nuts and homemade whipped cream.

She's making sugarwaffles, something she only makes a couple of times a year because they're so much work. And she has to make the batter the night before, so clearly she's been planning this from pretty much the moment Solana got here.

"What?" she asks when she catches me scowling.

"I know what you're doing."

"What am I doing?"

"Oh please." I grab one of the strawberries—which she dipped in freaking chocolate—and take a bite. "You never do all this when Isaac stays the night."

"That's because I've seen Isaac eat a cheeseburger that's been sitting in his car all day. Plus I know he likes burritos better. How's he doing, by the way? I never see him anymore."

"Don't try to change the subject. I get it. You like Solana."

"I *do* like Solana. She seems like a very nice girl, and I wanted to do something to thank her for staying up all night to help you sleep. I've been so worried about you, honey."

She reaches up and brushes my damp hair out of my eyes, and I notice she has a deep crease pressed between her brows.

"I'm fine, Mom."

"Are you? Because all I see is you racing off on secret missions and being dragged home unconscious."

She's right. That pretty much sums up my last few weeks.

My mom sighs. "I know you didn't ask for any of this and I know you're trying to be careful. But I also just want to make sure you're *happy*."

"I am."

My mom puts the bacon she's been frying on a paper towel to drain. "Can I ask you something?"

I grab a slice and take a bite. "Maybe."

She doesn't look at me, focusing on the waffle batter she's stirring when she asks, "Where's Audra?"

"I've told you I don't know."

"I know. But . . . don't you think you *should* know—if she means as much to you as I think she does—"

I shush her, glancing down the hall to make sure my parents' bathroom door is still closed. It is. And I can hear the sink running, so I doubt Solana can hear. But still.

The Gales know my mom knows about Audra. I told them we used the girlfriend thing as a cover and that my mom still doesn't realize it was an act. I'm pretty sure they bought it. But the last thing I need is to give Solana another reason to feel jealous.

"I just think it says something that she's not back yet," my mom says quietly. "And I'd hate for you to pass up something that could be great just because you have your heart set on something that might already be over."

"It's not over."

It's *not*.

"And what do you mean, 'pass up'? What do you know?"

"Nothing," she insists. But her cheeks are too flushed and her voice is too squeaky.

"The Gales told you, didn't they?"

I never told my parents about the betrothal—why would I? I ended it. But I always figured my mom would freak if she knew—get all ragey and protective and *you can't control my son!* But apparently . . .

"Unbelievable. You talk to her for one night and suddenly you're Team Solana?"

She spins around to face me. "I'm Team *Vane*. All I want is to see you smile again. But every day I watch you look more tired and stressed—and I know a big part of that is because she left. And I hate that. I hate seeing her hurt you."

"She isn't."

We both know it's a lie. But she goes back to making waffles.

A few minutes later Solana enters the room with dripping wet hair and the world's skimpiest white dress. I think a tube sock might have covered her more—and I grin when I see my mom's jaw drop.

How you liking Team Solana now?

Solana tugs at the thin fabric, pulling it a fraction of an inch down her suntanned thigh. "It's because of my gift."

"What?" my mom and I both ask at the same time.

Solana gestures to her skimpy dress, and I have to force my eyes to not linger.

Again, why *does she have to be hot?*

"My body can store the wind if I let it. Sort of like a cache. And the Gales think it will help in the next battle, giving them an arsenal the Stormers can't destroy, so I'm trying to gather as much as I can. Which means I need to have as much of my skin exposed as possible."

I'm not sure what freaks my mom out more. The idea that wind is swirling around under Solana's skin or talk of another battle.

Whatever it is, all she does is clear her throat and say, "You look beautiful."

"Thank you," Solana mumbles, tucking her hair behind her ear and glancing at me.

I look away.

My mom pulls the first sugarwaffle out of the iron and puts it on a plate. "So how do you like your waffles, Solana?"

"Oh, um." Solana stares at her feet. "I can't eat anything either."

My mom's smile fades and it's hard not to smirk at her.

Strike two for Solana.

"I'll take everything on mine," I tell my mom, sitting down at the table.

Solana fidgets for a second before she takes a seat across from me, and my mom says nothing as she hands me a plate heaped with so many berries and so much whipped cream I can barely see the waffle—exactly how I like it.

"I thought the not-eating thing was only for guardians?" I ask Solana before taking an enormous bite. It's even better than I remember. Sweet and crunchy, but somehow melty like butter, too.

Solana stares hungrily at my waffle. "It is. But anything I eat takes up space that could hold more energy. And right now the Gales need all the extra wind we can get."

"I guess," I say, wondering what it feels like for her to have the wind constantly swirling inside her. "But couldn't you—"

Frantic pounding on the door interrupts my question, and I run to answer it, with my mom hot on my heels.

Gus stands there, wide-eyed and out of breath. His hair is halfway unraveled from his braid and his uniform is soaked with sweat.

"You have to come with me," he says, dragging Solana and me outside. "We're under attack."

CHAPTER 20

AUDRA

I have to get inside that mountain.

I don't care how dangerous it is, or how much the vanished winds and the screeching air warn of something indescribably evil.

Raiden is *here*.

I doubt Aston knew that Raiden would be making a *rare* excursion from his fortress, but this must be why the Easterlies dragged me here. And even if it's just a lucky twist of chance, I have to take advantage of it.

This is not a time for caution.

This is a time to lay it all on the line.

I watch as Raiden leads his Stormers into the mountain, surprised that none of them remain outside to stand guard. It seems like a mistake—though I'm grateful they've made it. But then I remember that this is *Raiden*.

He's not some prince who inherited the crown at birth. He fought for it, killed for it, clawed his way up from the bottom to become the most powerful sylph alive.

He doesn't need his Stormers to protect *him*. Only to do his dirty work.

Which makes me more determined than ever to take him down.

I can feel the worry in my Westerly shield, but I whisper for it to stay calm as I count the seconds, waiting until five hundred have passed before I dart out of my hiding place. I scan the basin as I run, half expecting a Stormer to jump out of the shadows. But when I reach the entrance it truly is empty. No signs of life except the fresh footprints on the ground.

All I have to do is follow them.

My head screams at me to abort—call for backup—or at least give myself more time to prepare. But I can't risk losing this chance.

I reach up and unravel my braid, knowing it will be safer not to look like a Gale. Then I take a deep breath and step into the darkness.

The path turns narrow as it slopes into the earth, and the sound of muffled scraping fills the dark void. There's no light to guide me, so I walk with one hand on the sandy wall, surprised when I feel the coarse grains shifting under my fingertips. The entire tunnel is somehow rotating around me, like I'm walking through a cyclone that's been sucked into the ground.

A Maelstrom.

I've heard rumors of Raiden's evil prisons, but I'd always hoped they weren't true.

Now I understand why the winds are so skittish.

Maelstroms devour the wind.

My Westerly shield trembles, but I promise to keep it safe. If the Maelstrom could detect its presence, the draft would've already been consumed. Still, the breeze on my skin keeps resisting, trying to drag me back to higher ground with every step I take.

The air turns cool and damp, and I'm starting to think the pathway has no end when a dim yellow light fades into view. I press myself as tightly against the wall as I can and listen for signs of life. It's hard to tell over the scraping sand, but I don't hear any voices or footsteps, and I see no flickering shadows.

I creep forward, making my way into a small, round room where I have to cover my mouth to block my scream.

Dark chains dangle from the ceiling, each one shackled around a body—though they really aren't bodies anymore. They're gray-blue withered shells that hang shrunken and shriveled in their dingy Gale Force uniforms, their faces so wrinkled and twisted that I can barely tell they're sylphs. I've never seen this kind of decay. It's like they're raisins in the sun, like they've been sucked dry or . . .

I gag when I notice flecks of dust breaking off their contorted limbs and sinking into the slowly spinning walls.

The Maelstrom is eating the prisoners alive.

I have no words for that level of evil—and this has to be what Aston wanted me to see.

I've never felt so hopeless.

Especially when I realize I know one of the victims.

It's impossible to recognize his rotted face—but Teman always pinned a golden sun above the Gale Force symbol on his sleeve.

He was my Southerly trainer.

We . . . didn't get along.

Teman was all about joy and rest and ease—every longing I didn't want to have. He even tried to convince me that I should wait to become a guardian. Take a few years for myself before I swore an oath to serve.

And yet, four years later he was the first Gale to vote in my favor at my guardian hearing and my staunchest advocate when my mother voted against.

He believed in me, trusted me, and as I stare at his gnarled, crumbling corpse, I feel like I failed him.

If I'd pushed Vane harder—taken more risks to get him to have the breakthroughs earlier—would it have mattered?

Would Teman still be alive?

I smear my tears away as I shove the dark thought out of my mind.

I can't focus on what-ifs.

All I can do is learn from my mistakes and keep trying harder.

Still, I whisper an apology to Teman as I bow my head in mourning. And that's when I notice the other bodies.

Strewn along the edges of the room in careless piles like fallen leaves. Ordinary Windwalkers in regular clothes. We've always been an isolated race, scattered through the high places of the world, where the winds flow free and the groundlings rarely go. But Raiden must be hunting down every sylph one by one, forcing them to swear fealty or die.

A few even look like children.

I have no idea how long I stand there, staring at the indescribable cruelty. But voices coming from another hallway yank me back to reality.

Close voices.

I don't have enough time to run to safety—and when I hear Raiden's deep, booming voice, I don't want to. I can't understand what he's saying, but I manage to catch one word.

"Vane."

I want to cry when I realize there's only one place to hide, but I force my legs to carry me to the tallest pile of bodies and wriggle my way inside. Sickly gray dust crumbles around me, and I hold my breath, hoping it doesn't make me cough.

Or vomit.

Please let this be quick.

Please let them not see me.

And if I live through this, please erase this moment from my memories.

The footsteps draw closer, and I pick up more snatches of their conversation—words like "prepare" and "demonstration"—but it's all too vague and choppy for me to make any sense of. And by the time they reach the room, all I can hear is deep, throaty laughter. It echoes off the cavernous walls, so cold and cruel in this place of death and despair that it twists everything inside me with rage.

I hold still as the chains clatter and someone with a low, nasal voice asks, "Can I help you, my liege?"

"Yes, I want this one's pendant for my collection."

I don't know which makes me sicker: knowing that Raiden's

collecting the blackened pendants of the guardians he's murdered— or the fact that he's only a few feet away and there's nothing I can do to end him. I can't make a move in a place where he holds all the power.

The footsteps draw closer, making the ground tremble beneath me.

"Something feels off," Raiden murmurs.

"Off?" a new voice asks.

"Yes." Raiden takes several steps away. Then moves closer again. "There's something over here. A hint of life."

He knows I'm here.

I curse my stupidity as the footsteps thunder closer.

It's over.

He'll find me and feel the Westerly wrapped around me and that will be the end. I'll fight until my dying breath but I'll still be the next withered body dangling from the ceiling.

"This one, over here," Raiden says, his voice agonizingly close. "That one's still alive."

"You're right," the Stormer says, moving closer as well.

The load on top of me gets lighter, like someone is grabbing bodies and tossing them to the side. I wait for the burly arms to reach out and snatch me—but they drag a different body away.

"I'll string her back up," one of the Stormers offers.

"No need to bother," Raiden tells him. "We're almost done with this place. Just set her on the ground and I'll take care of it."

I hear a thud as the Stormer obeys, and then I hear a couple more footsteps.

Then a sickening crunch.

I bite down on my cheek, hoping it will distract me enough to stop me from throwing up.

Somewhere in the panic and pain I hear Raiden say something about a gathering and a long-awaited prisoner. Then I hear their footsteps walk away.

I should count to five hundred to make sure they're truly gone, but I barely last another minute in the dust and decay. I claw my way out of the pile, smothering my coughs with my fists as I crawl across the floor, hating how close I am to Raiden's newest victim.

Her hands are stretched out like she was reaching for freedom. But her skull's been crushed in the center. Stomped in by one of Raiden's boots.

My chest tightens and my eyes burn, but I manage to fight back my sobs as I pull myself to my feet.

I want to run, attack, tear Raiden apart piece by piece for every horrible crime he's committed.

But now is not the time.

Soon, I promise myself as I start the long climb back to the surface.

The path gets brighter as I walk, and when the sunlight starts to blind me, I press myself against the wall and check for guards. I see no sign of any Stormers, but I still slide slowly toward the exit, keeping to the shadows as I slip into the empty crevice.

The air is hot and still, but I gulp it down, grateful to be free of the tainted Maelstrom. The screeching wail has quieted, replaced by the low hum of a crowd, and when I creep to the edge of the crevice, I can see Raiden standing in the center of the basin. His back is to me, and he's balanced on one of the tallest stones, facing a group of

Stormers. A quick head count tells me there are at least fifty, and from the white bands on their arms, I'd guess they're his top soldiers. Maybe even his leaders.

It's strange to see them gathered so openly. Standing in the middle of a groundling valley, with no concern for anyone spotting them.

I can't see Raiden's face, but I can see the faces of his Stormers. Their eyes are wide with awe—and maybe a little fear.

My Westerly shield tugs at me, begging me to flee to safety. I offer the draft release instead. I'm not going to force it to suffer along with me. But it stays by my side, tangling tighter.

"I know you're growing restless in the heat," Raiden says, his sharp voice echoing off the valley walls. "The winds tell me there's been a delay. Apparently, he tried putting up a fight. When will they ever learn?"

The crowd's muffled laughter makes me want to throw something, but one glance at Raiden's pant leg freezes me in place.

The white fabric is splattered with red.

"I can assure you, this will be well worth the wait," Raiden promises. "And in the meantime, let me ease your discomfort."

He hisses a strange curl of words, part growl, part wheeze, and a fleet of grayish Northerlies fills the air, making the temperature drop at least twenty degrees. I duck back into the Maelstrom to avoid the winds as they dip and dive and race around the basin. If they touch me they'll give away my location.

"Is that better?" Raiden shouts as the winds vanish as quickly as they appeared.

The Stormers murmur their agreement, and I slip back outside as Raiden tells them, "All our hard work—all our years of patience and perseverance—have led us to this day. Some of you may have doubted that it would ever happen. I myself at times wondered the same. But this is the turning point I've been working for—searching for. We've tried and failed before—but today we finally have what we need. In just a few short minutes, you'll see. I now have the key that will give me the power not only to snuff out the last of this pitiful rebellion but to control *the entire world!*"

There's scattered applause as the Stormers process this information, and I wonder if some of them are as terrified as I am. But when Raiden stamps his bloody foot and shouts, "Who's with me?" they all raise their right arms straight in front of them and then sweep them back toward their foreheads in a waving gesture.

"Tell me this," Raiden calls. "Who's tired of living in the shadows of the groundlings—weak, pitiful creatures who cannot even stand in a storm? Who's tired of letting them hold the prime lands while we hide out of sight?"

More murmurs of agreement before everyone repeats their strange salute.

"The winds have turned wild against the groundlings, storming their lands and tearing apart everything they own. The sky has chosen to get rid of them—but it needs our help. They've been too resilient, relying on their technologies and their evacuations and their sheer power in numbers. But not for much longer. This is the day we join the winds' fight to reclaim the earth, and we won't stop until every last one of these useless creatures has been returned to the ground where they belong! Are you with me?"

This time the crowd erupts immediately and the sound makes me shiver under the scorching desert sun. But something else in Raiden's speech was far more chilling—something I want to pretend I didn't hear because then I won't have to decide if it's true.

The way Raiden keeps talking about having "the key" and "the power" he's been "searching for."

It almost sounds like he . . .

But he can't.

I don't believe it.

I press my hand against my chest, trying to feel the burning pull of my bond—but my heart is pounding too fast.

I can't tell.

I can't think.

"Any minute now my long-awaited prisoner will arrive, and then I will show you how we will win this war," Raiden shouts. "Today we will change the future!"

He throws up his hands and the crowd goes wild. Cheering and clapping and chanting, *Bring out the prisoner. Bring out the prisoner!* Feeding off one another's energy.

Each repetition crushes me more.

There's only one prisoner who could grant Raiden that kind of power.

The key he's been searching for.

The one he's tried and failed to catch before.

Raiden must've finally captured Vane.

CHAPTER 21

VANE

This can't be happening.

I know the Gales have been preparing me for this moment—but as Gus drags Solana and me across the grove, I can't remember a single thing Fang taught me. I can barely remember my own name.

All I can do is stare at the splotch of blood on Gus's hand, trying not to think about where it came from or who it came from or how much more of it I'm going to see today.

"Stop!" my mom screams as she chases after us. "Where are you taking him? What's going on?"

"We don't have time for this right now," Gus tells her.

"You have time to explain where you're taking my son," my mom insists, grabbing my arm and starting a Vane-tug-of-war.

"Okay, ow!" I jerk away from both of them, wrenching my wrist in the process. "Come on, Gus. You can't drop the 'we're under attack' bomb and not tell us what's going on or what we're supposed to do or where my family's supposed to go or—"

"Honestly? I don't know," Gus admits, staring at the cloudless sky—which seems way too clear and blue for an *attack*. "Feng sent me a piece of cactus covered in his blood. All the message said was 'ambush.'"

His voice cracks and he looks away.

My mom reaches for my hand, squeezing so hard it cuts off my circulation.

"Has there been an echo?" Solana whispers.

Gus shakes his head.

She places her hand on his shoulder. "Then there's still hope. And we both know there's no better fighter."

Gus stares at her hand, a few tears running down his cheeks as he nods.

I never realized he and Fang were so close.

Feng, I correct.

"Anyway, that's all I know," Gus adds after a second. "Os took a fleet of Gales up to Joshua Tree, where Feng had been patrolling. The rest of our force is divided between the Borderland Base and the Clear River Base, which also sent us alerts this morning. So Os told me to get you both underground in case Raiden's next move is here."

"That's your big plan—hide him underground?" my mom asks, pulling me back to her side. "Let me take him. I'll drive him any-where you want. The car has a full tank of gas and—"

"It doesn't work that way, Mom." I cover her hand with mine, hating that I can feel her shaking. "I know you want to help, but if they're really coming for me, I won't be able to outrun them. Especially not in our beat-up old Honda."

I can tell she wants to argue, but all she asks is "Where will you go?"

"Os said you knew a place," Gus tells me. "Somewhere near the desert's center?"

My skin itches just thinking about going back to the Maelstrom—and the last thing I want is to spend a few more hours with Arella. "But what about my parents? Someone needs to stay with them."

"I told you—*everyone* is gone."

Solana sucks in a breath and my stomach gets all churney. Suddenly, hiding in the Maelstrom seems like a pretty good idea. Except I have no idea if it's safe to expose my parents to those creepy winds—and I'm definitely not exposing them to Arella. . . .

"I'm not leaving my family unprotected, Gus. If there's no one else, then I'll stay with them."

"That'll only put them in more danger, Vane. You're the one Raiden wants."

"But at least I can defend them."

Gus snorts. "You really think you can take on the Stormers by yourself?"

"I'll be fine," my mom interrupts—though her voice sounds anything but. "Go with Gus. Don't worry about me. I'll just . . . I'll grab your dad from work and we'll head out of town again."

"There may not be time to get far enough away," I tell her.

"Well, then I'll . . ." She doesn't finish the sentence, because there's nothing *she* can do. This one's on me.

"I have to go with them," I tell Gus, straightening up so he knows I mean it.

He sweeps back his loose hair, smearing a thin stripe of blood across his forehead. "I have my orders, Vane."

"Yeah, well, this is my *family*, Gusty."

His eyes flash when I full-name him. Guess he thinks it sounds as stupid as I do.

"And let's not forget that I'm the only one who knows where you're supposed to take me," I remind him. "So . . . you're kinda screwed."

"How about this?" Solana asks, stepping between us as Gus lunges for me. "I'll go with Vane's parents to keep an eye on them, and you can take Vane underground."

"You don't have to do that," my mom tells her, but it's actually a pretty good idea.

Gus doesn't seem to agree, though. "You're not a Gale—"

"I know how to fight," Solana insists.

She *does* have muscles to go with her curves. I could see her beating the crap out of a few people. Though it's hard to imagine her doing it in that dress. Well . . . without something popping out.

Gus still doesn't look convinced, though. Not until Solana adds, "I've been without a guardian for two years now. And the only reason I survived that attack—"

Gus holds up his hand and she falls silent.

I can't tell if he looks like he wants to strangle something or curl up in a ball and cry. All he says is "My orders were to take *both* of you underground."

"Screw your orders."

"I think what Vane means," Solana says, jumping in, "is that sometimes it's better to protect the most people we can. Let me do this. And keep in mind that this is probably the only way you're going to get Vane to cooperate."

I can't help grinning, and when I meet Solana's eyes, I kind of want to hug her. But that would be ten thousand kinds of awkward so I just mouth *thank you* and leave it at that.

Gus throws up his hands. "*Fine!* If you want to go with them, *go with them.* But don't come back until you hear the all clear, and keep an ear to the winds."

"I will," Solana promises.

"And call Dad and tell him to come home from work *now*," I tell my mom.

She nods and smothers me with a hug. "And *you* be careful. Do you have your phone? Can you text me when you get there safe?"

"I'm pretty sure I won't get cell service where I'm going," I tell her, hugging her tighter.

I don't even carry my phone with me anymore. I don't have anyone who calls me. I've cut off my friends, and the Gales aren't exactly big on technology.

"Are we done wasting time?" Gus asks.

I let my mom go. "For now."

"Good. Then tell me where we're going."

"Why? Aren't you the expert at following me?"

I coil a few Easterlies around me and launch into the sky before he can respond.

Gus catches up a few seconds later and we head east. But every few miles I notice Gus glancing north.

I don't see any sign of the storm. The sky is clear and the clouds are feathery and the winds feel steady and normal. If Gus didn't have Feng's blood on his hand, I never would've thought there was any danger.

"So . . . how do you know Feng?" I ask, remembering Gus's earlier tears.

He's quiet for so long I wonder if he heard me. Then he says, "He's my father."

Whoa—how did I not know that?

"I'm sorry," I mumble, hating how lame it sounds. "I didn't realize."

"That's because I look like my mother. She was the pretty one."

He forces a grin, flashing perfect dimples. I want to smile back, but I can't help noticing that he used the word "was."

"And your mom, she's . . ."

"She was Solana's guardian."

Oh.

Oh.

Well . . . that explains why he reacted so strongly to her mentioning that attack.

"So that's what you meant about your families having a history?"

"Yeah. My mom sorta left us when she took the role as Solana's guardian. Feng had begged her not to. He knew Solana's last guardian

had been killed and that it was only a matter of time before the Stormers tracked Solana down again. But that's what my mom wanted. She
was angry and she wanted to *do something big.*" He sighs. "I guess it
doesn't make much sense unless I give you the whole tragic history.
You ready for it?"

I nod—stunned at how little I know about Gus. He seems like
such an easygoing guy—but I guess I should've figured he had some
darker crap. Why else would he be a guardian so young?

"My mom was ambushed by a Stormer when she was eight
months pregnant with my sister. He left her alive, but the baby . . ." He
clears his throat. "The worst part was, my mom wasn't even a guardian.
Feng was, and he'd just won a big fight against Raiden—one of the
only victories the Gales have ever had. And, apparently, if you make
Raiden look weak, he comes after you personally."

He's quiet for a minute and I struggle to figure out something
to say. I mean, I thought what happened to my family was tough
but . . .

"Anyway," he says, "not surprisingly, my mom never got over it.
All she wanted was revenge. She joined the Gales, signed up for
every risky assignment she could. She actually volunteered to protect
you, but the Gales went with Audra. So a few weeks later, when
Solana needed a new guardian, my mom jumped all over it. By then
I'd already enlisted in the Gales, so she left me there with Feng,
promising us she'd be careful. But she only lasted two years before
the Stormers caught up with them." He glances to the north again.
"Feng never got over it."

Listening to him talk makes me realize why I never guessed

the connection—besides how different they look. "Your dad doesn't mind that you call him Feng?"

"Actually, it was his idea. After what happened to my mom, he wanted to make it as hard as possible for Raiden to know who his family is."

"I guess that makes sense."

I watch him glance north for the dozenth time and realize what he must be thinking. "You should be with the Gales right now."

"I should be following my orders."

"That's dumb. You did your job. You told me where to go and I'm going there—I don't need a babysitter for the rest. Go help your dad."

Gus looks tempted, but he shakes his head. "The Gales had a reason for not bringing me with them."

"Yeah, and your dad had a reason for sending his message to *you*."

Gus stares at the dried blood on his thumb. Then he wipes it away on his pants. "He sent it to me so I could protect *you*."

"Ugh—I'm so sick of that."

I don't want to be the useless weakling everyone has to protect.

I'm the last freaking Westerly.

I should be out there leading the charge.

Isn't that what they've been training me for?

I'm still not sure how I'm going to handle the whole violence-makes-me-vomit thing, but if I'm ever supposed to take down Raiden, I'm going to have to start standing up and fighting.

"What are you doing?" Gus asks as I dive and touch down in the middle of the desert. "Is this where we're going?"

I don't answer, calling one Easterly, one Northerly, and one Southerly to my side and coiling them around each other to make a wind spike. It's different from the way Audra taught me, but over the last few weeks I've learned they're stronger this way. One of each wind.

I reach out my hands and call the Westerly I'm missing.

"So you *can* control the fourth wind," Gus says, staring at the draft as it swirls around my waist.

"You thought I couldn't?"

"I'd been starting to wonder."

I roll my eyes and weave the Westerly around the wind spike, ordering the drafts to *converge.*

The gusts spin to a blur, twisting out of my grasp and hovering above my head as a crack splits down the center. Gus covers his head like he expects the spike to explode. But the dull outer shell simply rolls away, leaving a gleaming deep-blue spike with sharp points at each end and a glinting sheen.

"Whoa," Gus breathes as he reaches slowly toward it. "Can I?"

I nod and he hesitates a second before he curls his fingers around it. "Crap it's like . . . solid."

I can't help laughing. "That's the power of four."

"I guess." He slices it through the air a few times before he turns to me. "You realize I'm never giving this back, right?"

"Oh, really?"

I whisper, *"Come,"* in Westerly and the spike launches out of his hand and floats straight into mine.

"You were saying?"

Gus blinks. "Okay, wow. That's freaking awesome."

"I'm glad you think so, because I'm going with you to the Gales. I'm tired of being fussed over and shuttled around like I'm some delicate little flower they have to shelter."

"No one thinks you're a flower, Vane. We've all smelled you after training."

"Maybe so, but I'm not going to hide in the sand anymore either—and you can try and talk me out of it, but we both know that's a waste of time. So let's just skip that part and go get your dad."

He still doesn't look convinced, so I offer the one thing I *know* will win him over. "I'll make you your own special wind spike. You won't be able to command it, but I'll keep track of it for you."

I hurtle the spike into a cactus and the thorny plant explodes, showering us with slimy cactus goo.

"It didn't unravel," Gus mumbles, pointing at the wind spike lying in a puddle of greenish slime.

I call the spike back to me and hand it to him.

He stares at it for a few seconds before he slips it through the strap of his windslicer scabbard. I weave another spike for myself, wishing I'd worn a belt with my shorts. I guess this is why the Gales keep wanting me to wear a guardian uniform.

"Okay," I say, ripping a hole in my pocket and slipping the spike through. "Armed and ready. Now let's go find Feng."

Gus nods and tangles himself in a group of nearby Easterlies. "This time you follow me."

He leads me into the mountains, over a forest of spiky, gnarled Joshua trees.

I keep searching for a change in the winds or a storm in the distance. But everything stays bright and clear and normal.

Until Gus spots a smear of red on the ground.

He takes us down to an area I remember hiking in with my family. A garden of weird green, tubey plants that look kinda like what would happen if palm trees and cacti hooked up and had a bunch of bristly babies. I'm careful to avoid the white thorns that almost seem to reach for me as we make our way to the red-stained cactus.

"It's his blood," Gus says quietly as he reaches up and touches a broken stem. "This must be where he grabbed the piece he sent me."

"But I don't hear his echo in the air," I remind him as he turns away to wipe his eyes. "So he's still alive."

Gus nods, sucking in a breath. "We should find the Gales. Os chased the Stormers southeast."

I can hear the nearby drafts whispering the same thing—and the wind isn't supposed to lie. And yet . . .

There's one draft singing a completely different song.

I call the Westerly to my side, letting it fill the air with its warning about a hostage heading north into a valley of death. And when I listen to the other winds again I realize there's no melody to their song. They whisper the words with no life or energy.

"I think the Stormers did something to the winds," I say, double-checking the Westerly to make sure I'm not going crazy. "This Westerly says Feng was taken to Death Valley."

Gus turns his palms northward, concentrating so hard that a deep line forms between his brows. "I can't find his trace that way. Can you?"

I search the nearby air for the *feel* of Feng. The hint of cool energy around the bloody cactus has to be him, so I hold on to that sensation and reach further, concentrating on the Westerlies coming from the north until I find a draft carrying the same chilly rush.

I gasp when I realize it's not the only trace the wind carries.

"What's wrong?" Gus asks as I call the draft to me, but my head is spinning too fast to answer.

The tingly warmth gets stronger as the wind gets closer. And the sparks feel more like a punch to the gut when the Westerly wraps around me, singing about a girl who found more than she was looking for in the valley of death.

"He's definitely that way," I whisper to Gus.

And so is Audra.

CHAPTER 22

AUDRA

R*aiden has Vane.*

The thought makes me want to tear through the basin, tackle Raiden to the ground, and scratch at his skin until there's nothing left but bone. But all I can do is curl my legs into my chest, wrap my arms around them as tight as I can, and rock back and forth as Raiden carries on with his speech.

I'm glad his back is to me so I don't have to see his cold, arrogant face—though the excitement in his Stormers' eyes is equally sickening.

Focus.

Think.

Maybe I'm wrong.

I concentrate on my heart, taking slow, deep breaths. The pain of my bond is definitely there—so Vane is still alive. But . . . it's weaker.

The searing heat is now a soft warmth, and the shredding pull is now a gentle tug.

That would happen only if I was moving closer to Vane.

Or if the Stormers are bringing him here . . .

My head spins and I lie down, pressing my cheek against the brittle ground. I could stay here, never get up, never have to face the possibility of Raiden having Vane in his clutches.

Or I could pull myself up and figure out a way to save him.

I choose option B.

Whether it was random luck or the will of the Easterlies that guided me, *I'm here*. Which gives me the chance to make sure Vane doesn't end up as another shriveled lump dangling from the ceiling of the Maelstrom. All I need is a plan.

I stand and scan the valley, searching for some miraculous idea that will allow me to steal a prisoner from the clutches of the most powerful Windwalker on earth *and* fifty of his top soldiers—without any winds to help me fight.

The dark mountains have potential. Their weathered, dusty slopes would easily crumble if I trigger an avalanche. But the falling rocks would never reach where Raiden stands. At best it would cause a distraction—which could be useful. I could rush in and grab Vane and . . .

Be defeated before I even take a few steps.

Raiden has all the advantages. My only assets are surprise and a single Westerly shield. It won't be enough.

If I had a way to call the Gales and let them know I'm here and that Vane has been captured, maybe they could get here in time to—

A horrifying thought stops me cold.

The Gales would never let the Stormers take Vane.

They would fight to save him until their final breaths . . .

So if I'm right, and Vane's been captured, I'm probably all he has left.

I'm shaking now, clinging to my Westerly shield the way I clung to Vane after the storm that stole our families and changed everything.

"Ah, here comes our guest now," Raiden says, pointing to a gray streak barreling toward us from the southern horizon.

A tornado.

"Clear a path," Raiden shouts, and his Stormers scramble over one another to get out of the way.

The massive funnel roars into the valley, pelting everyone with sand and rocks as it tears across the basin, destroying the careful trails etched by the sailing stones. It comes to a stop directly in front of Raiden as the clouds swell above, blocking out the sun.

I clench my fists so tight my nails make my palms bleed.

The boy I love—the only thing that's ever mattered—could be tangled inside that storm.

I have to save him.

Have to.

But as I stare at the power-hungry faces of the Stormers, I realize something even more frightening.

I have to stay alive.

Vane will never surrender to Raiden's interrogation. He'll protect the Westerly tongue until his dying breath. So if Raiden has him, and I can't rescue him . . .

I will be the last Westerly.

I wish I could strip the language from my mind—go back to being a worthless Easterly who can sacrifice myself to save him.

But the language is part of who I am now.

I have to protect it accordingly.

The crowd crushes forward as the tornado unravels and three figures step out of the funnel. Two Stormers with splashes of red staining their angry faces. And a bloodied, limping prisoner in a black uniform, his hands bound in ruined yellow winds.

His face is covered with a hood and I try to tell myself it's not him.

Vane hated the Gale Force uniforms. I can't imagine he'd be willing to wear one.

But the pain of our bond feels more like an empty longing. Like all I would need to do is reach out and hold him and everything would be okay.

It would feel that way only if Vane were *here*.

The last of my hope fades when Raiden pumps his fists in triumph and shouts, "Behold—the beginning of our ultimate power!"

He coils a draft around Vane's bleeding leg, yanking him into the sky and waving him back and forth like a tattered flag.

The Stormers cheer, shouting insults and pelting Vane with rocks.

A boulder clocks him in the head and Vane's shoulders fall limp. I can't tell if he's unconscious or dead.

He can't be dead.

Raiden needs him alive.

I repeat the reminders over and over, but it's hard to believe as I watch Raiden shake him harder and still he doesn't stir.

"*This* is what they call a mighty warrior," Raiden shouts, flipping Vane around. "This pathetic excuse for a Windwalker is who they've dared to defy us with?"

Vane finally jostles awake, letting out a deep, mournful groan that shreds everything inside me.

I sink to my knees, wishing I could cover my ears. But I have to hear what's happening. I have to find a way to fix this.

Raiden holds Vane steady, waiting for the crowd to quiet before he says, "And yet, we're just as vulnerable."

He snarls a command, and a sailing stone flies off the ground and smashes into one of the Stormers holding Vane, tearing the Stormer's body in half.

Red leaks into the cracks on the ground and the crowd falls deathly silent, their faces no longer holding smiles for their leader as Raiden stalks toward his murdered soldier.

"*This* is why we haven't succeeded!" Raiden yells, kicking the body like he's trying to make sure it's dead. "We're slow and vulnerable— and some of us let important missions be delayed." He turns back toward the other Stormer who brought Vane. "I could end you. But I've already made my point. In one fell swoop, *anything* can finish us. Even a weakling like him."

He points to Vane's body hovering in the sky. This time no one cheers.

"But I finally have the solution," Raiden tells them. "Gather around."

Slowly, carefully, the Stormers form a tight circle around him, stepping over their fallen comrade.

Raiden's back is still to me, but I can hear the smile in his voice as he says, "The Maelstrom has done a brilliant job of keeping our prisoners subdued during interrogations and disposing of them when we're done. But we so rarely learn what we want, and I've always found the process to be a bit wasteful. All those perfectly good soldiers being fed to the wind like scraps of meat. So I've been working on a better solution."

I'm on my feet without deciding to stand.

Everything about this feels wrong. Raiden's supposed to interrogate Vane—not do this, whatever this is.

Has Raiden finally found a way to claim any secret he wants?

I turn and run deeper into the crevice and start to shimmy up the mountain. Maybe if I get to higher ground there will be a few winds and I can weave a wind spike and . . .

And what?

Take Raiden—the villain we've been trying to kill for decades—down in one perfect shot?

Probably not.

I'm sure he has all kinds of defenses I can't see.

But I could take out Vane . . .

My hands shake so hard they lose their grip on the rocks and I slide several feet before my legs stop my fall.

There has to be another option.

Has.

To.

Be.

Raiden starts hissing a string of commands, and I climb faster, searching the air for any drafts I can use. I still can't feel any—but the wind responds to Raiden's call.

Thick gray gusts unravel out of nowhere and I watch in horror as they cocoon around Vane, entombing him inside their cloudy shell.

I start to tremble as I remember the *drainer* the Stormers trapped me in when they attacked a few weeks ago. I'll never forget the way the drafts sliced and tore, breaking me down bit by bit. If Vane hadn't shattered the shell with a wind spike, the drainer would've consumed me completely.

I fight my way to the top of the mountain, feeling my first glimmer of hope when I reach a few scattered breezes. They're weak and reluctant to answer my call, but finally a Westerly feels the presence of my shield and decides to trust me—and once it does, the other winds follow. I weave them into a wind spike and add the Westerly, ducking as the winds twist and crackle and form into the pointed spear of air. I trace my finger near the sharp edge.

Now I have a shield *and* a sword. Maybe it will be enough.

My hope fades when I turn back to the basin.

The mass of winds has swelled so large that it casts a physical shadow, covering the entire circle of Stormers.

"You might want to step back for this part," Raiden warns as he growls another command and the dull gray winds start to rampage.

The Stormers duck out of the way as the mass triples in size and the winds tear and howl. It's a catfight—a snarling battle—and I can't move, can't think, can't do anything except watch the winds tear and devour and wonder what's happening to the person trapped inside.

The outer shell finally crumbles and the winds spin inward, twisting into a tornado that swells taller and wider with each passing second. I lose track of Vane's body as the vortex tilts and crashes toward the ground in an enormous funnel of swirling, dark gray winds. Two smaller funnels branch off the top, stretching toward the ground but stopping before they reach it, and a small orb of winds crowns the top center of the mass. Shadows seep between the shapes as the winds continue to tighten until the storm almost looks like . . .

I gasp.

He can't . . .

It isn't . . .

My fears are confirmed a few seconds later when the winds finish their final twist and a crack ripples down the center of the storm. Scraps of broken wind crumble away, cementing the rest of the winds into a beast of a tornado with a head and arms attached to its torso.

The Stormers retreat from the monster towering over them, but Raiden moves to its path, his blond hair whipping in the wind as he shouts something I can't understand.

The monster raises an arm and salutes.

"Behold the first Living Storm. The beginning of our new army," Raiden announces, turning to face his soldiers. "Built from the blood of our strongest enemy and merged with the power of our darkest winds. I am its master and it will obey me blindly. But it can fight like a soldier and rage like the wind."

Each word feels like a bruise, but I choke back my sob and force myself to accept this cold new reality.

I stare at the wind spike in my hand, realizing it's time to let it serve its purpose.

Vane is a Living Storm.

And it's my responsibility to kill him.

CHAPTER 23

VANE

've never been inside a villain's lair before, but I'm pretty sure Death Valley meets every cliché requirement.

Creepy name—check.

Stuck in the middle of nowhere—check.

Miserable *why would anyone want to come here?* conditions—oh, definitely check.

And bonus points for the ominous winds swirling around, singing about monsters and devils and mountains where the wind goes to die.

At least I know we're in the right place, but still. Next time I'm rooting for a mansion on a private island or something.

We stop every few miles so I can check the Westerlies for Feng's trace, and I search for Audra, too.

Her trace always pulls me in the same direction.

Our connection feels strong, so I'm hoping that means she's not in any serious danger. But, clearly, whatever trouble Feng found, Audra's somehow in the middle of it.

Gray clouds appear on the horizon, and the winds turn more frantic as Gus has us land near a lookout point on a mountain pass.

"I can feel Feng's trace on my own now, so I'm guessing they're on the other side of this range," he tells me as he unravels his hair from his braid and removes his guardian jacket. "We should prepare here."

"Are we getting ready for battle or dancing at Chippendales?" I ask as he takes off his black tank.

"Until we know what we're facing, it's safer if I don't look like a Gale." He unclasps a blue necklace with a silver feather pendant and tucks it into his boot. "And you might want to remove that."

He points to the compass bracelet Audra gave me. I never take it off, but he's right. It probably screams, *I am a Westerly.*

Then again, we're carrying crazy blue wind spikes, so I'm betting they're going to know something's up.

I unfasten the clasp, hating my hands for shaking as I shove it into my pocket.

I know we're walking into a war zone and might have a hard fight ahead, but I'm honestly more nervous about what happens after that.

What am I supposed to say to Audra?

The last I heard from her was the vague apology she sent across the sky—and that could very well have been the Windwalker equivalent of a breakup text.

I'm not sure what I'll do if it was.

Probably grab her ankle and not let go until she agrees to give me another chance. But first I have to make sure she's safe, and we have to rescue Gus's dad and get out of this valley alive. Not really things I planned to be facing today when I woke up—but hey, I also wasn't expecting to have a hot girl in my bed, so it's been a day of surprises.

I strip off my T-shirt and toss it on the ground.

"You can keep your clothes on. You're not wearing a Gale uniform."

"Yeah, but it's freaking hot out here. So what's the plan?"

"We fly in, grab my dad, and get the crap out of there. And if anyone comes near us we use these." He makes a stabbing gesture with his wind spike.

"I like it," I say, even though my head is spinning and my heart is racing and I'm not sure how I'm going to be able to stab someone with a wind spike.

Or multiple someones . . .

"Ready?" Gus asks, calling the only Easterlies to his side.

I send them away. "I think we should fly with Westerlies. The Stormers won't be able to feel our trace on them."

"Good point." Gus steps closer and wraps his arms around my shoulders.

I'm suddenly wishing I'd left my shirt on.

Gus clears his throat. "Think this would be less awkward if I stood behind you?"

"Uh, I don't see how it would."

He repositions so he's holding my elbows as I call every nearby

Westerly and ask them to form a wind bubble around us.

The drafts seem nervous to obey—and I have to ask twice before they do. But they finally float us into the sky, whipping as fast as they can to hide our forms as we fly in the direction the traces are leading me.

"Are we crazy?" Gus asks as the clouds block out the sun.

"Probably. But what else are we supposed to do?"

"I could've followed my orders, instead of risking your life to save my father. He wouldn't have wanted me to do this."

"I had my own reasons for coming, Gus. And it's going to be fine. I've faced worse."

I really want to believe that's true, but the ground below us has a wide rut running down the center that looks a lot like a fresh tornado path. And the closer we get to the valley, the more frantic the Westerlies in our bubble turn. It takes all my focus to keep them under control.

So when Gus shouts, "My father's trace is gone!" it breaks my concentration and the winds unravel.

The good news is, I manage to convince one of the Westerlies to catch us.

The bad news is, it's not strong enough to carry us both, and all it really does is slow our fall.

We hit the ground hard—though the landing was probably much softer for Gus since the dude landed on top of *me*. I groan as he rolls away, trying to be grateful that nothing feels broken.

Gus jumps to his feet and moves to the edge of the cliff.

"What's going on?" I ask as I stumble to his side.

My jaw drops when I take in the scene.

The valley is filled with at least fifty Stormers—with some blond guy who has to be Raiden standing in the center. But terrifying as that is, it's nothing compared to the gigantic tornado with a head and arms that's looming over everything.

I watch in a daze as it picks up a giant boulder and hurls it at the mountain.

Half the rock face crumbles away.

Holy.

Freaking.

Crap.

"What are you doing?" Gus snaps as I grab my wind spike and line up my aim.

"I'm getting rid of that—whatever that is." I test my swing, feeling dizzy when I realize I'm about to kill something.

But it's not a person.

It's . . . well . . . I don't know what the hell it is, but it's not human or sylph—that's for sure.

It's a force for death and evil and nothing else—and I'm not going to let Raiden use it.

"Wait," Gus says, grabbing my elbow and stopping me midthrow.

"We don't have time to wait, Gus. Think of what that thing could do if it gets out of this valley."

"Yeah, but you can't give away our location and use up one of our only weapons until we have my father and are ready to get out of here."

I hate him for being right.

And I have to find Audra, too.

But we have to be quick because I have a feeling Raiden didn't just bring his new toy for show-and-tell. We have to destroy it before it's too late.

"You won't be able to find him," Gus tells me as I close my eyes and search the air. "Feng's trace is completely gone."

Audra's is too.

All the winds have vanished—and our bond has faded too much for me to follow.

But there has to be a way to find her.

I force myself to focus, begging my instincts to guide me as I stretch out my hands and search with every ounce of concentration I have. My brain feels like it's going to explode, but the pain is worth it when a warm itch prickles my palm, telling me there's a Westerly somewhere on the other side of the basin.

I try to call it to me, but the stubborn wind won't budge, almost like someone else is controlling it.

Could that be Audra?

Sweat drips down my face as I try to lock on to the draft's location, but all I can tell is that the pull is coming from one of the narrow cracks in the badlands.

"Where are you going?" Gus asks as I make a break for the nearest clump of rocks.

"There's someone down there in one of those crevices."

"Do you think it's my dad?"

I hate myself for forgetting all about Feng. "I don't know. I can't even tell which crevice it's coming from."

SHANNON MESSENGER

"Well then, let's check them all—but we better move quick." We both glance back to the giant storm thing, which is flinging more rocks at the mountains.

Gus draws his wind spike and we race toward the next outcropping. But halfway there I freeze.

I saw something move in one of the crevices, but it was too quick to tell what it was.

I squint into the shadows and it moves again—and this time I catch a glimpse of dark hair and pale skin.

My elation lasts about .0004 of a second. Then Audra steps out onto a narrow ledge in the middle of the mountain, standing in full view of the Stormers as she raises a special wind spike and hurtles it at Raiden's beastly storm.

CHAPTER 24

AUDRA

Throwing that wind spike was the hardest thing I've ever done. I know Vane would rather die than serve as a mindless mercenary for Raiden—but as I watch the pale blue spear streak through the sky, I can't make myself run away like I'd planned.

The dark patterns in the Living Storm look so much like eyes, watching me as I end him forever—and the ache of my bond still remains in my chest.

What if there's a small part of Vane left?

"Divert!" I scream in Westerly, holding my breath until the spike alters course. It misses Vane by inches, whisking by his head and landing on the ground a few feet away.

Right at Raiden's feet.

"Come!" I hiss at the spike, and it zips to my waiting hand.

For a second Raiden and I just stare at each other, his fury obvious even from this far away.

But I can also see his *hunger*.

He knows the power I have.

And he *wants* it.

"There are two ways we can do this," Raiden shouts at me as his Stormers turn to him, awaiting his order. "We both have our tricks." He calls the Living Storm to his side. "But *I* also have my army. And you?"

He waits, like he's expecting a fleet of Gales to pop out of the shadows.

"That's what I thought. So you can surrender now. Or we can see which one of us has the stronger weapon—though I get the impression you don't really want to destroy this." He runs his hand along the funnel of the Living Storm, his voice heavy with mock sympathy as he asks, "Was he a friend?"

I aim my spike at Raiden's head.

"Suit yourself," he says as his Stormers launch into the mountains above me, trapping me in the canyon.

Raiden snarls a command I can't understand, and I feel my insides drop as the Living Storm swells to three times its already enormous size, looming over the valley in a tower of shadow and wind.

I duck back into the crevice I'd scaled and slide down the sides, grateful my Westerly shield protects my skin from shredding against the sharp rocks. As soon as I'm back on the ground, I race for the Maelstrom, hoping the hungry, swirling drafts will shield me from the Living Storm long enough to come up with a plan. But I make it only a few feet before an arm of thunderous wind tangles around me and drags me back to the open air.

"Don't do this, Vane," I scream as I stare into the raging winds, trying to find the shadows that looked like eyes a few minutes before.

All I see is a cold, frenzied Storm.

The fist tightens, crushing the breath out of me, and I try to pull my wind spike free but I can't breathe and the pain is so sharp, like all the bones in my body are splintering from the pressure.

Light flashes behind my eyes and I feel my consciousness start to slip. But in the gray space between nightmare and darkness I see a blur of deep blue streak past me and crash into the shoulder of the Storm.

The winds howl and writhe and twist as a shadowy gray fog seeps out of the Living Storm's wound, making the air taste salty. I gag as I wriggle free from its weakened grip—realizing my mistake when I drop like a broken-winged bird and there are no winds to float on or call to my aid.

I brace for impact, but at the last second my Westerly shield surges, coating me in a thick shell of air that absorbs the bulk of the crash.

The Living Storm's giant fist hurtles toward me and I scramble to my feet seconds before it crushes where I'd been lying. I stumble toward my lost wind spike, but the Storm grabs my legs and I have to cling to cracked ground with all the strength I have left.

I'm about to lose my grip when a blur of blond hair charges toward me and slashes through the wrist of the Storm with a spear of deep blue.

The Storm's arm crumbles into a thick gray fog that makes it impossible to see as its roar of pain shakes me down to the deepest parts of my essence.

I fight my way through the flying debris as the Storm howls again and more fog explodes around me.

Before I can take another step, a streak of blue shoots past me, slicing through the thickest mass of fog. The sickening gray mist parts for the briefest second and I get a glimpse of the blond warrior as he raises his spike and launches it for the Storm's head.

"No!" I scream—but it's too late.

The spike hits its mark and the world explodes.

The choking cloud turns everything black as the earth shakes and rocks rain down and a high-pitched squeal sears into my brain. I know I need to run, move, breathe. But I can't.

The Storm is gone.

Vane is gone.

Strong hands grab me from behind, shocking me with tiny sparks when they spin me around.

"Hey, calm down," a familiar voice tells me as I kick and thrash and fight to break free. "It's me."

I freeze, squinting through the fog to stare into a face that's every bit as perfect as it is impossible.

"Vane?" My knees give out and I collapse into the warm arms that shouldn't be here, soaking up the electric tingles I wasn't supposed to feel again. "You're dead."

"I am?"

He takes my face in his hands and tilts my chin up, forcing

me to look into his eyes—vivid and blue even in all this darkness and chaos.

I don't know if this a dream or a delusion—but I know what I want to use it for. I pull his face down to mine and kiss him with every ounce of the love and longing that I've held on to all these weeks.

He tastes sweeter than I remember, and the heat between us is more intense, surging through me like a desert storm as I part his lips and kiss him deeper. His sparks burn on my tongue as I let the last parts of myself pass to him—sharing everything. Making him *mine*.

This is all I want, and if somehow I get to live this dream instead of having it ripped away, I'm never letting go. Never letting fear come between us again.

I hear another explosion and Vane's hands slide to my shoulders and push me gently back.

We both gasp for breath and I shake with a giddy laugh.

He's still here.

Still warm and beautiful and—

"We're in a *crapload* of trouble—you do realize that, right?" he asks me.

I force my eyes away from his face and realize the fog has cleared enough to show the chaos and destruction all around us.

"I know, I'll explain later," Vane says to someone behind me, and I spin around to face the blond warrior, who I realize is a Gale I vaguely remember from my days in training.

"Looks like I get three for the price of one," Raiden calls, his deep voice echoing around the canyon.

I glance up and find Stormers crouched in the cliffs all around us, holding wind spikes aimed perfectly at our heads. Every possible path is blocked—even the entrance to the Maelstrom—and the air is filled with nothing but scratchy, broken drafts.

Raiden stands between two of his Stormers on the highest foot-hill, his stance oozing calm and confidence as he studies the three of us.

"I'd surrender now, if I were you," he warns.

Vane raises his wind spike as Gus sweeps his hair back and hands me the weapon I'd lost. He has another, darker blue spike clutched in his fist.

"You got any ideas?" Vane asks him.

He wipes away the blood that's streaking down his face from a cut near his eye. "Yeah. We fight."

CHAPTER 25

VANE

A huge part of my brain wants to celebrate the fact that *AUDRA JUST KISSED ME!!!!!!!* But this is *so* not the time.

"I'm being very generous with my patience," Raiden calls as the Stormers in the cliffs test their aim. "I'd prefer to bring all three of you with me—but I really only need *one*. So put aside your weapons, lie down on the sand, and spare yourself unnecessary losses."

"Or you could put down those pathetic things you call wind spikes," Gus shouts back, holding out the spike I made him so the sunlight shines along the sharp edges, "and spare me from having to pick you off one by one."

I grab his arm and pull him closer to Audra and me. "It's probably not a good idea to piss off the guy who could shout a kill order any second."

Gus wriggles out of my grip. "He's not going to kill us. He saw what I just did to his beastly Storm thing—he'll be careful until he sees how powerful we are. And pissing him off is the best way to get him to tell me where my dad is. People get sloppy when they're angry."

"Your dad?" Audra interrupts.

Just the sound of her voice makes my heart all race-y.

Dude—focus!

"The Stormers took him this morning," I tell her, surprised at how long ago that feels. "That's how we found this place. We followed their trail."

"How long have you been here?" Gus asks Audra. "Did you see where they brought him?"

"I did," Audra whispers, turning very pale.

Gus grabs her arm. "What? Where is he?"

She's wobbling so much I have to steady her against me. "What's wrong?"

"I . . ." Her voice cracks and she takes a deep, shuddering breath. "The Storm—"

"I'll give you until the count of ten!" Raiden shouts.

Gus leans closer. "We're running out of time. Where is my dad?"

"Nine!" Raiden calls.

Audra shakes her head, her eyes glassy with tears as she holds Gus's stare. "The Storm that you . . . I watched Raiden make it. He took a prisoner and he tangled him in dark winds and made them swell into a giant mass, like a cocoon. And when the drafts finally unraveled, all that was left was . . ."

I watch all the blood drain from Gus's face, and I'm sure mine's doing the same.

So . . . the weird Storm thing with a head and arms.

That was . . .

And when Gus destroyed it, he . . .

"Seven!" I hear Raiden shout as Gus drops his wind spike and backs away, like he can actually see his father's blood on it.

"What did the prisoner look like?" I ask Audra.

"He had a hood over his face. But he had a Gale Force uniform on and Raiden said the Stormers just captured him today—and that he put up a fight and delayed them."

"Six!"

"God, Gus—I don't even . . . ," I say as Gus's eyes get cloudy and he starts to sway. "I'm so sorry—and I feel like a jerk for saying this, but . . . you have to hold it together right now. We're in a serious mess here."

I pick up his wind spike and he jumps back like it has the plague.

"Please, Gus. If we don't do something, Raiden's going to get exactly what he wants."

"I'll give him what he wants," Gus screams, snatching Audra's spike from her hands.

I guess I shouldn't be surprised when he turns around and launches it straight for Raiden's heart—but I am.

And so is Raiden.

He shouts a garbled command and some of his ruined winds slam against the spike. But it slices through them like butter, and the Stormer next to Raiden has to yank him out of the way—and the spike still tears a thick gash in Raiden's arm before it embeds in the mountain's face.

Everyone freezes.

Raiden glares at the red seeping onto his pristine sleeve, and I'm guessing it's been a while since someone actually got one up on him. The Stormers seem shocked too, watching their leader with wide eyes and open mouths, like they can't believe he actually bleeds.

"Okay, time to go!" I yell as Raiden orders his Stormers to attack.

The broken winds rage to life, making the air feel thick as they claw and tear at our skin. We shove our way through, trying to zig and zag to make ourselves harder targets as dozens of wind spikes explode around us.

Now would be a really awesome time to form a pipeline and blast ourselves out of here—but there are no usable drafts to call.

"Over there," Audra shouts, pointing to a huge boulder that will give us at least some cover.

She barely makes it another step before a wind spike slams into her shoulder, knocking her to the ground.

I hear myself scream, and tears blur my eyes, but Audra stumbles to her feet and runs to the shadow of the boulder. Gus and I follow and I drop to my knees, pulling her close and checking her for injuries.

She doesn't have a mark on her.

"How is that possible?" I ask, running my hands over her perfect skin. Warm sparks make my hands tingle, but I can also feel a soft breeze.

"It's a Westerly," Audra explains. "It's wrapped around me like a—"
The rest of her words are smothered by an explosion.

A batch of wind spikes hammers our shelter and the boulder cracks down the center as rocks and dust shower around us.

"We need a shield," Audra shouts before she whispers the same plea in Westerly.

I watch in wonder as the draft around her stretches into the air above us, spreading thinner and blanketing us in a silky dome of cool wind. I've never seen anything like it.

I guess I shouldn't be surprised that Audra already knows more about my language than I do—she's sort of the queen of I Am Better than Everyone Else at Everything. But it's strange to see how naturally the Westerly responds, not caring at all that it's being ordered around by an Easterly.

I push against the thin wall of air and my hand slips right through. "Uh, is this going to be strong enough?"

"I guess we'll find out," she says, as a wind spike crashes into a nearby boulder, pulverizing it into itty-bitty pieces. "But it's kept me safe so far."

"Thank God," I whisper, brushing my hand over her perfect shoulder again.

She reaches up and wipes my forehead.

"I'm fine," I tell her as we both stare at the blood on her fingers.

She nods. Then she pulls me closer and kisses me—so quickly it's over before I can even process it. But I can still feel her heat in my lips.

"What was that for?"

"I've lost you twice in the last few days. I don't want any more regrets."

Well, I'm definitely a fan of *that* kind of thinking. But . . . "Wait—twice? When was the other time?"

"We'll talk about it later. Right now we have bigger things to worry about."

We both glance at Gus.

He looks sweaty and pale and is clearly in the middle of some sort of meltdown—not that I blame him.

I grab his arm and shake him as another spike pummels our hiding place. "Stay with us, okay?"

He nods, but it's a weak nod, and I can tell by the way he closes his eyes that we'll be lucky if he can manage to run on his own.

"There has to be a way out of this," I tell Audra. "I mean, we have the power of four. Aren't we supposed to be unstoppable?"

"Raiden plays by different rules."

The rock we're hiding behind explodes, but the shards and pebbles bounce off our shield. I try to tell myself that means it'll protect us, but when I spot two wind spikes headed straight for us, I can't help pulling Audra behind me to shield her myself.

We both duck and cover as the spikes hit their mark, and the ground vibrates from a shock wave that makes my ears ring. But when I lift my head, the Westerly is still covering us, creating a pocket of clear air in the thick wall of dust.

"A most impressive trick," Raiden shouts from somewhere across the basin. It's impossible to see through the chaos, but it sounds like he's getting closer. "You'll have to teach it to me when you're ready to surrender."

"Yeah, I don't think we're going to be doing that," I shout back—though I'm very aware that our safe little bubble leaves us very much trapped and outnumbered. "Any chance this thing is portable?" I ask Audra.

She runs her hands along the draft. "I can't think of a command that would do that, can you?"

I close my eyes and whisper my request, trying to let my instincts take over. But the wind's song turns quiet. Almost sad. Singing of burdens that are too heavy to carry alone.

"I think we'd need one for each of us," I tell her.

"We'd have two more Westerlies if we unraveled our wind spikes."

True . . .

"But then we'd have no weapons, no plan, nothing but a shield—and we have no idea how strong that shield is. Can it really hold up against a windslicer?"

"I don't know," Audra admits. "I don't even know if a Westerly would be willing to shield Gus, since he doesn't speak their language—and none of the other winds have a command that works like that. I think it's a Westerly thing. They're defensive winds, not offensive."

Three freaky-looking balls of dark, cloudy winds stick to our shield, and I pull Audra to the ground as they explode like grenades.

The poor Westerly screams as it suffers through the blow, but it still manages to keep its hold around us. It's the most stubborn, loyal wind I've ever seen. Probably why it likes Audra so much.

"Maybe we should fly, then," I say as Audra whispers soft words to encourage our faithful shield. "We could unravel the spikes and use the winds to get us the hell out of here."

"Do you really think we'll be able to outrun Raiden's entire army with a handful of tired drafts?"

"If we used the power of four."

She shakes her head. "There's a trick they can use that would hold us suspended in the sky—even with all four winds. I'm not sure how it works, but I've been trapped by it, and it left me spinning helplessly for hours. We need something too fast for them to interfere with, like a pipeline. But those require a very specific set of winds."

And they *suck*.

It's like voluntarily stepping into a tornado and letting it blast you somewhere at warp speed. But it's probably our best bet.

"We'll need a distraction," I decide. "Something that'll keep Raiden busy so we can get far enough away to find the winds to make a pipeline. Any ideas?"

Another round of freaky wind grenades attach to our shield, and Audra shouts at the poor Westerly to stay strong as they explode.

I've never heard a draft screech the way our shield does, like it's actually in physical pain. But still, it holds on.

"How many winds are in these wind spikes?" Audra asks, pointing to the two I made.

"Only one of each."

A giant boulder slams into our shield, but somehow the amazing Westerly rebounds it away. It crashes harmlessly next to us in a giant cloud of dust.

Audra sits up straighter. "What about a haboob?"

"I'm sorry, what?"

"A haboob. It's a massive dust storm that swallows everything in its path."

"Okay, I'm trying to think how that would work, but all I'm hearing is 'boob.'"

She glares at me as another wave of wind spikes smashes against us so hard I see our poor shield ripple. They must be almost on top of us, and I have a horrible feeling that when they get here they'll be able to reach right through our little dome of air, just like I can. Assuming the Westerly can even hold out until then.

"A haboob would work," Audra insists.

"Okay, you're going to *have* to stop calling it that."

She ignores me. "My father used to make them all the time. They're one of the best ways to cause mass confusion—which is what we need right now. My father always used Easterlies, but I bet we could do it with Westerlies."

"Okay, putting aside the haboob jokes—which I will be saving for later, by the way—how many drafts did your dad use for something like that?"

"Hundreds," she admits.

Another explosion of wind spikes rocks us, and we both whisper soothing words to calm the terrified shield.

"The three Westerlies we have might be enough, though," Audra says quietly. "Two in the spikes, plus the one wrapped over us. We need only a few minutes so we can get to higher ground and find the winds to blast out of here."

"Right, but in the meantime we'd have no weapons, no shield, no nothing."

"I don't see another option—do you?"

No.

But . . . "I've been training with the Westerlies, and it's very tricky to make them do anything *violent*. They're about peace and calm and shelter."

"I know, I've found the same thing. But haboobs are just a frenzy of force and dust. We're not hurting anyone. We're simply creating enough chaos to distract Raiden so he lets his guard down and a few healthy winds can seep in."

Another whammy of wind spikes attacks, and this time dust and rocks sprinkle through small gaps forming in our shield. The Westerly's not going to hold on much longer.

"So what do you want to do?" Audra asks me.

I can't make this decision.

If something goes wrong and Gus or Audra gets taken . . .

I take her hands, clearing my throat so I can force my next words out. "Listen. Raiden's not going to kill me. I could make a deal with him—"

"No, Vane. He's seen me speak Westerly too. And he'll kill Gus just for revenge—or keep him alive and . . ." She shudders, wrapping her arms around herself. "I've seen firsthand what he can do."

The greenish tinge to her skin and the tremble in her voice is enough to convince me.

"Well, then, I guess we'll just have to make this work," I say quietly. "And hope Westerlies have big haboobs."

CHAPTER 26

AUDRA

The Stormers are moving closer.

I can feel it in the force of the explosions.

In the fear surging through our loyal Westerly shield.

Raiden seemed shaken by Gus's attack. Thrown by the fact that he couldn't deter it. Furious that his army saw a hint of his weakness.

If he catches us now, it won't just be about learning our language. He'll also make sure we're punished violently and publicly so that there will be no question who reigns supreme. No doubt who holds the ultimate power.

My hands shake as I help Vane unravel our wind spikes, and I try to draw calm and peace from the Westerlies as I coil them around my wrist.

"What?" I ask when I catch Vane watching me.

A shy smile peeks from the corners of his lips, which seems out of place as the explosions echo around us.

"Sorry. It's just . . . every time the Gales ask me to teach them Westerly, I feel sick. I can't imagine trusting them with that responsibility. But when it's you, I . . ."

He doesn't finish, but his smile tells me what he's not saying. The same words I suddenly have to say, even though our time is running out—or maybe especially because of that. In case I never get another chance again, I have to tell him.

"I'm glad I chose you."

I counted on a goofy grin or the smug smirk I remember so well. Instead, his eyes turn glassy and he looks away.

He clears his throat. "So what's the command for a haboob? *Please* tell me it involves the word 'knockers.'"

I feel my lips smile, even though I'm panicking inside.

I saw my father make haboobs, but he never taught me what he was doing. And during my training in the Gales I was so focused on learning violent attacks that would take out the most soldiers that I never bothered learning anything else. I never knew there was power in restraint. Not until I started listening to Westerlies.

My whole life I was taught that the west wind was weak. No one realized how much power comes from winds that are willing to work *together*, instead of dominating, like the Northerlies. How caution steadies the drafts against the pitfalls that a brash Easterly might dive into. How they always stay swift and active, unlike the sluggish Southerlies. They're the most willing, compliant winds I've ever experienced—and whether that's because of their easy nature or a result of suffering so much loss and loneliness, I can't be sure. But I know I can convince them to do this. I just have to find the right words.

"Have you ever triggered a haboob?" I ask Gus, hoping the command might be the same in any language.

Gus shakes his head, his eyes still so blank I can't tell if he even understands me.

"You don't know how to make one?" Vane asks, sounding as nervous as I feel.

"I can figure this out," I promise, ordering myself to believe it.

I think back to the haboobs I've seen. My father always triggered a rapid downdraft that battered the ground so hard it kicked up the towering wall of dust. Most of the force came from how many winds he used, but if I can get my Westerlies to flow in a cycle—flying high and then crashing back down, over and over and over—they might be able to trigger the same effect after a few rotations.

But that's a complex command. A single word isn't going to explain that many steps. For that I'll need a chain of words, like when I call the wind.

The Westerlies swirling around my wrist feel too distracted— too overwhelmed by all the chaos to share their secrets. So I focus on my loyal shield, hating that I have to turn to it again. The draft feels weary and faded and its voice is hushed, its words now stuttered as it sings.

The sound breaks my heart, and I wish I could send the poor wind away, tell it to wander through the endless sky and never worry about me again. But I still need its help, so I whisper a soft apology and beg it for another favor.

The draft's song turns sad and sweet, whispering about carrying on when all else feels bleak. And one phrase stands out from the others.

The force of peace.

The harder I focus on it, the more I feel other words tingle inside my mind, swirling and building until I know what my instincts are telling me to say.

> *Surge and swell and rise to increase.*
> *Then fall and crash with the force of peace.*

The *rightness* of the command makes my tongue feel heavy, desperate to whisper the words and put them to work. But not yet. Not until the Stormers are closer and I can be sure the chaos will affect them the way we need.

Vane reaches for my hand as the ground shakes again, and I can feel the poor shield fighting to hold on, clinging to the three of us with any strength it has left.

"I want you to promise me something," Vane says, waiting for me to look at him. "If something goes wrong and Raiden captures me, I want you to make a run for it—no, don't argue." He presses my palm against his cheek, closing his eyes as the sparks dance between us. "I'm strong enough to handle whatever Raiden does to me. But I'm *not* strong enough to watch him hurt you."

"Vane—"

"No, really, Audra. Raiden's been messing with my head these last few weeks, giving me nightmares, making me imagine that he had you and he was . . ." He shudders. "I *never* want that to be real. So I need you to promise me that if you can get away, you will. Even if it means leaving me behind. And try to take Gus if you can."

I glance at Gus, who's clearly in shock—not moving or blinking. I can barely tell if he's breathing. The thought of saving him instead of Vane makes me want to scream. But I can tell Vane needs this, so I nod. "Hopefully, I won't have to."

"But if you do?"

"Then I promise."

He grabs me and kisses me. Still electric and hungry and addictive. But there's a sadness this time and I realize he's saying goodbye.

I won't let him give up hope like that.

I press closer, trying to let him feel my confidence, trying to show him he can believe in me again, trying to—

"So these are the warriors who think they can defeat me? Two lovesick teenagers and a guardian who looks ready to soil himself?"

Vane and I break away and find a circle of Stormers surrounding us. Raiden stands in the center, so close that I can see the slate blue of his eyes. The angles of his jaw. The loose strands of hair that flop across his forehead.

There's something almost charming about his smile as he says, "The two of you will get to be my *very* special guests. Especially you." He points to me, and I feel Vane's grip tighten on my hand. "As for you"—he turns to Gus—"you will get the honor of replacing the Living Storm you destroyed. And I'll make sure the process is *especially* painful this time."

The taunt snaps Gus out of his daze, and in one blur of motion he dives for Raiden and—

Crashes into the wall of our shield and slams back to the dirt.

"Fascinating," Raiden says as he steps forward, running his hands along the edge of the Westerly.

I see Vane holding his breath and realize I'm doing the same. But no matter how hard Raiden presses, his hand cannot pass through the shield's barrier.

"Once again, your abilities are very impressive. And yet, your carelessness betrays you." He reaches behind him and pulls out the wind spike Gus attacked him with. "I suspect I could use this to blast right through your little shelter—much the way you used it to shred my Living Storm. But I'd hate to risk wrecking my new toy."

He runs his palm along the precise edge and I have to stop myself from lunging for him.

"Come!" Vane shouts in Westerly, and the spike launches out of Raiden's grip and slips straight through the shield.

Before Vane even catches it, the Stormers draw their windslicers and charge—but they're knocked back by the shield, which is still miraculously holding strong.

Raiden laughs, tossing his head back so far I can see down his throat. "Bravo. But what's your move now? Are you going to run me through? The winds told me how well it went for you the last time you got violent. But maybe you think you're stronger now." He steps forward, holding out his arms and baring his chest. "Go ahead, then."

"Do it," Gus begs him.

"Don't," I whisper.

There's no way Raiden would take such a risk—even if he thinks Vane is too peaceful. He must have a defense we can't see, and if Vane attacks, it'll backfire against us.

Vane looks at Gus. Then at me.

His grip loosens on the spike.

Gus shakes his head as Raiden laughs again. "That's what I thought."

"I'm not going to kill you," Vane says, his voice darker than I've ever heard it. "Because death would be too easy."

"Really? Is that what it was for your parents?" Raiden asks. "Easy?"

"No. They had something to live for. But you?" He whispers the command to uncoil the wind spike and smiles when Raiden's jaw falls. "All you have is power. And I'm going to take it away. Make you live out the rest of your days knowing you came *so* close and still managed to fail. And then you can die, alone and useless."

"If I don't kill him first," Gus growls.

Raiden leans down to Vane's eye level. "I know what you have to live for too"—he glances at me—"and I'm looking forward to making you watch as I break her apart piece by piece."

Vane's shaking as he reaches for my other hand. I start to twine our fingers together, but he resists, coiling the Westerly he unraveled from the wind spike around my wrist.

Our eyes meet and I feel a shiver in my core when I realize what he's telling me.

It's time.

I soak up one last rush of warmth from Vane's touch to steel my courage as I concentrate on the four Westerlies we now have. I'm tempted to keep our shield and use only the three from the wind spikes—but the drafts are so timid and weary, I know they won't be enough.

Even with the shield working with them, they *still* might not be enough.

But we have to risk it.

One deep breath calms my racing heart. Then I shout the Westerly command and the shield unravels, tangling with the other winds as they streak into the sky.

The Stormers raise their windslicers and jump back, bracing for the winds to attack. But when the drafts crash to the ground, they don't even kick up enough dust to make a cloud.

Raiden laughs so hard it echoes around the canyon. "And thus ends the final stand of the last living Westerlies."

The Stormers drag us to our feet as the winds return. But when they crash again they barely stir up more dust than the first time.

Raiden laughs harder, shouting a word that makes his draining gray winds tangle around Vane and Gus as he grabs my wrist with one hand and unsheathes his windslicer with his other. The blade is a dull black color, and when he presses the needled edge into my side, the hundreds of razor-sharp points burn and sting with an energy I've never felt before. I'm sure being struck by lightning is less painful.

Vane thrashes to get to me—but the Stormer holds him too

tightly. And when the Westerlies touch down again, their crash is almost weaker this time, only scattering a few pebbles.

"Now who's the powerful one?" Raiden asks as he presses the blade deeper into my side.

This time I bite back my scream, but I feel blood running down my skin and I can see Vane watching it. He wrenches himself free from the Stormer, but with his arms and legs still bound by the draining winds, he crumples to the dry, cracked ground in a heap.

Raiden kicks him in the shoulder so hard it leaves a welt immediately. "I could split her in half right now and there's nothing you could do to stop me. Though it does seem like such a waste."

He runs his fingers over my wounded hip, making my skin burn with the salt of his sweaty touch.

Tears stream down Vane's face as he struggles forward, but Raiden kicks him again, this time in his side. I hear the crunch of bone as Vane collapses and doesn't move. The sickly winds binding him have turned him pale—and when I turn back to Gus I see he's already passed out.

"Please," I beg the Westerlies when I feel them crash down again. "Please fight harder. Please help us."

Three of the winds don't respond. But my loyal shield sweeps to my side, coiling around me, easing the pain of my wound with its cool breeze. I close my eyes, and as I sink into the calm, I feel two words burn my tongue.

Get help.

I shout them and the draft races away, gathering with the others before they whip into the sky.

"Looks like your winds have abandoned you," Raiden whispers in my ear. "Such is the folly of giving them a *choice*."

He pulls his windslicer away—cutting me one more time in the process—and tangles me in his wicked winds. The sharp, draining drafts drag across my skin and I feel my energy fade. My ears start to ring and my vision turns dim and I'm about to surrender to the darkness when a clap louder than thunder erupts all around, rocking the ground so hard, Raiden loses his grip on me.

I collapse to my knees, coughing from the cloud of dust that burns my eyes as I fight to breathe. The thick brown air blurs everything, but I can make out a dark splotch on the ground nearby and scramble toward it, feeling my first real hope when I see that it's Raiden's windslicer.

The earth shakes again and I realize it's the Westerlies. Dozens of them—maybe even hundreds—crashing in unison and kicking up so much sand the sky turns black. I hear coughing and screaming as Raiden and the Stormers command their broken winds, but the ruined drafts only swirl the dust and debris more.

I wriggle in my bonds, twisting until I free my right hand. I can barely bend the wrist, but I manage to grab the hilt of the windslicer and tilt the blade up enough that when I lean against it, the winds binding me unravel in a puff of smoke. Then I grab the windslicer and stumble to my feet, groping through the blinding dust, unable to tell if I'm moving toward Vane or away.

My progress is slow, and twice I bump into Stormers and barely duck the sweep of their blade. I shout for my loyal shield and the draft rushes to my side.

When it drapes itself around me, I can finally breathe and see again, and I take off running, searching for Vane and Gus—hoping the Stormers haven't dragged them away. I find Gus first—cast aside like a pile of trash. His head falls limply as I move him, but when I sever his bonds, his eyes flutter open—and then immediately close from the dust.

I call another Westerly and beg it to shield him. The draft doesn't want to obey, but it finally agrees to coil around Gus's face, clearing the air enough for him to breathe.

"Where's Vane?" he asks when he's done coughing and hacking.

"I don't know." I pull Gus to his feet and he reaches for Raiden's windslicer. My training screams for me to resist, but I remind myself of what happened when I attacked Aston. Better to have the weapon in the hands of someone capable of killing.

"Please," I whisper to my Westerly shield. "If you know where Vane is, help me find him."

The draft doesn't respond, leaving Gus and me on our own.

Gus grabs my hand so we can't get separated and we wade into the thickest part of the storm.

"You and Vane are bonded, right?" he shouts as we run. "I didn't imagine that part?"

My face burns as I nod, but I hear no judgment in his tone when he says, "Then can't you feel where he is?"

He slashes at a Stormer who crosses our path, and I close my eyes, trying not to think about the spray of red. "The pull of our bond weakens when we're this close to each other, but I'll see if I can feel it."

I ask my Westerly to leave me for a minute so I can search for Vane's trace.

The dust is so thick it coats my tongue, but I force myself to concentrate, searching for a hint of warmth or some sign of contact in the other winds. I feel like I've swallowed half the desert before I finally feel the electric tingle I need.

I tighten my grip on Gus's hand and we take off running, him slashing anything in our path and me following the heat in the air until I crash into a bare chest.

"Thank God you're okay," Vane says as I wrap my shield back around me and call one for him.

I wait for the Westerlies to blanket us like second skins. Then I fall into Vane's arms and cling to him as tightly as I can.

Vane squeezes me back, but his arm bumps the gash in my side, and I hate myself for wincing.

He pulls away, staring at the blood on his hand. "I'll kill Raiden."

"No—he's *mine*," Gus insists.

"Actually—you're both wrong," Raiden calls, parting the dust enough to show where he's been hiding. He's coated in sickly gray winds and he looks pale and green from their effects. But they seem to let him breathe in the storm. "Once again, you've managed to impress me with your powers. But it's time to stop these foolish games. Call off this ridiculous haboob and I promise I'll let you all live."

"Or we kill you now," Gus says, holding up Raiden's windslicer.

"Try it, see what happens."

I put my hand on Gus's shoulder to stop him. I'm sure Raiden isn't bluffing.

The Westerlies crash again, but Raiden doesn't even flinch.

We won't be able to get away from him—not unless we do something new. And that's when I realize that my Westerly has changed its song again.

Every verse now ends with the same word—like it's begging me to listen to the clue. The command doesn't make sense, but this draft hasn't failed me so far.

I tighten my grip on Gus and Vane and shout, *"Fuse!"*

The Westerlies shift direction, collecting together, swelling thicker and stronger. I'd thought the storm was chaos before, but now it's an impenetrable wall of choking dust that traps all the Stormers—even Raiden—in the heavy air that Gus, Vane, and I are allowed to move through with ease. Our Westerly shields must be telling the other winds to let us pass.

We run as fast as we can, not looking back as the ground gets steeper. And the higher we climb, the more the air clears until we're finally able to gather the winds we need for a pipeline.

"Wait," Vane shouts, adding a Westerly to the mix before I give the final command.

Then he takes my hand, grabbing Gus with his other as he shouts *"Enhance!"* and the vortex expands around us, blasting us out of the valley.

CHAPTER 27

VANE

I can't believe we're alive.

Well . . . for now.

I don't know how long that crazy wind-sludge stuff will trap Raiden in Death Valley, but I'm betting it's asking too much for it to last a few hundred years. Odds are, we have a couple of hours. Maybe less.

The vortex spits us out into the open air, and I do useful things like scream and flail while Audra unravels the pipeline and Gus gathers Southerlies and tangles them around us to slow our fall. At least I remember to release the Westerly shields. We owe our lives to those weary drafts. They deserve to be free.

The winds around Gus and me zip into the gray twilight sky. But Audra's shield tightens its grip, and from the smile on her face I can tell she wants it to stay. Only Audra could make a Westerly her new pet.

"Where are we?" Gus asks when we touch down in the middle of yet another desert. I'm starting to wonder if that's all there is in this freaking state when I realize we're not actually in California anymore.

The skyline in the distance has a castle, an Eiffel Tower, and a blinking neon pyramid. Leave it to me to blast us all the way to Vegas.

"Looks like we're at least three hours from home. Unless someone wants to hit the buffets first? Or maybe get married by Elvis?"

I realize the awkward mess I've stepped in the second the joke leaves my mouth.

"That's not a proposal," I tell Audra, wondering if her cheeks are as red as mine feel. It's hard to tell in the dim moonlight. "I would never—well, I don't mean *never*—I just mean . . . I would do it way better than that—not that I'm thinking about proposing—at least not *now*—I just . . ."

Please, somebody kill me now.

Then Gus clears his throat and I realize there's a whole other level of awkward to this situation.

I sigh. "Listen. I know I can't ask you to—"

"Don't worry, I'm not going to tell anyone," Gus interrupts. "This one's your mess. I'm staying out of it."

Well, that's good—I guess. I don't know, I'm kinda over the whole "hiding it" thing. But I'll have to talk to Audra and see how she feels about going public.

"But just so I'm clear," Gus adds, "*she's* the one you were sneaking off to the mountains to check for all the time, right?"

"All the time?" Audra repeats.

"Every chance I could," I admit. "Finding your trace was the only thing that kept me going."

Her face falls and I reach for her. "Hey—I didn't mean it like that. I just missed you. I—" My hand brushes something wet on her side and she flinches. "You're still bleeding?"

I lift the side of her shirt, and my head starts to cloud when I see the dark, jagged gash that starts above her hip and stretches onto her stomach.

"I'm fine," she insists as I search for something I can use to cover the wound.

I try to tear off the bottom of my shorts, but the thick cargo fabric refuses to rip.

Why did I have to take off my stupid shirt?

"Hey," she says, coiling her Westerly around her waist, "It's okay, see? The wind helps us heal."

I can't tell if the cool breeze is actually stopping the blood or just whisking it away—but I guess it'll have to do until we can get home.

"Do you feel any threat?" Audra asks Gus, who has his hands stretched out, searching the air.

"No. I don't feel anything."

He stalks off into the desert without another word.

It's hard to see in the dim light, but I hear him unsheathe his windslicer and start hacking the crap out of something.

Audra looks at me, and I know she's waiting for me to go talk to him. But what am I supposed to say? I'm assuming this is about his dad, and I suck at emotional things like this.

Several minutes pass and Gus is still going to town, so I finally make my way over.

"Hey," I mumble, off to a brilliant start. "Um . . . you okay?"

"Oh yeah, I'm awesome." He takes another swing, slicing the top off a dry, scraggly bush.

"Look. I know you're angry—and I don't blame you. What happened to Feng was—and I don't mean what *you* did to the Storm thing . . . I mean what Raiden did. By the time you got there he . . ."

Wow, I *really* suck at this.

"I know that *thing* wasn't my father," Gus growls, slashing another plant. "And I always knew I would probably lose him. It's what happens to guardians—it's in the oath we all swear. It's just"— he sighs and stares up at the stars—"there's really nothing left. I can't even find his echo."

"I never found my father's either," Audra says, coming up beside me. "And I know it probably sounds crazy but . . . sometimes I wonder if that's because he's not *really* gone. It feels like there's still part of him left—a small hint of his presence carried on a breeze, that finds me when I need him most."

Her voice cracks and I reach for her hand.

She never told me that—and I have no idea if it's possible. But I hope it's true.

Gus must too, because he takes a deep breath and slides the dark blade of his windslicer back in its sheath.

Raiden's windslicer.

I want to grab it and hurtle it into the desert as far as I can—bu a scarier thought stops me cold.

We took Raiden's weapon.

And we escaped.

And I taunted him in front of everyone.

If Raiden went after Gus's mom to punish Feng for his victory— how much more will he want to retaliate against me for all of that?

"I have to get home," I say, kicking myself for not thinking of this sooner. How many minutes have we already wasted?

Solana's with my parents—and I haven't told them to come back, so they shouldn't be home yet. But I bet Raiden has a way to track them down.

Audra must know what I'm thinking because she puts a hand on my shoulder. "The Gales will protect them."

I nod, hoping she's right—but when we left, the Gales had all been called away. And even if they're back, protecting my family has never been a very high priority. . . .

"We should use another pipeline to get back," I say, cringing as I suggest it. Hurtling through one feels like getting launched from a slingshot, blasted through a giant vacuum, and then flung back toward the ground at rocket speed.

Audra shakes her head. "Pipelines should only be used for emergencies."

"This *is* an emergency!"

"No, she's right. They're pretty unstable—especially over a lon distance," Gus tells me. "And if they collapse while you're in ther there's nothing you can do."

Funny how Audra never mentioned that when she taught me how to make them.

"But we made it to Vegas," I remind them. "Maybe the fourth wind makes pipelines safer."

"Or we got lucky," Gus argues. "I thought my head was going to explode, didn't you?"

Actually, I thought my skin was going to tear off—but I don't want to admit that. I *have* to get home.

Audra squeezes my hand. "Flying with the power of four will get us there in half the time. And I don't think Raiden's going to make a move yet, anyway. He called the Living Storm the first of his new army—I can't see him attacking until he's made more. But even if we *are* racing toward another battle, we need time to come up with a strategy, and we can do that along the journey."

She calls drafts from all four winds and weaves them into a wind bubble around the three of us. "I think we should fly together. Everyone hold tight."

Gus moves behind me and grabs my shoulders. I can tell he's trying to avoid where Raiden kicked me, but the bruise covers my whole freaking shoulder blade. The one on my side is even worse, and it aches every time I take a deep breath. I wouldn't be surprised if Raiden cracked a few ribs.

But it's nothing compared to what he did to Audra. I try to find a spot on her waist that's safe to grab, but it's all too raw and bloody. She takes my hands and slides them lower.

"Don't get any ideas," she mumbles when we both realize that I'm practically cupping her butt.

If Gus weren't here and my family wasn't in danger—and she weren't *bleeding*—I would have *lots* of ideas. But under the circumstances, all I want to do is get back to my valley as fast as we can.

Audra shouts, "Rise," and we blast into the sky faster than I've ever flown before. The stars turn to a blur and I hear Audra whispering adjustments, keeping the winds in check as we fly. But her voice sounds tired, and the shadows under her eyes are almost as dark as my bruise.

"Hey," I say, pulling her closer. "Let me take over. You need to rest."

She smiles. "It probably wouldn't be a good idea to let us plummet to our deaths."

"Uh—I *can* windwalk. How else do you think I got here? Took me a few tries to get it right, but once I figured out how to hear the wind's undertones, it was easy."

"Undertones?"

"Yeah. Like right now, the Easterlies are longing to spin to the left. So I would coax them back on path."

She sucks in a breath.

"What—does something hurt?"

"No, it's just . . . that's my father's gift . . ."

"Is it? Well, I guess you must've shared it with me when we bonded."

Audra shakes her head. "I've never heard of gifts passing during a bond. My parents' didn't. My mom had hers—my dad had his."

"Mine too," Gus mumbles.

Audra's quiet for so long I have to finally ask, "Are you okay?"

"Yeah, I'm just trying to figure out what it means. I've never heard of bonds sharing languages either, and yet . . ."

I pull her even closer, feeling an explosion of heat rush between us as I whisper, "I think it means we were meant to be together."

"If you two start making out I will fling you out of the wind bubble," Gus warns.

I can't help laughing.

"Later," I whisper to Audra, loving when I feel her shiver.

I still can't believe she's here. Back in my arms after all these weeks.

"Aren't we supposed to be coming up with a strategy?" Gus asks, and I totally hate him for being right.

We need something better than his grab-and-stab plan, since that didn't exactly go well in Death Valley. Not that Audra's attack-the-Living-Storm-all-by-herself plan was much better.

"Why were you there?" I ask, realizing she never explained. "Did you know Raiden was going to be there today?"

"No. Aston told me I should go to Death Valley—but I doubt he knew Raiden was going to be there."

"Aston?" I want to snuff out the sudden wave of jealousy—but that totally sounds like one of those preppy British guys that girls are always fawning all over.

It doesn't make me feel any better when Gus asks, "Wait—Aston as in . . . *Aston?*"

Audra nods.

They both don't say anything else for so long that my mind has time to turn Aston into the sylph James Bond. Then Audra tells me he's a crazy ex-Gale who held her hostage in a cave up north, and by the end of her story I'm biting my inner cheek so hard I taste blood.

"Did he . . . ?" I can't even say it.

She reaches out and strokes my face. "He didn't hurt me. I think he was mainly just . . . lonely."

I don't like the way she says that word—like she almost feels sorry for the guy who tied her up and threatened to kill her. Ex-Gale or not, that's an automatic qualification for the You Are Dead to Me list I've started making.

"You really don't think he knew Raiden was going there?" Gus asks.

"No, I think that was a fluke. I do believe the Easterlies who coaxed me there knew that Raiden was on his way. But I think Aston sent me because he wanted me to see the Maelstrom."

This time Gus shivers. "I've heard of those."

Audra stares into the darkness. "It was much more evil than the rumors."

Evil.

The word gives me a strange flutter in my stomach.

I still haven't decided how I feel about Arella being trapped in a Maelstrom. But it doesn't feel like a good sign that Audra sounds so freaked out.

I wonder how she'll react when I tell her about her mom—not that I have any idea how to do that. I'll have to find the right time to bring it up.

Not tonight. We have enough going on—and even if we're safe, I can think of lots of better ways to spend our first night back together.

We whiz past the glowing hotel of a massive Indian casino, which means we're finally getting close. Audra slows the winds when the weird Cabazon dinosaurs blur by. Then she changes course, steering us into the mountains and setting us down on one of the lower peaks.

I hold my breath as we all listen for signs of a storm.

The sky is clear. The winds calm.

"All the drafts coming from the northeast say nothing about an attack," Audra says, closing her eyes. "And I feel no unrest in the valley."

"Me either," Gus agrees.

We all push our senses as far as they can go, but everything is quiet.

A little too quiet.

"Where are the Gales?" Audra whispers.

"They went to find my father." Gus's voice hitches on the word, and he has to clear his throat before he continues. "The Stormers made a false trail, and I guess the Gales haven't figured it out yet. I'll use the emergency call to get them back and bring them up to speed."

"Do you want us to stay with—"

"No," Gus cuts me off. "I really need some space."

I nod.

Audra nods too. Then she wraps her arms around me, sending tingling waves of heat through my aching shoulders as I tangle us in Westerlies and fly us back to my house.

All the windows are dark as we touch down on the grass, so my family must still be on the move like I thought. I know I should call them and tell them to come home, but they're probably safer out there. Plus, Audra and I could use some time alone. We have a lot to figure out.

"So . . . ," I say after I've tested the air to double-check that we're safe. "Now what?"

"I don't know."

She stares at her feet and tucks her hair behind her ear.

It's bizarre to see her look so shy. Even more bizarre to think that she's here, standing outside my house, holding my hand.

We're not broken up.

In fact, I'm pretty sure we've never been more together.

All that's left to figure out is "Your place or mine?"

Her nervous laugh rings through the night.

I pull her closer, wrapping her arms around my neck, and I suck in a breath as the heat of her body sparks against me. I sorta forgot I was shirtless—but I'm *very* aware of it now.

Very aware of how tiny her tank top is too.

I clear my throat. "Seems like a pretty simple decision to me. On the one hand, your place has scratchy palm leaves. And bugs. And dead things."

"Dead things?"

"Gavin's been busy. He's pretty pissed at you, by the way. He may tear out some of your hair when he sees you."

"I wouldn't blame him." She leans her head against my chest, triggering a new wave of sparks that makes it very hard to breathe.

"So then . . . my place?" I whisper. "No psycho bird. Everything we need to get cleaned up. Then a nice soft bed . . ."

She leans back to look at me. "I don't think that's a good idea."

"Actually, I think it's a *very* good idea. Pretty much the best idea I've ever had."

She smiles and steps up to her tiptoes, pecking me on the lips before she pulls away.

I grab her hands to stop her from leaving. "I promise, I'll be a perfect gentleman."

She doesn't look convinced.

I drop my eyes to our hands, twisting our fingers together. "I just . . . I feel like if I let you out of my sight, you might disappear again."

Sadness seeps into her features and she lifts my hand to her lips, kissing the center of my palm. "I'm not going anywhere."

"Then stay with me."

I can hardly believe it when she nods, and my legs get all weak and wobbly as I lead her toward the house.

I forgot to bring a key to the front door, so we head toward my bedroom, and I can't help turning toward the date grove—where Feng will never wait for me again.

I swallow the lump in my throat as I try to open my window. It's locked too.

Audra laughs and nudges me aside, sending a draft under the sill that clicks the lock and slides open the window in one go, like she's done it a thousand times before. I smile when I realize she has.

But this time is different.

This time I'm not asleep, and she's not sneaking around.

She climbs in first and I copy her steps, for once making it inside without scraping my skin on the thorns. And as soon as my feet hit the rug, I pull her against me, kissing her forehead, her cheeks, her—

"I thought you were going to be the perfect gentleman," she whispers against my lips.

"Well, maybe not *perfect*."

I feel her mouth twist with a smile as she slides her hands up my neck and tangles her fingers in my hair. "I was hoping you'd say that."

She kisses me then, and the sparks are so hot, so bright, I swear they almost blind me—but when I open my eyes, I really am blind and it has nothing to do with the kiss.

The lamp by my bed is now switched on, and as I squint through the glaring light, I see a movement in the covers.

I have just enough time to think, *Craaaaaaaaaaaaaaap.*

Then Solana tosses her hair and says, "I guess this is the real reason why you canceled our betrothal."

CHAPTER 28

AUDRA

I don't know what to feel as I watch Solana untangle her long, tanned legs from the covers of Vane's bed.

She's prettier than I remember. Soft curls and bright eyes and toned, graceful limbs.

And Vane only seems a little surprised to see her.

Mostly, he looks *guilty*.

I try to pull my hands away but he tightens his grip. "It's *not* what it looks like."

"Really?" Solana snaps, before I can form a coherent reply. "Because it *looks* like you're bonded to another girl."

Vane turns around to face her. "Well, okay, I guess it *is* what it looks like to you—and I'm sorry you had to find out like this." He turns back to me. "But I promise, she's only here because she offered to protect my parents while I was gone. And she wasn't even supposed to be home," he adds, turning back to Solana. "You said you'd take them somewhere safe."

"I did. And then I heard on the winds that the Gales had turned back, so we did the same."

"That doesn't explain why you're in his bed," I say, wishing I didn't sound as jealous as I feel. She has just as much right to be there as me—probably more, since she's the one with the promise link on her wrist.

Still, an irrational rage makes me want to claw at her face when she crosses her arms and says, "Vane and I have been sleeping together."

"*Just* sleeping," Vane corrects—glaring at her before he turns back to me. "And only because I was desperate. I told you Raiden was giving me nightmares, right? Solana knows a trick that blocks them."

I want to nod—want to make the pieces of his story fit together into a truth that washes away the sour lump in my throat.

But I can't stop staring at the dent in Vane's pillow, imagining Solana lying in the dark, waiting for him to crawl into bed next to her.

Is that what he wanted?

"Hey," Vane says, turning my chin toward him and forcing me to look in his eyes. They're wide and worried and focused only on me. "I promise, I dreamed about you the entire time."

"You did?" Solana and I ask at the same time.

I'm mildly triumphant when he ignores her and tells me, "I dreamed about the day I tried to run away when I was seven. Do you remember that? It was snowing and I got lost in the woods and then I fell and couldn't get up and I thought I was going to die out there all alone. But you found me, and you called your dad and he brought me home. And even though we weren't friends, you stayed with me that night by the fire until I fell asleep. I asked you to stay and you stayed."

I hear Solana mumble the word "stay," but I can't pull my eyes away from Vane.

I'd blocked out that moment with everything else about that time in my life. But I do remember finding him in the woods, trembling like a fallen fledgling and clinging to my hand like I was the only thing that mattered in the world. And I remember staring at him later that night, as the firelight danced across his skin, and thinking he had a nice face.

I was seven and I didn't even know what that thought meant.

But it was there.

Before Raiden's Stormer broke our lives apart and the Gales made their grand plans for Vane.

"Vane—is that you?"

Vane grumbles something under his breath as his mom bursts into the room. "Thank God—I've been so worried. . . ."

Her words fade away when she notices me.

"Oh." Her eyes dart from Solana to Vane. Then back to me. "Oh."

"Don't start, Mom," Vane warns as he reaches for my hand. "It's been a long day."

Start what? I wonder as his mom steps closer to examine the bruise on his shoulder. It looks so much more painful in the bright light—though the one on his side is worse. I can't even look at the wide blue-black splotch without feeling my eyes burn.

"What happened?" she asks, her hand shaking as she reaches for the cut on his cheek. "I thought Gus was taking you somewhere safe—where is he? And when did Audra—"

"Can we save the twenty questions for later?" Vane interrupts. "I'm fine. Gus is waiting for the other Gales, and the rest is a really long story I don't have the energy to tell right now. But it involves Raiden. And a giant haboob."

"You saw Raiden?" Solana whispers.

He nods and she shivers and wraps her arms around herself— which makes her dress cut even lower on her chest.

I glance at Vane to see if he noticed, but he's not looking at her. He's looking at me—at the wound on my side.

He leans down, lifting the hem of my shirt, and even I can't help gasping when I see the gash in the light. The Westerly is keeping it clean for me, but the cut is deep and the jagged skin is practically shredded.

I try to cover the ugly wound, but Vane grabs my hands to stop me. "Do we still have a first aid kit, Mom?"

"She needs to go to the hospital. You both probably do. I'll go wake your dad—"

"We can't do that, Mom. The doctors would have all kinds of questions about how we got hurt. Plus human medicine makes us sick, remember?"

"Right," she mumbles. "Not human."

She stares at the three of us, looking lost and helpless.

"I'll be *fine*," I tell everyone, lifting Vane's hands and draping his arms around my shoulders, which I know he won't resist. He takes my cue, pulling me against him, and I can't help glancing at Solana.

She glares at me before she looks away.

She still wants him.

"Please let my mom treat the cut," Vane whispers, his breath grazing my cheek. "I'd rather not have it turn into a giant, gangrene-filled hole in your side."

I shudder, unable to stop myself from thinking of Aston.

"We have to do something," his mom chimes in. "Come on, I'll get you the gauze and ointment."

I hate the idea of leaving Solana and Vane alone. But I feel better when I see Vane's sweet, worried eyes focused completely on me as I follow his mom out of the room.

She leads me to a cluttered bathroom that has to be Vane's. Everything about it screams "guy," from the musty clothes and towels piled on the floor to the streaked mirror speckled with dried flecks of water.

"Sorry about the mess," she says as she bends and removes a white box marked with a red cross from the cabinet under the sink. "You know how Vane is."

I don't realize she meant it as a question until she turns to face me, waiting for my response.

"I . . . do" is the best I can come up with.

Her face is impossible to read as she soaks a clean white towel with steaming water from the faucet. I reach to take it from her but she doesn't let go. "Don't worry. I've treated plenty of scrapes and cuts over the years. Vane was a very accident-prone kid."

"Yes, I remember."

"Oh. So . . . you knew him back then?"

I nod.

"What about before his parents were . . . ?"

"Vane didn't tell you?"

"He hasn't told me *anything*."

I'm not sure how much I should say. But I can tell she's desperate for me to fill in some of the blanks. "I've known Vane since he was six. My parents were in charge of protecting his family."

Her eyes widen as she processes that.

"Did your parents survive the storm?" she whispers.

"My mother did."

I leave out *why*. It's safe to assume she wouldn't be looking at me with sad, sympathetic eyes if she knew I was the daughter of a murderer. And I can't say I'd blame her.

I clear my throat. "Anyway, after that, I volunteered to be his guardian, and I've been watching him ever since. Trying to keep him safe."

"I can't decide if that's sweet or kind of . . . weird," she says after a second.

"Me either, honestly."

She smiles. But it's a hesitant smile. A tired smile.

"Did Vane know you were watching him?"

"I think he wondered. There were a few times when he accidentally saw me—but they were too quick for him to tell if I was real.

He didn't know for sure until about a month ago, when the Stormers found us and I had to show myself so I could protect him."

She nods, wringing the towel in her hands. "And now . . . you're back?"

This time I don't miss the question in her tone.

I wait for her to look at me before I tell her, "As long as he wants me to be."

I can't tell if she's happy with that answer. It shouldn't matter, but . . .

I want his mom to like me.

It's silly and childish and probably impossible. But seeing how fiercely she loves her son makes me ache for a small sliver of acceptance—something I could hold on to, to tell myself I deserve the beautiful boy I've stolen. Maybe it would ease a tiny bit of the guilt that swells inside me every time I think about the angry betrayal I saw in Solana's eyes.

"Can you lift up your shirt a little more?" Vane's mom asks, holding out the towel.

I do, leaning against the counter as she squats down and touches the skin around my wound.

Her fingers are gentle but confident as she smoothes the jagged edges of the cut. "This looks really painful."

"I've had worse."

She frowns, and I think she's going to ask me what I mean. Instead she says, "Is there a *breeze* swirling around your skin?"

"Oh—yes. It's been keeping the wound clean for me."

"Uh-huh," she mumbles as I unravel the draft and carry it to the

window above the shower. I have to balance on the edge of the tub to reach it.

I can tell the Westerly doesn't want to leave, but it's time to let it go. "Stay safe," I plead as I stand on my tiptoes and slide open the glass. The draft whips around me, singing a song about drifting through the dunes, and I hope that means it will stay nearby—but I'm not going to tell it to. The wind deserves a *choice*.

I hold it up to the screen, letting it slip through the tiny holes as I whisper a final thanks and tell it to "Be free."

"Sometimes I have to remind myself that I'm not crazy," his mom murmurs as I watch the draft float away. "I mean, you talk to the wind. And you fly. And you bring my son home bruised and bleeding and . . ."

Her hands are shaking so much that she drops the towel.

I step down from the tub and pick it up for her.

She leans against the counter, twisting the ends. "I'm sorry, I know it's not your fault. I just . . . I feel so helpless. Nobody taught me how to raise a sylph king."

"Well, you're doing an incredible job. And we all know how difficult Vane is."

Her lip trembles, and even though she smiles, tears slip down her cheeks. "Promise me you'll keep him safe."

"I'm doing everything I can."

She clears the emotion from her throat, wiping her eyes as she kneels closer to me. "Right, I'm supposed to be helping you."

I grit my teeth as she presses the rag against my cut.

"Does that hurt?" she asks, lightening the pressure.

"It's just different from what I'm used to." When the wind cleans a wound, it feels more natural. But the real difference is the concern in her eyes. I'm not sure my own mother has ever looked at me that way.

Fresh blood seeps from the gash, and his mom wipes it away before spreading a thick, clear balm over the wound. She presses a square of soft cotton over my side and tapes the edges to hold it in place. I trace my fingers along her handiwork when she's done, surprised at how much better my side feels.

"Thank you."

She smiles, but it twists into a frown when she takes another look at me. "Do you want to clean up a bit? You look like . . ."

"I've been drowned in the ocean and trapped in a sandstorm?"

Her eyes widen, and I'm glad I left out the part about the pile of dead bodies I hid in. Just thinking about it makes me want to burn everything I'm wearing.

"I don't think you should shower until the wound heals a bit more. But you can wash up with these." She pulls a stack of clean white towels from the cabinet and points to the sink. "And I'll see if I can find you a change of clothes. I'll wash your . . . is it a uniform?"

"It used to be. And I'm hoping it will be again."

"Well, I can wash it for you tonight."

She leaves me then and I strip down, surprised at how good it feels to be out of my clothes. The wind keeps them mostly clean, blowing away any filth that settles into the fibers. But a thorough wash would be a nice, fresh start.

I lean into the sink, rinsing the sand and salt out of my hair and

scrubbing my face clean. My skin turns pink as I wipe it with warm, soaked towels, then fades to its normal pale color.

My scars are even paler.

Thin white lines scattered across my body, each one a souvenir from training or battles I fought.

Protecting *Vane.*

I trace my fingers over them, remembering the pain from every wound.

I'm not tanned or soft or nearly as beautiful as Solana—and I may not be the one the Gales chose.

But I *earned* him.

And if I have to fight for him, I will.

CHAPTER 29

VANE

I keep waiting for Solana to leave—or at least say *something*. But she doesn't. She just stands there twisting the gold cuff with our initials on it. Over and over and over until I'm sure the skin underneath is raw.

It probably says something that she *still* hasn't taken off the link, but I don't have the energy to think about what that means.

I should walk away and leave her with all of her complicated, girlie emotions. But this is *my* room.

Plus . . . I feel bad.

I know I didn't *actually* do anything wrong. The Gales made the promise to her—not me. And I've made it very clear that I'm not interested.

But still. It had to suck finding out that way.

"Hey," I mumble when I can't stand the silence anymore. "I . . . I'm really sorry I didn't tell you sooner. I just didn't feel like I could say anything until Audra was back."

She closes her eyes and takes a slow, deep breath. "So did you guys just . . . ? Or were you before . . . ?"

I'm not great at deciphering vague girl-talk. But I *think* she's asking how long Audra and I have been bonded. "We, uh, made it official about a month ago."

She nods like that doesn't surprise her, then turns her back on me and walks to the window. "So there was never a chance," she whispers.

I sigh. "The thing is—Audra and I have always had a connection. Even when we were kids. I don't know how to explain it, but it goes back way before you and I were supposed to . . . you know."

"And yet, she still left," she says, turning back to face me. "That doesn't bother you?"

"Well, I missed her, if that's what you mean."

"What about the pain?"

My hand automatically darts to my chest, but the burning ache is gone, replaced with the heat of Audra's touch—like every spark that shot between us filled the empty space that used to be there.

"It was brutal, wasn't it?" Solana asks quietly. "That's why you were such a mess the night the Gales called me to help you sleep, isn't it?"

Actually, it was because I thought Audra had ended things with me—but I have a feeling telling her that is only going to make this worse. "I was fine."

She doesn't look convinced. "One of my guardians was separated from her husband—and every day she stayed away, every mile she put between them, the more their bond tore her apart inside. There were days she could barely breathe. I used to watch it and wonder how she could bear it. And I worried for her husband, suffering every day and knowing she could spare them both the agony if she just went home."

"I guess when you love someone, you don't mind making sacrifices," I say, making sure to emphasize the word "love."

I have a feeling she's talking about Gus's family—and his mom had pretty darn good reasons for needing her space.

Just like Audra did.

"You *really* love her?" Solana whispers.

I can hear the plea in her voice, but I can't give her what she wants. "I do."

Her eyes well with tears and she turns away, spinning the gold cuff on her wrist again.

Why won't she just take it off?

Probably the same reason I wouldn't even consider the betrothal.

I wish there was something I could say to make it better. But all I have is the same lame thing I've already said. "I'm sorry. I never meant to hurt you."

"But you did. I doubt you have any idea how much." She reaches up and starts tracing lines on the window with her finger. "Do you know what this is?"

It looks kinda like a trippy clover, with the four leaves made out of four spirals.

"No."

"It's the Southwell crest. The mark for my family that was woven into the gates of Brezengarde. Or it was, before Raiden invaded the capital and replaced the symbol with his storm clouds. I've been dreaming of the day I would see it restored. The Gales have a huge celebration planned, so our whole world can see that things have been set right. And now I'll get to stand there on the sidelines at the coronation, watching my family's legacy be handed over to someone else."

My insides get all tangly.

All the times the Gales have talked about making me their king—I never thought about the fact that I'd be taking that role from someone else. No wonder they decided it would be simpler for me to just marry Solana.

"Look, Solana. I don't even want to be king. I'd be more than happy to hand it all back."

"They won't let you." She reaches up and smears away the squiggles on the glass, leaving a big, blank streak. "You're the last Westerly. The one everyone's been waiting for. I'm just the girl you didn't want."

Her voice cracks on the last word, and then her shoulders are shaking and . . . crap—I can't just stand here and let her cry.

I move to her side, wondering what I'm supposed to do. A hug seems super-inappropriate given the mountain of complications between us. But how else do you comfort someone who's crying?

I finally settle for putting my hand on her back. She doesn't flinch at my touch, but she doesn't stop crying, either, and it feels wrong just leaving my hand there, like this stupid dead weight. So I sweep her hair out of the way and rub her shoulders. It's what my mom used to do when she was trying to calm me, and I figure she's probably way better at this than I am.

"I really am sorry, Solana. If I could change anything, I would. I'll even talk to the Gales, see if there's something they can do. I don't know if there is, but it's worth a try."

Movement near the doorway catches my eye, and I jerk away from Solana when I find Audra standing there in my favorite Batman shirt.

In *only* my favorite Batman shirt.

I know I should probably be wondering how long she'd been there or if she was bothered by seeing me rub Solana's back—but all I can think about is how much I love having her in my shirt, in my room, like this is exactly where she belongs.

"How's your wound?" I ask when my voice is working again.

"Better now." Her hand darts to her side, rubbing where the bandage must be—which makes the shirt hike even farther up her legs.

I forgot how long they were. And smooth. And . . .

Audra must notice where I'm looking, because she blushes. "Your mom's washing my clothes, so she gave me this to wear in the meantime. She gave me some of her pants, too, but they slid off my hips. I hope you don't mind."

Mind?

The only thing I mind is that Solana's still standing there, refusing to leave us alone so Audra and I can get started on all the making-up-for-lost-time-by-making-out that I've been planning.

"I brought you some ice for those bruises," my mom announces as she comes back into my bedroom. I notice her double take when she sees what Audra's wearing, but she doesn't say anything. Probably because Solana's dress is way shorter. "And I set up some blankets for Audra on the couch."

"Audra's not sleeping on the couch, Mom."

"Oh, really? Then where *is* she sleeping? Because she's not sleeping *here*, Vane."

"We'll play by your rules—one of us on top of the covers and we'll keep the door open."

"That's not good enough."

"Why not? It was good enough for Solana."

"Yes, but you aren't dating *Solana*."

"Dating," Solana mumbles. "They're a little past that now."

My mom's eyes narrow. "What does she mean?"

"Nothing," I say quickly, but Solana won't let it go.

"You're not going to tell her?" she asks me.

"Tell me *what*?"

I can only imagine what kind of crazy theories my mom's coming up with, but I have a feeling the truth is going to be just as bad.

Still, I can't think of a lie to fix this, so I take Audra's hand, focusing on my feet as I say, "Audra and I are bonded."

The room falls painfully silent, and I swear all the air disappears, because I can't breathe anymore. My mom must not be breathing either, because her voice sounds superstrained when she asks, "What does 'bonded' mean?"

"It means that we're connected to each other now," Audra explains when I don't answer. "Kissing is different for sylphs than it is for humans. It forms a connection between us. A physical bond."

"And it's *permanent?*"

I close my eyes as I nod, wishing I could fast-forward through the epic freak-out that I know is coming—but sadly I can only control the wind, which is feeling like a pretty useless power right now.

"How could you do that?" my mom asks, her voice so high-pitched I'm surprised it doesn't shatter glass.

My palm turns sweaty and I feel like I'm shaking—but then I realize it's Audra's hand shaking, not mine. I glance at her, hating the hurt I can see in her eyes.

"How could I do *what?*" I snap.

"Vane," my mom says, squeezing the ice packs so tight they crackle. "I know you think you're in love with her—and maybe you are. But you're *seventeen*. Do you really think that the things you want now are the things you're going to want *forever?*"

"Yes."

My mom shakes her head. "She's your first girlfriend, Vane. You haven't even considered . . ."

She doesn't finish the sentence, but her eyes are focused on Solana.

I'll give Solana credit, she looks *almost* as uncomfortable with my mom's insinuation as I feel. But she also looks a tiny bit hopeful, like part of her is wondering if I'm realizing I made a mistake.

I tighten my grip on Audra. "I know this is going to be hard to believe, Mom, but I *know* I will always love Audra."

"You say that now—"

"No—you don't get it. I've loved Audra for as long as I can remember. I never told you because, well, that would've been weird. Especially since I didn't know if she was real. But yeah, Audra's always been the one—and she always will be. You know me—you know I would *never* say that if I wasn't sure. I'm *sure*."

"I . . . don't know what to say."

"Say you trust me. I chose the right girl—I promise."

"Excuse me," Solana says, pushing past us and practically running out of the room.

"Well, I guess that settles that," my mom says, watching her disappear down the hall.

I can't tell if the regret in her tone is because Solana looked hurt or because Solana's *gone*. Either way, I can't take it anymore.

"Look," I say, pressing on my forehead, trying to shove back my headache. "I have a *lot* going on right now and I just . . . I need you to trust me—please? I need someone on my side or . . ."

My voice cracks and I look away.

I shouldn't be this upset, but I need my parents to be okay with this. I can't take on them *and* the Gales *and* Solana *and* Raiden *and* . . .

"Hey," my mom says, stepping forward and wrapping me in a hug. Somehow she manages to avoid all my bruises and not touch me with the ice packs as she whispers, "Okay, Vane. I'll trust you."

"Thank you," I whisper back.

I soak up the hug long enough for us to both take a deep breath. Then she lets me go and turns to Audra.

"I . . . guess I should be saying, welcome to the family!"

I smile as she gives Audra the most awkward hug of all awkward hugs—complete with an uncomfortable back pat.

"We're not *married*, Mom. Not—" I stop myself, deciding not to say "not yet." That should be Audra's decision.

My mom lets Audra go and turns to me. "Well then, as long as she's *not* your wife, I'm going to hold to my one-of-you-sleeps-on-the-couch policy. I'll let you guys decide who gets the bed."

"Come on, we're not going to do anything with you and Dad down the hall. And I thought you said you trust me."

My mom sighs—one of the dramatic kind that shakes her shoulders. "Fine. But you *will* keep the door open and I *will* be checking on you guys all night."

I can't believe she caved. And I can't help laughing as I tell her. "Sounds awesome—and not creepy at all."

A tiny smile cracks her lips as she glances at Audra. "See what you've gotten yourself into?"

"I know," Audra says quietly. "I guess it's a good thing I love him."

It's the first time she's used the *L* word since she's been back, and I swear my heart skips a beat. My mom's eyes get a little watery, and her voice sounds thick as she reminds us that we're not *really* alone. Then she tosses the ice packs onto my bed, pushes my door as wide open as it can go, and tells us to get some sleep.

"So . . . that was interesting," I say after a few seconds of silence.

"Yeah," Audra mumbles.

I can see dozens of questions swimming in her eyes—and I kiss her before she can ask any of them.

I meant it as a slow kiss, just to reassure her that everything's going to be okay. But as she presses closer and I feel her bare legs against mine, the kiss deepens until I'm gasping for breath and her fingers are digging into my back and my hands are sliding—

"I said go to *sleep*," my mom snaps, and we break away—both of us blushing but neither of us looking particularly sorry.

My mom stomps off, and I can't help laughing as I sit on the bed, feeling a little weak in the knees. Audra hesitates a second before she lies down next to me, automatically taking the side I don't sleep on.

"Do you want to be on top or bottom?" I ask, earning myself raised eyebrows. "I meant the blankets."

"Oh. Top."

I was hoping she'd say that. Now I can stare at her legs.

I slip under the sheets, and Audra covers my bruises with the ice—I hate myself for yelping, but it's freaking *cold*—and I switch off the light.

"Are you comfortable?" I whisper as she shifts a few times.

"Not really." She scoots closer, nudging her head into the space between my neck and nonfrozen shoulder. "Better."

I grin. Who would've thought Audra was a snuggler?

Her heat races through me and I realize there might be a flaw to this sharing-a-bed-with-Audra plan. How am I *ever* going to sleep?

I'm not even sure if I should, in case Raiden sends any more creepy winds. But then Audra whispers the call for a few nearby Easterlies and weaves them into a whirl of soft lullabies, like she used to send me every night. The peaceful calm of their song always kept me safe, and I sink into the feeling, relieved that everything is finally back to the way it used to be.

Audra's face rushes into my dreams, letting me stare into her eyes. Her dark hair blows wild, tickling my skin as she leans in and whispers that everything will be okay. She sings a song of love and peace, but the words turn sadder, fading into an apology. A promise that she will never leave me again.

I want to tell her that I believe her, but then a dark shape passes over her, stealing her songs and her smile. She turns away from me and screams—a horrible, bone-chilling scream that makes my body thrash as I pull myself upright.

My burning eyes are too blurry to tell me if anything is real, but I see red and black—blood and shadow—mixed with Audra's desperate cries.

And wind. So much wind.

A tempest of dark drafts, raging and roaring and swallowing everything they touch until there's nothing left but storm and chaos, ripping at my skin, trying to drag me under. I fight to hold on as haunting laughter drowns out the winds, worming into my brain and making my head throb with every sharp beat.

The storm unravels, growing a head and arms and wild shadowy hair—a Living Storm of Audra that joins an army of others, howling and laughing as they rampage into my valley, tearing apart roads, houses, cars, people—anything that gets in their way.

The Gales rally against them, standing in the line of the Storms as Gus races forward, raising Raiden's windslicer to slash and shred—but the winds toss him into the sky and tear him apart piece by piece. His agonized screams mix with the thunder of the storm as he crumbles to dust and is lost on the breeze. The rest of the guardians turn and run but the winds swallow them whole, splattering the ground with red as their bodies are twisted into new Storms—an army that keeps growing stronger, feeding off anyone who dares to stand against it. Heading straight for me.

My parents try to run—try to scream—but the Storms are too fast, too merciless as they scoop them up like paper dolls and spit them to the ground in crumpled heaps. Leaving only me, standing in a circle of dead trees as the Storms unravel and Raiden marches forward with an almost gleeful smile.

"I know how to break you," he tells me, and I want to run somewhere safe.

But everything's gone.

There's nowhere left.

He laughs, tossing back his head as he says, "Now you die."

Searing pain rages through my head, and I feel my body thrash, but I can't pull away, can't pull my mind back from the horror as Raiden binds me in his wicked winds. Not until a warm breeze whisks inside me and melts away the thick fog.

I tear open my eyes and jump out of bed—so relieved to be in my undestroyed bedroom that my brain barely registers that it was Solana leaning over me instead of Audra.

I collapse to the floor, shaking my head to shove away the dream or nightmare or whatever it was. But as the images replay in my mind I realize it wasn't any of those things.

It wasn't even a warning.

It was a *promise.*

CHAPTER 30

AUDRA

Vane wouldn't wake up for me.

I tried screaming his name. Tried shocking him with the heat of our connection, like I've done in the past. Nothing helped.

Not even a kiss.

Then Solana heard my panicked screams and rushed in, shoved me aside, and crawled on top of him. She sent a Southerly into his mind, whispered a command I'd never heard and . . .

Vane woke up.

His dad cheered and his mom cried and all I could do was stand in the corner like an outsider, wondering why he wouldn't wake up for me.

"Are the Gales back?" Vane gasps, rubbing the sides of his head as he pulls himself up off the floor and leans back against his bed.

"I heard Gus arrive in the grove about an hour ago," Solana answers, and Vane whips his head toward her.

"Oh," he mumbles, "I thought you'd left earlier."

"No. I started to, but . . . I had nowhere else to go."

Even *I* can't help feeling sorry for her. Though my sympathy turns to unease when Vane asks, "You brought me out of the nightmare, didn't you?"

She blushes as she nods. "Your mind put up more of a fight this time, but I found a way to entice you back."

"Thank goodness," Vane's mom whispers, her voice thick.

"Yeah, we owe you," his dad adds.

Solana practically glows from the praise—or maybe it's just the tears I feel burning my eyes. But all Vane says is "We need to tell Gus to call everyone."

The pain in his tone snaps me out of my wallowing and I move to his side, feeling everyone watch me as I try to figure out what to do. Touching him almost seems wrong now, but when I reach out my hand, he grabs it and clings to me like I'm the only thing tethering him to the earth.

I drop to my knees on the scratchy gray rug and wrap my arms around him, surprised to feel that he's trembling. I catch Solana watching us before she runs to the front door to call for Gus—but I'm too shaken to feel triumphant.

Why did he wake up for *her*?

I know we're bonded—but that only means he *shouldn't* care about someone else. Not that he *can't*.

And they clearly have some sort of connection.

And when I first came back in the room last night, I heard them whispering about him talking to the Gales—seeing if anything could be done. . . .

"What's wrong?" Vane asks, pulling me into his lap.

I shift my weight, struggling to keep the too-short shirt I'm wearing adjusted. "I'm just worried about you. You . . . wouldn't wake up."

I manage to stop myself from adding "for me."

He reaches up, tucking my hair behind my ear. "I do that sometimes, remember?"

I force myself to return his smile, but the words only make my chest heavier.

I used to be the one he needed.

He leans his forehead against mine and I can feel the hum of our bond rushing through me like a jet stream. I soak in the warmth, promising myself that I will not be one of those silly girls, worrying about a boy. Especially a boy holding me on the floor of his messy room, looking only at me.

"What's going on?" Gus asks, making Vane and me jump as he runs into the room, slightly out of breath from his sprint across the lawn. "Another nightmare?"

"This time it felt more like Raiden was talking straight to me. . . ." Vane's voice trails off and he pulls me closer. "He's coming."

Gus grips the hilt of his windslicer. "When?"

"I don't know. But I doubt he'll wait long."

His mom covers her mouth and leans against her husband.

"But . . . that doesn't make sense," Solana says after a second. "Why would he warn us? Why give us time to prepare?"

"The same reason a cat plays with his prey," Gus says, looking like he wants to punch something.

"Fear is one of the most powerful weapons," I add quietly. "Though I wouldn't be surprised if there's a trick, too."

"Probably," Gus agrees. "What exactly did he show you, Vane?"

"Just your basic *I'm going to destroy everything you care about with my army of Living Storms* nightmare."

I try to fight back my shiver, but it rocks my shoulders anyway.

Raiden talked about building an army, but in order to do that he'd need . . .

"Os said the Stormers captured twenty-nine Gales yesterday," Gus tells us, like he knows what I'm thinking.

"Holy crap," Vane whispers.

"How did they get that many?" I've never heard of such a crushing defeat.

"I guess they thought they were only chasing two Stormers, but when they entered a canyon, a third Stormer ambushed them and gave some command that chased off all the winds they were flying with. Some of the Gales crashed to the dunes, but most were able to call a draft to stop their fall, and apparently the drafts seeped into their minds and lulled them all to sleep. Then the Stormers shouted something and the drafts turned red and blasted everyone away before the others could do anything to stop it."

"Raiden wanted to make sure he caught the strongest," I mumble. Though I'm surprised Os wasn't among them.

"Twenty-nine Living Storms," Vane says, and the quiver in his voice mirrors the one in my stomach.

"What are they?" Solana asks quietly.

"Trust me, you don't want to know." Gus fidgets with the sleeves of his uniform before he looks at me. "When he turned Feng into . . . how long did it take?"

The moment was such a blur it's hard to say for certain. But I know it wasn't long. "Only a handful of minutes."

Vane straightens. "So he could already be on his way?"

Gus leans out the window, turning his face to the stuffy breezes sweeping through the soft dawn light. "I feel no warning yet."

"But we all know how quickly the winds can shift," I remind him.

"What does that mean?" Vane's mom asks, and we all fall silent. She turns to Vane. "Do we need to leave again?"

"Probably," he admits.

I've never seen her look so tired as she nods and says, "And I'm assuming you can't come with us?"

"No, they'll need me here." He pulls me closer so he can whisper in my ear. "But I want you to go with them."

"I'm staying with you."

"You could keep them safe for me—and then I wouldn't have to worry about you."

"I'm *not* leaving you."

"I'll go with them," Solana offers. "I'll do whatever you need."

I don't know which I hate more, how grateful Vane looks or how bad I feel for not being the one who made him look that way.

But Gus steps forward before Vane can agree. "If we're taking on twenty-nine Living Storms, we're going to need every soldier we can get. I know you want to protect your parents, Vane. Believe me,

I *understand*. But I don't think we can afford to spare anyone this time."

"Yeah, we'll be fine," Vane's dad jumps in. "I'm getting good at outrunning storms. Haven't gotten a speeding ticket yet!"

Vane looks torn as he turns to his mom, who's twisting her hands so tightly her fingers are turning white. "Are you sure you'll be okay alone?"

"I'm not worried about *us*, Vane." She glances at me. "You'll take care of him for me?"

The question feels like a calming breeze.

She could've made that request to anyone in the room. But she asked *me*.

"I've been protecting him for ten years," I tell her. "Nothing's going to happen."

Vane tightens his hold on me.

Solana looks away.

"I guess I should go make some coffee for the drive, then," Vane's mom says quietly, taking one last look at her son before she rushes out of the room.

Vane's dad forces a smile. "At least I like road trips. Maybe we'll do the Grand Canyon this time."

"No—go south," Vane tells him. "Last we knew, Raiden was in Death Valley."

His dad's smile fades. "Okay. Well, then—Mexico it is. A margarita sounds pretty good right now, actually. Extra heavy on the tequila."

Vane sighs. "Sorry this keeps happening."

"Hey, we knew adopting a son was going to be an adventure. I didn't expect wind warriors, but . . ." He runs a hand over his shiny head. "You'll really be okay? That bruise . . ."

"I'll be fine."

Vane probably sounds less confident than his dad would like, but his dad leaves it at that, turning instead toward me.

Then away.

Then back again.

He finally steps forward, offering his hand. "I guess I should, um . . . offer my congratulations."

"Ugh, you guys are so embarrassing," Vane whines as my cheeks burn.

Part of me wishes I could bury my face against Vane's chest and hide. But I force myself to lean forward and shake his dad's hand. "Thank you."

He nods, his eyes slightly glassy as he clears his throat again and says he's going to go pack.

"I take it this means you told them?" Gus asks when he's gone.

"Yeah, it sorta came up." Vane glances at Solana, then away. "I'll tell Os when this is over."

"Tell me what?" Os asks, making everyone jump as he stalks into the room.

I've seen the captain of the Gales only once, standing outside my mother's house as I swore my oath as a guardian. At the time he'd looked equal parts proud and nervous—the way they all did as they put their most important assignment in the hands of a thirteen-year-old.

Now the scar under his eye is twisted with anger as I try to scramble out of Vane's lap.

Vane holds me in place, whispering, "He's already seen."

"What madness is *this*?" Os demands. "What are you—"

"Raiden's coming," Vane interrupts.

Os's eyes widen and he turns toward the window, staring at the calm sky. "You're sure?"

"Positive."

He mutters a curse under his breath and pulls his hands through the loose hair around his braid. "So what are we facing?"

"Did Gus update you on everything that happened yesterday?" Vane asks him.

"*Almost* everything. He failed to mention that our deserting guardian had returned—I take it you weren't able to track down the third Stormer?" he asks me.

"Really, that's what you want to focus on?" Vane snaps before I can ask what that means. "Raiden's coming to destroy us and you want to talk about Audra?"

"The biggest mistake any leader can make is keeping a traitor in his midst."

Vane slides me to the side and stands. "You're seriously calling her a *traitor*?"

I know I should stand too—say something in my defense—but my heart is pounding too hard and my head is spinning too fast and all I can do is stare at the floor and tuck my stupid bare legs underneath me.

Os stalks closer. "Did she or did she not abandon her duties as a guardian—break her oath—"

"Audra didn't abandon anything," Vane interrupts. "She took a few weeks to clear her head—and after everything she's done for us and everything she'd been through, she deserved it."

"Yes, well, the families of the guardians who lost their lives while caring for *her* responsibilities might disagree."

He turns to Gus, but Gus shakes his head. "My father was honored to serve his king."

I can tell that Gus means every word. Still, the weight of his father's loss feels like a stone in my heart.

"His *king*," Os repeats, turning back to me. "And am I safe in assuming that *this* is who you intend to make your queen?"

"Well, we haven't really talked that far into the future—"

"But you *have* bonded?" Os interrupts.

I wish we could wait until Vane's not shirtless and I'm not pantsless with unbraided hair and it's not so incredibly humiliating. But it's already too late.

"Yeah," Vane says, reaching for my hand. "We have."

Os groans, muttering something about foolish teenagers.

I pull myself to my feet, trying to look more confident than I feel as Os takes in the full effect of my ridiculous outfit.

He rolls his eyes and turns to Vane. "So this is the kind of king you're going to be? One who blatantly disregards our wishes and does whatever you please?"

"When it comes to my personal life, *yeah*."

"You don't have a *personal* life—that's what being king means! Your life is about serving others, not yourself. Otherwise you're no different from Raiden."

"Uh, I don't murder innocent people, so I'm pretty sure that gives me a big one-up on him. And how does who I date have *anything* to do with 'serving others'?"

"Because your people are searching for safety and stability and you've bonded yourself to the daughter of a murderer!"

I'm too numb to feel Vane's warmth as he drapes his arm around me. But I notice he doesn't say anything.

There's nothing to say.

Os turns and starts pacing. He's crossed the room three times before he says, "We arranged for you to marry the daughter of our fallen king and queen—two heroes who not only were known for their strength and kindness but who sacrificed themselves so the royal line could have a chance to live on. That future is something our people have been waiting for, hoping for. Fighting for the day they'd see the royal symbol once again adorn the gates of Brezengarde with a member of the Southwell family on the throne. And now you want me to tell them that instead, they need to embrace a queen who stole the king from his betrothed when she was supposed to be guarding him—who then abandoned her post, only to return weeks later and ruin everything we'd been planning for years? And the only notable claim she has for her pedigree is that her mother is one of the most infamous criminals our world has known—second only to Raiden?"

He pauses and I realize this is where I'm supposed to argue, prove that I'm worthy of Vane and all the responsibility that comes with him.

But every word that Os has said is true.

"You're right," Vane says quietly.

They're two small words, but they hurt more than anything Os has said. I turn to look at Vane, but he's looking at Solana and it feels like something inside me withers as he says, "Solana *should* be queen."

I close my eyes, choking back my tears and reminding myself that I knew this could—should—happen all along.

But as I'm waiting for Os to bind me and drag me away, Vane pulls me closer and says, "I just shouldn't be king. I wish I could fall in love with the princess and make everyone's life easier. But I love Audra. So if I have to choose between being with her or being king, I will happily hand back the throne."

I open my eyes, seeing nothing but the beautiful smile on the beautiful boy I will never deserve but want so much it makes me ache.

Os laughs—a sharp sound that spears my few seconds of happiness. "You think it's that easy?"

"It can be if you want it to be," Vane tells him.

Os shakes his head and goes back to pacing. "Our world is broken, Vane—and when we're finally free of Raiden and struggling to rise from the dust, we're going to need strength to bring our people back together. We need our new leader to be the warrior who harnessed the power of four and destroyed the villain. Not the pretty girl who stood on the sidelines during the battle."

"Hey, I'm going to fight right along with you," Solana argues.

"No, you'll be defending yourself and storing winds for the rest of us to use—which is a very useful tool," Os tells her. "But it's *not* the same as being the *hero*."

Solana's eyes narrow, and I can understand her fury. I know what it feels like to be underestimated.

But I also agree with Os.

Solana's a trophy, meant to be paraded around and admired.

Not respected and loyally obeyed.

Not that I deserve respect or loyalty either.

"Raiden stirred the seeds of rebellion among our people," Os adds quietly. "Even when he's gone, there will be some dissenters who remain. So we need a ruler who is as feared as he is respected. Someone so powerful that no one would dare try to steal the throne again." He turns back to Vane, sizing him up with his stare. "I'm still not convinced that you can be that warrior. But you're the best chance we have. The throne *will* fall to you."

"Well then, I guess I don't need this," Solana mumbles as she unclasps her gold cuff and sets it on the floor, backing away from it like it carries a disease.

"Not necessarily," Os tells her, bending down and retrieving the link. "This matter is far from settled."

"Uh—yeah it is," Vane corrects.

"Trust me when I tell you it isn't." Os walks over to Solana and clamps the bracelet back on her wrist.

Her *left* wrist this time, like their commitment is already sealed.

Solana frowns. "But . . . they're *bonded*."

"Yes," Os says, looking straight at me. "And bonds can be broken."

CHAPTER 31

VANE

I know I'm new to this Windwalker stuff—but one of the few things I was pretty sure I had figured out was that bonds are *permanent*.

I thought that was why Audra spent so much time ruining my dates and turning me into a huge joke at school—and why it took so freaking long to convince her to finally kiss me.

And yet, Audra doesn't seem *nearly* as surprised by this revelation as I am. If anything she looks . . . worried.

"Is that true?" I whisper, giving her the cue to tell me it's a mistake.

The fact that she won't look at me says it all.

I sink to the edge of my bed, my head spinning too much to stay standing. "You told me bonds couldn't be broken!"

"I thought they couldn't," she admits. "But Aston said—"

"Wait, you saw Aston?" Os interrupts. "He's alive?"

She nods.

Os gazes into space for a second—then reels on Gus. "Why didn't you tell me?"

"I guess I forgot. A *lot* happened yesterday."

"Yes . . . I suppose it did." Os sighs and turns back to Audra. "When did you see him?"

"About two days ago."

Os steps closer, grabbing Audra's wrist. "Can you take me there?"

She pulls her hand free and sits next to me on the bed. I can't help noticing how high my shirt creeps up her thigh, but the mood is kind of killed when she whispers, "He's *not* the Gale you remember, Os. Raiden tortured and twisted him into someone incredibly unstable—and incredibly powerful. He conquered me without ever having to step out of the shadows of his cave, and if he hadn't chosen to let me go, I would still be his captive."

"But he *did* let you go, didn't he?" Os asks.

"He did," she admits. "And I'm still not sure why."

She stares at a faint blister on her wrist, and I don't think I want to know how she got it. If he hurt her I'll—

"We need to find him," Os says.

Audra shakes her head. "He told me he would kill anyone who comes near his hideout—and believe me, he's capable."

"All the more reason why we need to get him back on our side."

"Okay, can we back up a second?" I interrupt. "We can deal with psycho cave boy *after* you explain what the crap you mean about bonds being broken."

"Actually, we should be planning for Raiden's attack," Os corrects.

He's right—we should. But he can't just drop that kind of bombshell and not explain. "We'll plan in a minute."

"I thought it was pretty self-explanatory," Os says after glaring at me for a few seconds. "Bonds can be broken. Simple as that."

"But . . . how?" Gus asks, and I'm glad to see that he and Solana look as confused as me.

Meanwhile, Audra's staring sadly at the floor. . . .

"What do you know?" I whisper.

She steals a glance at Os before she turns to me. "Aston told me that *anything* can be broken if you're willing to harness the power of pain."

My mouth goes dry. *"Pain?"*

"I'm sure the process is rather unpleasant, yes," Os agrees.

"Well then, fun as that sounds, I'll pass."

A sad smile peeks from the corners of Os's mouth. "I never said it would be your choice, Vane. We let you believe we were canceling your betrothal because we thought it would make you less resistant to Solana, and that once you got to know her you'd change your mind. But just because that didn't work doesn't mean we're changing our plans. You may be king, but your opinion isn't the only one that matters—not when it comes to what's best for our people. And it's better for everyone if you're with Solana."

"So . . . what? You're going to chain me up and torture my bond out of me?" I feel dizzy just saying it—and he can bet I'll go all power of four on him if he tries.

Os looks away. "If you leave us no other choice."

"Whoa," Gus breathes.

"Is there a problem, Guardian Gusty?" Os asks.

Gus swallows, looking like he wishes he hadn't said that out loud. "That just sounds . . . kind of cruel, sir."

"Cruel?"

"Yeah. Torturing two of our own because they fell in love sounds more like something Raiden would do."

"The pain only lasts a few minutes."

I snort. "Right—because *that* makes it better."

Os ignores me. "Have you ever broken a bone, Gus?"

Gus nods. "My left ankle, when I was first learning to windwalk."

"Ah, yes, I remember. That was quite a fall. And tell me this, did it hurt when they set the bone?"

"Yes, sir."

"And yet, it made your ankle heal properly, didn't it? Otherwise you wouldn't be able to walk now, right?"

"Yes, but"—Gus shifts his weight—"that's not the same as what you're saying."

"But it is, Gus. Sometimes pain is necessary to fix a problem that cannot otherwise be corrected. It's unpleasant and unfortunate, but then it's over and everything is set right."

"Do you hear yourself?" I shout. "I bet that's the kind of crap Raiden spews out to his Stormers to try to justify the evil things he does."

Os stalks toward me. "Raiden cares only for his own selfish needs. *I* am thinking about the good of our people. Trying to bring together the shattered pieces of our world."

"And who put *you* in charge?"

"Nobody." He steps back, clutching his blue guardian pendant. "This matter will be brought to the full force of the Gales, and *they* will decide. I'll simply be one vote. However, they're a very reasonable group of soldiers. I have no doubt they'll decide what will benefit everyone."

"Everyone except me and Audra.'"

"With time you'll see that isn't the case. You two were not meant to be."

"Can I say something?" Solana asks, her voice shaking as much as her legs as she steps forward. "I don't want to bond with someone who's being *forced* to do it. If Vane loved me"—she clears her throat—"or if there were a way to keep my family's heritage without us having to be together, well . . . that would be different. But if Vane really needs to be the king and I'm not who he wants to be with, then . . . I guess that's how it has to be."

Her eyes dart to mine, so sad and broken that a part of me can't help wishing I could love her.

But I just *can't* feel that way. Not when I know what *real* love feels like.

"Another young person thinking they have a choice in all this," Os says through a sigh. "Though I notice you're being awfully quiet, Audra. Feeling guilty now that you're seeing the consequences of your selfish actions?"

"Actually, I'm trying to figure out how you know about the power of pain. Aston gave me the impression it was one of *Raiden's* tricks, and not something the Gales knew anything about."

Os steps closer, pointing to the scar under his eye. "It's no secret that I know Raiden better than others. Back when we were friends, he used to share some of his theories with me—it was partly how I knew to distance myself from him. And when he started attacking us with shattered winds, I knew it meant he'd proven at least one of his theories correct."

"And now you want to use it—knowing it's one of *his* tricks?" Audra asks, standing up to face him. "Don't you realize how it will affect you?"

"Affect me?"

She steps closer. "Aston told me the power corrupts anyone who uses it. It becomes an addiction you can't cure, can't fight, can't satisfy except to break and destroy more—and after seeing how he behaved, I believe him."

"Sounds like someone with a guilty conscience trying to blame his wickedness on another."

"Or perhaps you're just tempted by a greater power than you understand."

"Watch yourself," Os says, his scar twisting with his scowl so it looks more like an X. "Given your recent crimes, you would do well to be as polite and obedient as possible."

"Why?" I ask, stepping between them. "You already threatened to break our bond—what's next? Lock us underground in your Maelstrom?"

The word makes Os freeze, and for a second his mouth just hangs there, begging for a fly to zip in.

I'm just as stunned when I realize the mess I've walked into.

I turn to Audra, feeling my heart sink when I see the horror in her eyes.

"Do you mean the Maelstrom in Death Valley?" she asks me.

"No," I say, trying to choose my answer carefully. "Os built one in Desert Center."

I don't mention who he's keeping there, hoping she won't guess. But her whole body starts shaking.

"You built a *Maelstrom?*" she asks Os, leaning on me to stay standing.

"I had no choice!"

"Wait, when you say Maelstrom . . . ," Gus starts, but his voice trails off when I nod. "Whoa."

"Yeah." I pull Audra closer, silently begging everyone to drop this. *Now* is not the time to give Audra anything else to worry about.

But Audra isn't letting it go.

"How could you?" she yells at Os. "How could you do that to the wind? To innocent people?"

"Who said anything about *innocent?*" he snaps. "The only person trapped in my Maelstrom is a violent murderer who used her gift to nearly escape—twice—from our regular prison."

Audra sucks in a breath, and I tighten my arms around her, wanting to hold her steady as she puts the pieces together.

She pulls away from me, stumbling to my window and staring blankly outside.

I should've found a way to tell her before this.

She should've heard it from me.

But even now, I have no idea how to say it.

"What prisoner is he talking about?" Solana asks when no one says anything.

I open my mouth, trying to force out the words. But I can see in Audra's eyes that she already knows.

She reaches out her hand, letting a small mockingbird land on her finger as she whispers, "My mother."

CHAPTER 32

AUDRA

My *mother is in a Maelstrom.*

I . . . don't know what to feel.

I stare at the tiny bird roosting on my finger—drawn to me because of the gift my mother and I share—and try not to imagine her gray-blue, withered body dangling from the ceiling on a chain, her limbs twisted and tangled, her face contorted with agony.

I knew her punishment would be severe. But I never imagined . . .

"How long does she have left?" I whisper, wondering if I really want to know the answer.

The tiny bird tenses as Vane comes up behind me and puts a hand on my shoulder. "She was only guessing when I talked to her. But she thought maybe a few weeks."

Weeks.

My hand shakes so hard the bird flies away, and I grasp the windowsill to steady my balance.

"Did she look . . ." I can't even ask. I don't want to picture it.

Vane spins me around and pulls me against him. "She looked weaker," he whispers. "Kind of pale and greasy. But not like someone who's . . ."

"Dying," I finish for him.

My mother is dying.

A slow, painful, horrifying death.

But she's a murderer, I remind myself.

A cold, cruel monster who killed Vane's parents and cost my father his life and let me blame myself for all of it.

And if I'd been weaker, she would've killed me.

But . . . does that mean she deserves to be eaten alive by the winds?

The winds.

"How could you do that?" I ask, turning to Os. "How could you ruin the wind?"

I can still hear the Easterly's mindless wailing after Aston shattered it in front of me—still remember the restless spinning of the devouring winds in the Maelstrom.

"I thought my heart might break along with them," Os whispers. "But my first priority is to protect *our people*, and your mother was uncontainable without the Maelstrom. I used the absolute bare minimum of winds that I could, stopping the second I had enough."

"And how many was that?" I ask.

Os's hand darts to his scar, his fingers tracing the thin red lines. "Twelve."

Twelve.

Twelve times he called the wind to his side.

Twelve times he let them sweep around him like loyal friends, then watched them writhe and scream before their songs fell silent.

Tears blur my vision and I don't want to smear them away. I don't want to look at the man who could do something that horrible *twelve* times.

But the tears fall on their own when Os tells me, "Believe me, their cries will haunt me until my dying day. And I keep hoping that there's a way to restore them. Perhaps with the power of four, or . . . just, somehow. I refuse to believe they'll forever be this way."

I can hear his grief in every crack in his voice.

He doesn't seem like the power-crazed monster Aston described, but . . .

Hadn't he been threatening to break our bond only a few minutes ago?

Aston sent me to Death Valley so I could see Raiden's Maelstrom—see the depths of his horrors and the level the Gales would have to sink to in order to defeat him.

Is that what's happening?

My knees can't seem to hold me any longer, but Vane catches me and carries me to the bed. He lays me down and I want to pull the blankets over my head and pretend the rest of the world doesn't exist. I settle for pulling him next to me and leaning against his side, soaking up as much of his heat as I can.

"Are you okay?" he whispers.

I'm not sure how to answer.

I feel like I've just found out the sky is green, and can never see blue the same way again.

Os clears his throat. "We're wasting precious time. None of this is going to help us face down Raiden."

"You're right," Vane agrees after a second. "But we *will* be talking about all of this with the Gales when we're done. No more secrets— for any of us."

"As you wish, Your Highness," Os says, his voice almost sounding sincere as he dips his head in a bow.

That's when I realize why my world has turned sideways.

Not because of my mother. I lost the *real* her years ago in the same storm that stole my father.

Because of Os.

I don't trust him.

I've dedicated my entire life to the service of the Gales—sacrificed food, water, even my childhood.

But I believe what Aston told me about ruining the winds coming at a cost.

No matter how careful Os was, he will still have to pay it.

"So . . . I guess we're ready to go," Vane's mom says from the doorway, startling me back to the present.

She stands next to Vane's dad, suitcases piled at her feet along with a thick stack of books.

Vane smiles sadly. "I don't think you'll need the family photo albums."

"We thought it might be a good idea this time to bring the things we can't replace," she says quietly, and from the way she's staring at Vane I can tell she wants to shove him in her bag and take him with her.

Instead she runs over and strangles Vane with a hug until he reminds her that he needs to breathe and she finally lets him go.

I'm completely caught off guard when she throws her arms around me.

"Take care of yourself, too," she whispers.

Tears burn my eyes and I find myself hugging her tight before she pulls away. "We'll see you soon."

"You'd better," Vane's dad says before he wraps his arms around us both. "Try not to destroy the house."

Vane forces a laugh. "Dang, there go all my plans."

"Oh, I almost forgot," his mom says, lifting a tattered shred of black fabric from the top of her suitcase. "I'm so sorry. I guess your clothes can't go in the washing machine. . . ."

It takes me a second to realize the scrap she's holding is what's left of my uniform, and another after that to realize my mistake. I'd forgotten that groundlings use machines for their washing instead of water and air. Our porous fabric must not be able to hold up.

"It's fine," I tell her, even though I have no idea what I'll wear now. My shelter had nowhere to hide possessions, so I only had the one uniform. "I'll figure something out. Maybe the Gales have an extra—"

"We've been keeping all the supplies at the Dustlands Base," Os interrupts. "It's an hour away from here."

"I still have your jacket," Vane offers, pointing to a crushed pile of black on the floor next to his bed. "But that's probably not going to help much."

"I'm sure I can make your mother's pants work if I have a belt."

Solana lets out a slow, heavy sigh. "Or, I have a few extra dresses."

She doesn't *actually* offer them, but Vane still tells her, "That would be *awesome!*" and before I can argue, she nods like it's settled.

Vane's parents rush through a teary goodbye—making Vane promise he'll remember to text them this time. Then the house is quiet and Vane watches from his window as they drive away.

The tense line of his shoulders makes me want to hug him. But Solana turns to me. "My stuff's in the living room."

She looks about as thrilled with this arrangement as I am, which somehow makes it easier to follow her down the hall. Until she shows me my choices.

One is nothing more than a tube of shiny teal—and not nearly enough of that. Another is sheer peach and dips almost as low in the front as it does in the back. And the third is bright red.

I'm positive it would take the fabric from all three to actually cover me—especially considering I'm at least two inches taller than her. But, clearly, the point of these dresses is to be *seen*.

And to catch the eye of a certain Westerly king.

The thought has me reaching for the red one, though I tell myself it's mostly because it looks longer than the others.

I realize on my way to the bathroom that I'd forgotten about my black shifting dress, tucked away in the eaves of my old shelter. I want to believe that I don't switch to that because I don't want to waste any time—and *not* because I want Vane to see me in something new. But if I'm being honest, the thought *did* cross my mind.

Apparently, I *am* turning into one of "those girls."

I'm even more disgusted with myself when I slip the silky red fabric over my head and glance in the mirror. The V of the neckline dips low enough to make me blush, and the thin straps tie around my neck, leaving my shoulders—and most of my back—bare. The sides at least come up high enough to cover my bandage, and the skirt is longer than the other dress options—but only in the back. In the front it cuts much higher, and the flowy design has me wondering what I'm supposed to do if I catch an updraft.

But the truly horrifying part is that I can't help imagining Vane's reaction when he sees me. I want to believe he'll be pleased—but what if he isn't?

What if he thinks I look as ridiculous as I feel?

I'm this close to raiding his mom's closet—she's only a few sizes bigger than me, surely there's *something* I can make work—when I step under the vent in the ceiling. The air sinks effortlessly through the thin material, cooling my skin and giving me a boost of strength.

Sylph fabrics breathe better than groundling ones—and I'm going to need all the energy I can get. Embarrassing as it is, this dress is my best option.

I start to braid my hair, but that leaves *far* too much skin on display, so I smooth the strands as best as I can and force myself to walk away from the mirror.

Solana's waiting for me outside the bathroom, and her frustrated sigh makes my lips curl into a smile.

I must look better than I think.

It's an incredibly foolish thought to have when preparing for a fight, but Solana seems to bring out the foolishness in me. Maybe because she's changed into the even tinier flesh-toned dress, which almost makes her look naked.

"You have an interesting battle wardrobe," I tell her, pulling at the hem of my skirt.

"Not that I *need* to explain myself, considering I just bailed you out, but it's because of my gift."

"Your gift?"

"I'm a windcatcher. So I need to keep my skin exposed to the air so I can absorb as many drafts as possible."

That explains what Os meant earlier—and why she looked so frustrated at the way he belittled her. Those who can windcatch are especially rare, and the gift requires continual sacrifice in order to maintain.

We both know that's not the *only* reason for her dresses, though. But since we seem to have reached a truce, I bite my tongue as I follow her back to Vane's bedroom.

I can hear some sort of argument going on, but my heart is pounding too loud for me to pick out the words. I keep my eyes glued to the floor as I slink through the doorway, cringing when the room falls silent.

Someone finally coughs and I brave a quick glance at Vane.

I'm sure my face is turning as red as my dress, but I can't help smiling at the intensity of his stare.

"Okay, so, new plan," Gus says after a second. "Let's just let the girls fly out there dressed like that and give them all heart attacks."

Os sighs. "We're facing an army of Living Storms. Pretty girls are hardly going to be an effective distraction."

Gus rolls his eyes. "I was *joking*."

"Now is not the time for jokes." Os holds his hands toward the window. "The winds are starting to flee, and there's only one reason they would leave. And there's only one thing we can do to give ourselves a fighting chance." He turns back to Vane. "Are you *finally* ready to teach us Westerly?"

"How do you know it's going to help?" I ask, feeling extra exposed as Os's eyes narrow at me.

"Are you saying that you don't think the power of four is useful?"

"No, but"—my mind flashes back to my disastrous escape attempt from Aston's cave—"how do you know the Westerlies' aversion to violence won't be triggered with the breakthrough?"

"The same way I didn't become steady and sluggish when I learned Southerly," Os snaps back. "That's exactly why it's so crucial that Vane share his language. We'll harness his power in ways he'll never be able to."

I open my mouth to argue but stop myself just in time. He doesn't know I'm part Westerly now.

And maybe he's right. I learned the language through a *bond*. Maybe breakthroughs are different.

But the thought of Westerly words being whispered by the same man who shattered enough drafts to build a Maelstrom makes me physically ill.

I can see the uncertainty in Vane's eyes, and I want to grab him and run far away before he can say another word—or at least beg him not to share his secrets.

I stop myself from doing either.

Westerly is *his* heritage—and even though he shared it with me, this should still be his decision. It's his kinsmen who gave up their lives in Raiden's interrogations, his parents who were stolen because of Raiden's greed. And if anything happens to the sanctity of his language, no one will suffer greater than he will.

He runs his hands through his hair as he turns to Gus. "What do you think?"

"The only reason we escaped that valley alive is because you could control the Westerlies," Gus says quietly, "but you were also able to handle it without me."

I notice he doesn't mention anything about me, and when he glances my way I realize he did that on purpose.

Maybe I'm not the only one who doesn't trust Os.

Vane starts to pace.

Every time he crosses the room, Os's scowl deepens. "We don't have time for indecision, Vane. Only action."

"Fine." Vane turns back to me, and I can see his answer in his eyes.

It breaks my heart, but I press my lips together and keep silent as he says, "I'll teach you Westerly."

CHAPTER 33

VANE

Even as the words are leaving my lips, I can't believe I'm saying them—and the queasy feeling that follows doesn't seem like a good sign.

What else am I supposed to do, though?

Westerlies are the only winds Raiden can't ruin or send away. If I don't teach the Gales how to call them, they'll be completely defenseless in this battle. And I can't let any more guardians die for me.

But what about the Westerlies who gave their lives to protect this secret?

They trusted me to do the same, to keep our language safe from anyone who might abuse or destroy it. And now I'm going to hand it over to my entire army—some of whom I've never met—right after their captain basically threatened to torture me?

My ears ring and everything goes dim as I start to sway—but then someone's wrapping their arms around me and I can finally breathe when the rush of warmth hits me.

"Audra?" I whisper, trying to get my eyes to focus. I can only see a blur of red and skin—which wouldn't be such a bad thing if my stomach weren't flipping and flopping and making the possibility of throwing up on her feel very, very real.

"Hang on," she tells me, pulling me down to the floor and helping me put my head between my knees.

Calm down.

Breathe.

Do not hurl all over your very hot girlfriend.

"He needs space!"

Audra's voice sounds much too far away, considering I can feel her hand on my unbruised shoulder. The ringing is getting louder and my vision is completely dark and I collapse to my side, curling up in a ball and trying not to swallow as my mouth waters the way it always does right before I vomit.

"Okay, everyone out," Gus shouts. "Give the guy some air."

I reach for Audra and she squeezes my hand, just like that cold day in the snow. Everyone else stomps away, and when their footsteps are gone, Audra whispers a soft call in Westerly. A cool breeze sweeps into the room, circling around me.

"Try to relax," she tells me.

I concentrate on the wind brushing my skin and the whispers filling the air. The Westerly's song is peaceful and soft, but it's sad, too. About constantly trying to get back to the calmer skies it used to know.

I know how the draft feels.

Sometimes all I want to do is rewind back to the days when my biggest problems were convincing my dad to cough up some gas money or getting teased about how I messed up yet another date. Now I don't even need my car—and I have pretty much the hottest girlfriend on the planet, who's sitting here next to me in an absurdly sexy red dress, stroking my back even though I'm all gross and sweaty from almost passing out around her *again*.

But I also have to figure out how to protect my army and all the innocent people in this valley from the creepiest dude I've ever met.

If only I could keep all the perks and not have to deal with the other crap.

Especially since the only way I can think of to help everyone is the same thing that's making me stay crashed on the floor, counting my breaths and trying to figure out how to keep the promise I just made when the thought alone turns me into a useless Vane-lump.

I could make them all the special wind spikes, like I did for Gus. He didn't need to know any Westerly commands to use it to destroy the Living Storm.

But what if some of those fall into Raiden's hands?

If I don't teach the Gales the voice commands, they won't be able to call them back after they throw them or unravel them if the Stormers manage to steal them, and there's no way I can keep track of that many wind spikes on my own.

Another wave of nausea hits me, and I go back to concentrating on the Westerly, wishing its song would tell me what to do. The only clue it gives me is the verse "don't flee from the path"—but which

path? The promise I just made? Or the path I've been on all this time? It could be either, and if I guess wrong . . .

I tighten my grip on Audra's hand. "This is a lot tougher than I thought it would be."

"I know." Audra reaches up with her other hand, running her fingers through my hair and sending gentle ripples of heat through my head. "I feel sick thinking about it too—and I'm not really a Westerly."

"You kinda are. Shoot—you have better control than me, and I'm pretty sure that Westerly you brought home wanted to be your pet."

"Maybe." She sighs, pulling her hand slowly away. "But this has to be *your* decision, Vane. I can't be a part of it."

"Why? I thought we were in this together now."

"We are. It's just . . ." A painful stretch of silence passes before she says, "This is your heritage—and we may not be bonded forever—and if—"

"Uh, wait a minute," I interrupt. "Yeah we will."

My eyes sting when I open them and find my room filled with light—the sun must've risen while I was panicking—but it's worth the pain when I get another glimpse at her dress.

Holy freaking wow.

Right—*focus.*

"No *way* am I letting them break us apart," I tell her. "Not unless . . ."

I can't stop myself from remembering the look on Audra's face when Os threatened us. I thought she'd looked worried, but . . .

"Unless?" Audra prompts.

I force myself to sit up, careful to stare at her face instead of the many other places I would much rather be staring. "Do you *want* to be bonded to me?"

"I . . . want you to be happy."

"That's not what I asked." She looks away, and now I'm seriously getting worried. "You haven't changed your mind, have you?"

"No . . ."

Okay, it's the right word, but the way she drags it out—like there's supposed to be a "but" afterward—isn't exactly reassuring.

"If something's changed, you need to tell me. I don't . . ." My voice hitches and I clear my throat. "I don't want you to feel like you're stuck with me."

She turns back toward me, her expression impossible to read. "I don't want *you* to feel stuck with *me*. Now that you've met Solana—"

"Oh my God—is *that* what this is about?"

I'm so relieved I can't help laughing as I grab her and pull her close—which turns out to be a bad idea because I'm still shirtless and holy crap her dress is *backless*. I take a deep breath, trying to remember what I was going to say, and finally manage to mumble, "Solana's a nice girl, but she'll never be you."

"But . . . how can you want to be with the girl whose mother killed your parents?"

She dips her chin, but I tilt it back up, forcing her to look at me. "I will *never* blame you for that, Audra. I'm not even sure if I totally blame your mom anymore. Especially now that she's . . ."

Audra closes her eyes.

"I'm sorry I didn't tell you about that sooner," I mumble. "I didn't know what to say."

It's a weak excuse even to me, but Audra lets me get away with it. She just sits there, looking so heartbreakingly sad.

"Do you want to talk about it?"

"My mother?" She shakes her head. "No. She chose her own path. But . . ."

"But?" I prompt when she doesn't finish.

Audra sighs, dropping her eyes to the neckline of her dress. I try not to follow her stare—but it's *not* easy.

"What is it?" I ask quietly.

"I'm just . . . such a mess. Between my mother and the Gales and . . ." She sighs again and her whole body droops. "Solana's so perfect and pretty and—"

There's only one way to stop this insanity. I pull her closer and kiss her with everything I have.

She sinks into my arms, parting her lips as she presses her body against me. The rush of heat makes my head spin, or maybe that's from all the skin touching skin. Her lips trail down my neck and I realize that if I let this keep going I won't be able to stop—and we're kind of running out of time here. So with the last of my willpower I kiss her one more time and break away.

"*Now* will you believe that I want to be with you?" I ask, grinning when I see the way she's gasping for breath.

Her smile fades. "You could have anyone."

"Ha! I seriously doubt that. I was hardly a hit with the human girls—and not *just* because of you, though you definitely didn't *help.*

But more important, are you ever going to stop doubting me? Or do I need to, like, get your name tattooed across my body—because I'm really not a fan of needles, but I'll put a big 'I Heart Audra' right here if I need to."

I wave my hand across my chest.

She shakes her head and I pull her back, resisting the urge to kiss her again as I whisper in her ear. "I choose *you*. And if anyone ever tries to break our bond, I'll destroy them—and then I'll chase you down and beg until you to let me form it again."

She smiles against my neck, giving me goose bumps, before she tilts her chin up and whispers, "Then what are we going to do about Os?"

"I don't know. But I don't trust him," I whisper back, feeling better just saying it out loud.

"Me either," she admits after a second. "So you're not going to teach him Westerly?"

"I don't think I physically can. I feel like passing out just thinking about it. But what about the rest of the Gales? I don't know how I'll live with myself if I let more of them die for me—"

"It's not your responsibility to worry about the other guardians." She traces her fingers along the edge of my bruise, letting her sparks ease some of the ache. "You're putting your life on the line too—and they knew the risks when they took their oath. They all know their jobs could end in their own death."

The word feels like it casts a shadow over us.

A battle to the *death*.

I suppose I could send them away, but I really don't think Audra and I are strong enough to take all the Stormers on by ourselves. And if the Living Storms get loose in the valley . . .

I feel like I've been punched in the chest as I realize what I'm forgetting, and I stumble to my nightstand to grab my long abandoned cell phone.

"What's wrong?" Audra asks as I switch it on and dial, relieved that it still has a little battery left.

"Someone better be dead," Isaac says as he answers, which makes me realize what time it is. The clock by my bed says quarter to six.

"Hey," I mumble, bracing for how awkward this is going to be. "I know this is going to sound strange, but . . . I need you to head out of town for the next few days. Like now."

I can hear the covers rustle like he's sitting up in bed. "Are you high?"

"No—and I'm not drunk, either, if that's your next question. Just trust me when I say that you'll be much safer if you get out of the desert for a bit. Take Shelby and your family, too. My parents went to Mexico, so maybe you can meet up with them there."

"Okay . . . let me get this straight," Isaac says after an endless silence. "I don't hear from you for, like, two and a half weeks—and now you call me at the crack of dawn telling me to pack up and head to Mexico with your parents? And I'm supposed to believe that you're not on drugs?"

I don't blame him for not believing me. But he *has* to get out of town. "Look, all I can say is that crap is going to hit the fan, like, *soon*—and I don't want you to get caught in the middle of it—"

"What kind of crap?"

"It's . . . hard to explain." He'll never believe me if I tell him the truth. I certainly wouldn't. "But it's big, crazy, you-cannot-wrap-your-head-around-it kind of crap. So please, just get your family and Shelby out of here—don't you have relatives you could stay with in Ensenada?"

"Dude, quit tripping and go back to sleep."

"I'm not tripping, I—"

He hangs up on me.

I call back and it goes straight to voicemail. Same with the next time. And the time after that.

I'm tempted to call his house, but if I can't convince my best friend that I'm not drugged out of my mind, I doubt I can convince his paranoid mother. And his girlfriend, Shelby, hasn't spoken to me since the Hannah-from-Canada debacle weeks ago.

Which leaves me with only one option.

"You're going to get him?" Audra asks, proving how well she knows me as I grab the nearest shirt and throw it over my head.

"I have to try to get him out of here. If something happens to him, I won't be able to live with myself."

"You will do nothing of the sort," Os says from the doorway. "We have precious little time for you to teach us what we need—and *that* is the best way to protect everyone."

I glance at Audra and she nods. "Listen, Os, about that—"

"Don't you dare—you already agreed."

"I know. But I can't. You saw how sick I got."

"Then don't get sick."

"It's not that simple."

"Yes, it is."

"Not when I don't trust you!"

I can see Gus and Solana standing behind Os, looking pretty dang shocked that I would admit that. But it's the truth. Might as well lay it all out there at this point.

"You don't *trust* me?" Os growls. "I am your *captain!*"

"Yeah, and less than an hour ago you threatened to torture me and break my bond. I'm sure you can see why that might make you seem a little shady."

"Is that what this is about? Some sort of blackmail to force me into accepting your relationship?"

"Of course not—we don't need your approval. You don't get to—"

I stop myself and take a deep breath, focusing on the Westerly still floating around my room. It's singing that line again about not fleeing from the path, and I think I finally know what it means.

"Look," I say, trying to make sense of the chaotic thoughts in my head. "Everyone's always talking about how I'm the one with the power to fix everything. But I'm not. The *Westerlies* have the power. Every single time they've managed to save me it's because I stepped back and listened to what my instincts were telling me to do. And my instincts are telling me not to teach anyone else my language, so I have to trust them. I know it's scary—but it was pretty freaking scary when Audra was trapped in a drainer and my instincts told me to make an ultra strong wind spike and launch it at her, and it was even scarier when we were cornered by Raiden in Death Valley and we had to drop our only shield and unravel our only weapons and hope that the few tired drafts we had would come through for us. But they did. So fine, maybe you don't trust me and I don't trust you, but can we both agree to trust the *wind*?"

Os's mouth forms one word. Then another.

When he changes his mind again, I say, "You know you agree with me. You just don't want to."

He reaches up and smoothes the hair around his braid. "I *do* agree that your instincts are important, Vane. But that doesn't mean they're always perfect, either—or that you're properly understanding them. Yes, you felt ill thinking about teaching us, but how do you know that's not just nerves resulting from a life-changing decision?"

"Because it wasn't."

"But how do you know—and don't give me some pointless answer like 'I just do.' You've never given teaching us a chance. How do you know it won't feel differently if you try?"

"Because I didn't feel like that with Audra!"

Gus cringes, and I realize he never told Os that important detail—which was probably the right call.

"What does he mean?" Os asks, reeling on Audra. "Did he teach you Westerly?"

Say no! I want to beg her. *Lie to cover my mistake.*

But Audra squares her shoulders, glancing quickly at me before she turns to face Os and says, "Yes."

CHAPTER 34

AUDRA

I could've lied.

I almost did.

But in the split second that I had to think, I realized there's a bigger secret that I need to keep. And this is the best way to hide it.

"Yes, he taught me," I tell Os, silently begging Vane and Gus to go along with this. "After we bonded. He wanted to make sure I had extra protection, but I was only able to learn a couple of commands."

"That didn't trigger a breakthrough?" Os asks.

"I'd hoped it would. But no." I'm proud of how smooth the lie sounds. "I've memorized the words, and I know what they mean because he translated them for me. But the language is still a mystery."

Vane frowns, and I can tell both he and Gus are trying to figure out what I'm doing. Thankfully, neither of them corrects me.

If Os knew that Vane passed his heritage to me through our bond, I'm sure he would expect the same phenomenon to happen with Vane and Solana—and the possibility alone would sway the Gales to vote to break our bond and try it.

Maybe it would work.

Maybe it wouldn't.

But Vane is *mine*.

Solana has pretty dresses and a pretty gold bracelet and the pretty future the Gales promised her. But I have a lifetime of knowing Vane, protecting Vane, sacrificing everything to keep him safe. And he chose *me*.

I won't let the Gales take him away.

I won't let them know how powerful I am, either.

As much as I hate to be underestimated, it can also be an advantage. And if Os is harnessing the power of pain, I need all the advantage I can get.

"Did you know about this?" Os asks Gus.

Gus shrugs. "The battle was so chaotic it was hard to tell what was going on."

Os looks less than satisfied with that answer, but he turns back to Vane. "And you won't teach me the same commands you gave her?"

"I told you, my instincts won't let me."

"What about Solana? Her family was chosen as our royals for their kind, generous manner, and she's been the only one able to calm your nightmares—twice now."

The reminder of my earlier failure cuts deeper than a windslicer. So does the hope shining in Solana's bright eyes.

But Vane's words heal the pain. "I only trust Audra."

Os reels back toward me, his disgust so obvious it might as well be a sign around his neck. "And what commands have you been privileged enough to learn?"

"Why do you care?" Vane demands before I can answer.

"Because I'm trying to strategize! If you won't teach the rest of us, the least you can do is tell me her strengths so I can organize our formation accordingly."

I choose only things they would see me use during the fight. "He taught me how to call a Westerly. And how to weave all four winds into a spike."

"The same spikes Gus used when he defeated the Living Storm?" Os asks, stepping closer when I nod. "We need those for this battle. If you won't teach us to weave them, at least supply them for the others."

I'd thought of that earlier—and it seems like a fair compromise. But the idea of handing over that kind of power turns my stomach. Vane must feel just as torn, because when I look at him he shakes his head—but it doesn't seem like a no.

It looks more like he's leaving the decision up to me.

"Please," Os whispers. "I don't want to lose any more of my guardians."

For a moment he looks like the Os I remember—the valiant captain staring at me with a mix of fear and respect.

I don't understand or agree with his recent methods, but I know he's trying to protect our people.

That doesn't mean I can trust him, though.

I try to think through everything I've learned about the Westerlies, hoping there's some clue that will tell me what they'd want me to do. They're brave and loyal. Steady and peaceful. And yet, the command that finally allowed our escape from Death Valley was an aggressive word. I never would've thought to give that kind of command to a Westerly. But that was what my shield told me to use, like it knew there are times when we have to push beyond what feels comfortable and go with something more extreme.

I take a deep breath, looking at Vane as I say, "I'm willing to weave one spike for every guardian. Only one."

Vane hesitates for a second, then nods.

Os does too, though he looks less than satisfied. "How long will it take?"

"How many guardians are coming?"

"Nineteen, including myself and Gus. Twenty if you count Solana."

The numbers feel heavy in my head.

Twenty-nine Living Storms—plus who knows how many Stormers—against so small a band of Gales . . .

Os must read the worry on my face because he tells me, "You could teach us your commands."

"I can't."

"Really? And what if Raiden captures you? Have you thought of that?" he asks Vane. "You realize she could hand him the power of four now, don't you?"

"Uh, have you met Audra? If anyone's stubborn enough to resist Raiden, it's her." He flashes a small, sad smile at me, but that isn't what makes my breath catch. It's the absolute trust in his eyes.

Not since my father has anyone shown so much faith in me.

"But I'll never let that happen," Vane adds, his voice darkening. "Raiden won't get anywhere near her."

"If you really want to make sure of that," Os snaps, "you'd give more of us the power to protect you two."

"The wind spike was all I needed," Gus reminds him. "And if Audra's going to make them for us, she should get started—now. While we still have enough winds."

We all turn to the window. The sky is a clear, perfect blue, but the trees in the grove are mostly still. The morning breezes that usually stir their leaves are whisking away. Spooked by the change in the air.

Vane slips on his shoes. "Will you be okay without me for a few minutes?"

He's talking to me, but Os is the one who answers. "Your responsibility is *here*, Vane."

"Actually, I thought my responsibility was to every innocent person in this valley."

"And you think you're helping them by wasting time warning *one* groundling?"

"He's my friend."

"That's not good enough."

"For me, it is."

"Maybe you should let him go, sir," Gus interrupts. "You know he's going to do it anyway."

Os doesn't agree—but his silence is enough.

Vane pulls me in for the briefest of kisses—so light I'm not sure if our lips even touch—before whispering for me to stay close to Gus, then making his way to the window. I can't help smiling as he jumps outside and I hear the thornbushes crunch, followed by a high-pitched yelp.

"So smug in your betrayal," Os grumbles as soon as Vane's flown away. "You swore an *oath*—have you forgotten that?"

The words sting more than I want them to, and it takes me a second to find the right reply. "I've never stopped serving the Gales— but my loyalty lies with my *king*. As I thought it was supposed to be for all of us, now that he's stepped into his role."

"Has he now?" Os laughs without humor. "Do you know how many guardians we've lost since Vane *stepped into his role*? Forty-one." He kicks one of Vane's shoes across the room and it slams into the wall hard enough to leave a black scuff. "*Forty-one* loyal, dedicated soldiers who kept up the fight after you abandoned your duties. All while we have a leader who harnesses an ultimate power he refuses to share with anyone—except *you*. A leader who we thought had at least been trained for this moment by our most dedicated child prodigy. And yet Feng told me Vane knew almost nothing when he took over. Did you do *anything* besides seduce him?"

My eyes sting with shame, but I fight back the tears.

What Os is saying might be true—but I have to believe that Vane shared his heritage with me for a reason, and that with the Westerlies' help we'll be able to win the coming battle.

Voices outside break the uncomfortable silence.

"Excuse me," Os says, "I need to go lift the morale of my soldiers before the fight—not that there's much I can say. Without the power of four, we all know *someone's* going to die today. We just don't know who, or how many."

He stalks out of the room, followed by Solana. She doesn't look at me, but I can see her judgment in the straight line of her shoulders and the sway of her hips.

Gus sighs. "Well, *that* went well."

"I'm sorry you have to deal with all this—and thank you for not correcting me."

He nods, staring at the floor before he steps closer and whispers, "You *have* had the fourth breakthrough, right?"

I study his face, making sure I can trust him. "Yes."

He releases the breath he'd been holding. "Then maybe we have a chance. Vane's a terrible fighter."

"I know. I tried to—"

"Relax, I didn't mean that against you. My dad didn't get very far either—and he's one of the greatest fighters in the Gales. *Was*," he corrects.

Guilt surges inside me, hot and sharp. "I'm so sorry—"

"Please don't apologize. It's not your fault. And in a weird way, I think this was what he wanted. He never got over losing my mom. Now he doesn't have to miss her anymore."

The only thing I can say is what we're always supposed to say at a moment like this. But this time I force myself to believe it's true. "Now they're together in the sky."

Gus nods and looks away.

I leave him alone, heading toward the door.

"You don't have to stay with me," I tell him when he follows.

"Vane will kill me if I let you out of my sight. And it's probably better if I stay out of Os's way right now."

I can feel all the guardians watching us as we make our way to the date grove. It's strange to see so many of them gathered together. During my training they always worked in small groups. Bases of five or ten at the most, to make sure we never opened ourselves up to too many casualties. And once I was assigned to Vane, I was alone.

If Raiden's killed forty-one Gales—even if twenty-nine of those were his recent capture—he must've taken down most of the nearby bases. And if he wins today he'll have wiped out the bulk of our Pacific Fleet. I wish we had time to call the other fleets for aid, but I'm sure that's why Raiden is moving quickly. He doesn't want us to have a chance to regroup.

My legs feel heavy as we weave through the familiar overgrown trees, but I stuff my exhaustion away. I'm no stranger to sleepless nights.

Still, I wish I had time to steal away to the mountains for fresh air to revive me. Instead I head straight to the sun-bleached walls of my shelter.

Vane was right about the mess, and paired with the heat and the bugs swarming everywhere, it's hard to imagine that I actually lived here. I never truly thought of this place as my home, but as I cross into the small corner of shade under the few remaining eaves, I realize that, for better or worse, these crumbling walls know the story of my life.

I pull my windslicer from the slit I carved into the floor and

check the needles to make sure they're not bent or tarnished.

"This must've been a tough assignment," Gus says, kicking away a couple of date roaches. "I don't know how you did it. I mean, living in this piece of crap, having to stay hidden, putting up with Vane—though clearly that last one wasn't as challenging for you."

"Actually, having feelings for Vane was the hardest part. Despite what you may think, I did try to fight them."

"Hey, I didn't mean—"

"It's fine, Gus. You don't have to pretend that you don't think I'm a traitor for bonding to him."

"Good, because I don't."

I nearly prick my finger on a needle. "You don't?"

He crunches a few more roaches as he comes to stand beside me. "No. It's a mess—I'll give you guys that. But if this is what you both want, I don't think the Gales should have the right to interfere. And I will never support them if they try to break you apart."

I'm almost too stunned to speak. But I manage a weak "Thank you."

That's one vote in our favor at least. I wonder how many others . . .

"How does it even work?" he asks quietly. "Like, how do you *break* a bond?"

"Aston didn't say. He told me our instincts can guide us if we decide to do it ourselves, and that it's a bit like shifting forms. But if someone does it to you, all he said is that it would be very unpleasant."

Gus shudders. "Sounds like an understatement."

"Yes, it does."

The holes in Aston's skin flash through my mind.

Vane is so much a part of me now, I can't imagine I'd be any less scarred if someone ripped him away. But I shove my worries to the same place I shoved my weariness. I have a lot of wind spikes to make.

I build them the new way Vane used, with only one of each wind united together. They turn sleek and deep blue and even more deadly than I remember, and with each new spike, I whisper a silent plea that I'm making the right choice by sharing them with the Gales.

"Is that your bird?" Gus asks, pointing to the top of the tallest palm. "Because that would explain a *lot*. Freaking thing screeches his head off every morning at sunrise, and the only reason I didn't blast him across the country is because Vane wouldn't let me."

I smile sadly. "Gavin was used to me coming home at that time."

It takes several deep breaths to work up the courage to finally look where Gus is pointing.

I could've taken Gavin with me when I left, could've let him fly beside me for my journey, the way he did every day since he became mine. But after all the ways my mother lied and deceived me through him, all the misplaced blame and guilt—even though it wasn't Gavin's fault—I couldn't have him with me.

Even now, as I stare into his angry red-orange eyes, part of me wants to look away. But then I'd be as bad as *her*, turning my back on someone who needs me, simply because it hurts.

I hold out my arm and call Gavin to my side.

For a second he ignores me. Then he spreads his strong gray

wings and dives, landing on my wrist with an earsplitting shriek. His talons cut in just enough to let me know he hasn't forgiven me, but not enough to draw blood. A happy truce I'm willing to accept as I reach up and stroke the silky feathers along his neck.

"A storm is coming," I tell him, beginning to understand why Vane had to warn his friend. "You have to get somewhere safe. Head as far south as you can and don't return until the skies clear."

Gavin screeches again, and his wings don't budge. But when I repeat the command with a plea, he nips my finger gently and takes off, sweeping toward the south like I've asked.

"It's hard to believe we're really going to get through this, isn't it?" Gus asks as he picks up a wind spike, testing its weight in his hands.

He steps back, squatting into a sparring position before he launches into one of the Gale's advance practice routines. The way he moves is flawless. No wasted energy. Every swipe precise and perfect. I've seen Gales with decades more training fight with less ease.

And Vane trusts him.

And he kept our secret—without my even asking.

"Come," I say in Westerly, and the wind spike shoots out of Gus's hand, midslice.

He glares at me as I catch it. "No need to rub it in."

I hold his gaze and repeat the word again, slower this time. Making the syllables easier to understand.

His eyes widen. "Are you . . . trying to teach me?"

I nod, relieved when a wave of nausea doesn't hit.

"Will that even work if I haven't had the breakthrough?"

"It did for Vane as a kid. He used a command he'd heard his parents say, even though he didn't know what it meant. It's how he saved my life."

"Wow, you guys have a ton of history, don't you?"

"We do."

I repeat the word again, breaking down the intonations. Gus repeats it, fumbling over the sleepy hisses in the second part. But after four tries the spike launches into his hands.

"That is so freaking awesome."

He flings the spike toward a palm and hisses the command, snapping it back toward him like a boomerang.

"So I don't get to know what I'm saying?" he asks as he catches it one-handed.

"It's safer for you if you don't."

Breakthroughs are complicated things. Most of the time they require extreme measures to trigger. But it always comes down to learning one word and having all the pieces snap together. Sometimes just hearing it is enough.

Gus goes back to practicing slashes with his spike. He moves so fast his arms turn to a blur as he whips the sharp edge at a strange angle that ripples the air.

"I guess it would be a pretty big responsibility," he mumbles. "You just jumped to the top of Raiden's Most Wanted list."

"Second to the top," I correct, trying to copy his motion and not coming close. "Vane's still the only actual Westerly."

"All the more reason why you'll be at the top. Who's Raiden going to want more—the guy whose kinsmen have been resisting his interrogation methods for decades, or the *first* non-Westerly to have the fourth breakthrough?"

I slash again, still failing to copy Gus's skill. "Both."

"Maybe." He comes up behind me, grabbing my arm and guiding me through the motion. Halfway through the thrust, he slides his fingers to my wrist, showing me how I need to twist it at the tail end of my swipe. It's the same way all my trainers worked with me when I was learning blade technique, but it feels strangely uncomfortable this time. Probably because Gus still has no shirt on and I'm stuck in this ridiculous dress.

Gus must feel the same way because he clears his throat and steps back, raising his spike to challenge me to a spar instead. "All I'm saying is, be ready. If I were Raiden—and I knew there was a chance I might only be able to grab one of you—I know which one I'd make my priority."

I raise my spike to accept his challenge. "If that's the case, it's a good thing. Of the two of us, I'm far more ready to face down Raiden than Vane is."

"Well, *that* is definitely true."

Still, Gus manages to knock my spike out of my grip in only three thrusts—and when I challenge him to a rematch I barely last five minutes before he knocks me to the ground and sends my spike skidding out of my reach.

"My gift lets me pull strength from the wind," Gus explains, and I'm sure that's part of my problem.

But the bigger issue is that every time I go for a deadly swipe, a rush of dizziness weakens my arm.

Gus helps me to my feet, and I can feel him studying me as I dust the sand off my shaky legs.

"That question you asked earlier," he says after a second, "about picking up the Westerlies' aversion to violence. Did you . . . ?"

I can't look at him as I nod. "I'm not *as* bad as Vane, but . . ."

Gus sighs, and I want to crawl into a hole and disappear.

He squeezes my shoulder, waiting for me to meet his eyes. "I'll have your back the entire time."

I force a smile, trying to be grateful.

But as I stare at the sky, all I can hear are Os's words from earlier.

Someone's going to die today.

For the first time, I believe him.

CHAPTER 35

VANE

The flight to Isaac's street takes less than five minutes, and as I touch down next to his beat-up truck, I still have no idea what I'm going to say. I just know that I'm not leaving until he agrees to get the hell out of town.

His neighbors are still asleep—their blinds closed tight—and when I stare at the row of nearly identical single-story houses, I feel like I've swallowed something bitter.

Dozens of families are in there, just like Isaac's, all sound asleep, with no idea they're in any danger.

Same with the next street over.

And the one after that.

And the whole freaking desert.

But I don't have time to warn them all—and even if I did, it would only create massive panic.

I won't let the Storms reach the valley, I promise myself as I sneak in the gate to Isaac's backyard. His curtains are closed, and when I test his bedroom window, it's locked. Which leaves pounding on the glass and calling his name, hoping I'm not waking his whole family.

It takes at least a minute of solid banging before he slides the curtains apart.

"Gah—put some clothes on!" I shout as he throws open the window wearing only supertight briefs.

"Dude, Vane, I don't know what you're on—"

"Come on, you know me better than that—"

"No, I *used* to know you," he snaps, running his hand through his hair—or what little of it he has left. He buzzed it since I last saw him. And finally got rid of his scraggly mustache.

Now if only he'd put on some pants.

"Look," I tell him. "I know things have been weird lately—trust me, they have been for me, too. It's just . . . the world's not the way you think it is, okay? There's all kinds of other crap going on in the background that you don't know about—and some of it is pretty huge. Life-or-death huge. I don't know how else to explain it, but please, you have to trust me when I say you need to get your family out of here."

Isaac snorts and starts to close the window. I reach out and block him.

He pushes harder, but it makes no difference. After weeks of late-night workouts I'm way stronger than him now.

"I'm serious, Isaac. Look." I use one hand to lift my shirt, showing him the wicked bruise on my side. "Does this look like a joke? Am I imagining this?"

He winces and stops trying to shut me out. "What happened—did someone jump you?"

"It's way bigger than that. That's why you have to get out of here."

"No, that's what cops are for."

I almost want to laugh at the idea of a few out-of-shape policemen pointing guns at Raiden and telling him to freeze.

"This is so far beyond cops, man." I sigh, trying to figure out how to make him understand. "I'm talking about the kind of thing you only see in movies and stuff. Like Thor or—"

"Really? You're giving me thunder gods?"

Crap, there's no way to explain this without telling him everything.

And there's no way to tell him and have him actually believe me. Unless . . .

"You want the truth? Fine."

I'm already winning the prize for Biggest Rule Breaker at this point, so why not shatter the Gales' code of secrecy again?

I call the nearest wind to my side, tangling the cold Northerly around Isaac's waist. Before he can blink, I tell the draft to surge and it yanks Isaac into the air, floating him a few feet above his bedroom floor.

When he's done flailing and shouting words in Spanish that I can't understand—but I'm pretty sure I know what they mean—I set him down and twist the wind into a small dust devil. I tell it to suck up a pair of pants off his floor and launch them at him. "Seriously, dude, cover your junk."

Isaac barely manages to catch his jeans. He's too busy looking back and forth between the tornado and me. "What the—how the—you just—"

"I'm a sylph," I say, cutting him off. "Don't worry, I'd never heard of it either. I guess it means I can control the wind."

Isaac laughs. The hysterical kind where if he were out in public, parents would be pulling their kids to safety.

"How do you control the freaking *wind*?"

"It's really hard to explain, but it has to do with words." I whisper the command to release the Northerly and it sweeps around Isaac's room, fluttering all the papers on his desk before it streaks out the window and races back into the sky.

Isaac stares at me for a second. Then backs away.

"Dude, you don't have to be afraid of me. I'm still the same guy you know."

"Uh, the Vane I know could barely control his farts, much less the *wind*. And he didn't bang on my window at the crack of dawn covered in mysterious bruises, telling me to get out of town."

"Okay, so maybe a *few* things have changed."

I glance around his bedroom, which has stayed pretty much the same since I met Isaac when I was eight. Some of the football and video game junk has been shoved aside to make room for pictures of his girlfriend, Shelby, and all the papers on his desk look like college applications. But he's still the same guy who went out of his way to talk to the weird new kid at school.

If he knew what I was way back then, I doubt he would've bothered. And maybe that would've been better, because now he's in a crapload of danger.

"So, like, how did you find all this out?" Isaac asks quietly. "Did you just wake up one day and start talking to the wind?"

"No. Audra had to show me."

"Is that the hot chick who ruined your date with Hannah?"

"Yeah." I grin, remembering the way she stormed into the Cheesecake Factory and told Hannah she was my girlfriend. One of the most awkward—and awesome—moments ever.

"And you and her are . . . together?"

I nod, deciding not to get into the whole bonding thing. I'm sure Isaac's had all the weird he can take.

"Niiiiiice," he tells me, though he frowns. "Is she a sylph too?"

"Yep. There are a lot of us, actually. Well, not a lot compared to, like, humans but—"

"Wait. You're not *human?*"

I shake my head and he takes another step away.

"Come on, don't act surprised. I told you, I'm a *sylph.*"

"I know, but I thought that was like a title or something. Like Hawkeye or Batman or—"

"I'm not a superhero."

"I guess not. Which is good. If you start wearing spandex, I'm ditching you."

"This from the guy in tighty-whities."

He glances down and blushes before *finally* slipping on his pants. "Thank God."

"Shut up—you're just jealous of my sexy."

I'm tempted to shove him across the room with another draft. But I've already wasted too much time.

"You have to listen to me, Isaac. You need to get out of town."

"Why? What does any of this have to do with me? I haven't even talked to you in weeks."

"I know—I was trying to keep you out of this. But I can't anymore. It's a really long story, but there's this superscary guy who's coming here to get me, and he'd be happy to get his hands on my best friend, too."

"You're telling me you have an archnemesis?"

"I guess you could put it that way—except I'm being serious, Isaac. I hope you get that. Raiden's tortured and killed *hundreds* of people. Maybe thousands. And he's extra pissed at me right now." I lift my shirt again and point to my bruise. "He did this right before I got away. *No one* gets away from him. So he doesn't just want to catch me, he wants to destroy this whole freaking valley."

Isaac rubs his temples as he processes that. "Wait—the whole valley? How are you going to warn everyone?"

"I can't—there's not enough time. And do you really think they'd believe me?"

"But . . . there're a lot of people here."

"I know."

He starts mumbling in Spanish again as he turns and paces his room.

"So what are you going to do?" he asks after a few seconds.

"Fight."

"Uh, no offense, man, but my kid brother is tougher than you."

"Hey—I've been training for weeks. And I won't be fighting alone. My army—"

"You have an *army?*"

"I told you, it's a really really really *really* long story. And someday I promise to tell you anything you want to know. But I don't have time right now. I'm not even supposed to be here, but I couldn't let things start without warning you. So *please*. Grab your family, get Shelby, and head south, before it's too late, okay?"

"I don't know, man," he mumbles. "I don't know what do with any of this."

"I get that. But will you be able to live with yourself if something happens to anyone you love?"

That seems to snap him out of it, at least enough to ask, "What the hell am I supposed to tell them? They're not going to believe this sylph crap."

"I don't know—but I know you're awesome at getting people to do things they don't want to do. How else did you drag me on so many blind dates?"

He grins at the memory, and I feel myself smile too.

"So just . . . work that same magic. And don't waste any time. As it is . . ." I glance at the sky and feel my heart freeze.

A few minutes ago it was a clear, vivid blue. But the western horizon is now dark and gray. And now that I'm paying attention, I notice the air has a chill. Way too cold for the desert in August.

"Is that a storm?" Isaac asks, pointing to the clouds gathering above the mountains.

"Yeah." I'm barely able to make my mouth form the word. My head is too busy trying to figure out if Isaac has enough time to get out of town and if I have enough time to get back to Audra and if the Gales have enough time to put whatever plan they've scrambled together into effect.

I sure hope so, because it's too late to do anything else.

Raiden is already here.

CHAPTER 36

AUDRA

A horrible hiss echoes through the valley, coming from the mountains to the west, where an enormous storm is gathering.

Thick gray clouds swirl together like a hurricane, and when another hiss shatters the silence, the air turns achingly cold. I shiver in my thin dress and reach for any nearby Westerlies. All I feel is one, sweeping through the dunes a few miles away.

"You can't leave," Gus tells me as I call it to my side.

"I have to find Vane."

"No, you have to stay here." He grabs my arm when I don't listen. "Raiden's here for *you*, too."

He's right.

I know he's right.

But Vane is alone and unprotected and Raiden is so close and he's not attacking from the east like we thought and—

"You think Vane can't see that?" Gus asks, pointing to the wall of thunderheads cresting the mountains. "I'm sure he's just as worried about you, and if he's not on his way back by now, he will be any second."

But Raiden could already be in the valley. And if he catches Vane alone—

"Hey, deep breath," Gus says, shaking my arm until I look at him. "If he's not here in a few minutes I'll go after him—but you have to stay here. *I'm* his guardian now, remember?"

The words feel like thunder—or maybe that's my pounding heart.

I'm not Vane's guardian anymore.

I can't be.

But putting myself ahead of Vane makes me feel every bit the traitor Os accused me of being . . .

The wind I'd called sweeps into the grove, brushing against my cheeks and whispering a song about trust and hope. Tears prick my eyes when I realize it's my loyal Westerly shield, and as it drapes itself around me—without my even giving the command—I feel my heartbeat steady.

The Westerlies have accepted me as their kin.

I have to start accepting myself.

"You have to keep him safe," I beg Gus.

"I have to keep *both* of you safe. So come on, let's get back to Os and find out how he's changing his strategy. I can't believe Raiden's coming from the west."

I can't either, and I can't decide if he's doing it for some great poetic irony or if it's part of some trick we have yet to uncover. Knowing Raiden, it's probably both. The only thing we can rely on with him is cruelty.

I help Gus gather the wind spikes, and we race through the scraggly palm trees to find the rest of the Gales on the lawn. They stand in a wide circle around Os and Solana, and it's hard not to panic when I take a quick head count and realize the much-too-small group is all we're going to get. Especially when I see how thin and pale they are. Gray streaks pepper their braided hair and creases weather their faces.

Raiden definitely stole our strongest fighters.

"Vane isn't back?" Os asks when he sees us. His voice is eerily calm, though his lips are pressed into a hard line.

"I'm sure he's on his way," Gus tells him. "In the meantime, we brought you these."

He pushes through the circle and hands Os the first wind spike.

Os holds the sharp edge up to the fading sunlight and swipes it a few times before he turns to me. "Any special instructions?"

"Don't lose it."

He sighs. "Any *helpful* instructions?"

"That's the only instruction that matters. These spikes won't explode like the ones you're used to. It's what makes them so powerful—but it also means you can't use them the same way. If you throw them or lose your grip, the weapon could fall into the enemy's hands."

The Gales start to grumble at the news.

I can make out only snatches of what they're saying, but I hear the word "pointless" several times—and Os does nothing to quiet them.

"You dare to disrespect this gift?" Gus shouts, shaming them all into silence. "You hold the power of four in your hands—a power even Raiden doesn't possess—and you grumble and complain because you have to protect it?"

"We don't need more things to protect," a short, frail-looking guardian shouts back, tossing his spike on the ground.

The others in the group back away as Gus stalks forward, leaning in the rebellious guardian's face. "The weapon you've just cast aside was the *only* thing that allowed me to defeat the Living Storm I battled. Without it, you might as well surrender to the sky now."

The rebellious Gale glares at Gus, and for a second I wonder if he's going to turn and walk away. Instead he bends and recovers his spike from the ground, shoving it through the belt of his uniform, right next to his windslicer.

"That is a smart place to store it," Gus tells him, turning back to the others. "In fact, the best way to use these spikes is to think of them like a windslicer."

"You expect us to engage in hand-to-hand combat with these Storm beasts?" an old, tall Gale with a braided beard asks.

"Why not? I did. And I won." Gus's voice holds no arrogance. Only assurance. "I understand that things feel bleak—and I wish I could promise that no lives will be lost today—but that is no different from any other battle we've faced. And this is our *chance*. Raiden is coming to us, desperate to prove that he's the invincible king he

claims to be. But he is *not* invincible. I've seen him bleed. I've *made* him bleed. And the weapon that sliced him was one of these."

He holds up his spike and this time there are cheers.

Halfhearted and fleeting, but still, cheers.

"Guardian Gusty is right," Os says, like he's just realized that Gus is doing *his* job. "The tide is turning, my friends. If we stand strong against it, we could mark this day in our histories as the day this war swung in our favor. Perhaps even the day we end Raiden's reign forever!"

Louder cheers this time, mixed with applause.

Gus moves back to my side as Os continues to prep his soldiers.

"Do you really think Raiden will come here?" I ask, keeping my voice low so that only Gus hears.

Raiden may crave power and prestige, but he usually stays away from the action. And I saw the fear in his eyes when Gus's wind spike sliced his arm. I can't see him risking further injury in a battle with this many variables.

"I don't think he'll be able to stay away," Gus whispers back. "Though I wouldn't be surprised if he hides in the mountains. And you can bet I'm going up there to find him."

His grip tightens on his wind spike, and I have a feeling if Gus gets another shot, he won't miss again.

If only it could be that easy.

Os switches to discussing their strategy and I try not to cringe. It sounds like he's reciting straight from the basic-training guide. Divide and conquer. Clean, direct attacks. No one works alone.

"This isn't a time for basics."

I don't realize I've said it out loud until everyone turns to look at me.

"What was that, Ms. Eastend?" Os asks.

I notice that he doesn't call me Guardian Audra. Though at least he doesn't call me Your Highness.

I clear my throat, hoping my cheeks aren't as red as my ridiculous dress as I say, "I'm sorry—I didn't mean to interrupt. But I've seen Raiden fight, and nothing about his method is basic."

"Ah, I see," Os says, and the circle parts as he stalks closer to me. "So perhaps you think *you* should be captain?"

"I didn't say that."

"And yet, you thought it was perfectly acceptable to second-guess me in front of my guardians."

"I didn't mean—"

"I agree with Audra," Gus interrupts, earning himself a death glare from Os—and a grateful smile from me. "The plan you explained to me earlier was a stronger plan. Just because Raiden's coming from a different direction doesn't mean we should abandon it."

"Another person thinking they're an expert on battle strategy. Tell me, Guardian Gusty—how many battles have you actually fought?"

"Three," Gus replies without a hint of apprehension. "And one of those was against a Living Storm."

"Yes. *One* Living Storm, Gus. Which is entirely different from facing down an army of them—something you would know if you understood anything about battle tactics. But Feng was the brilliant strategist in your family, and from everything I've seen, you take more after your mother. A strong fighter and a loyal Gale, but far too impulsive and reckless—and we all know how that turned out."

"Ravenna didn't die because she was reckless," Solana shouts, surprising everyone with her fury. She wraps her arms around herself, staring at Gus as she whispers, "She died because I failed her."

"What do you mean?" Gus asks, but Solana shakes her head and looks away.

Os puts his hand on her shoulder. "Ravenna was *your* guardian, Solana. Her job was to protect *you*—and the fact that she left any part of her strategy up to her charge only proves my point about her recklessness."

Gus's hands curl into fists, and I can feel mine doing the same. Trusting your charge is the hardest call a guardian can make. No one would *ever* make it recklessly.

"My mother was not—"

"Now is not the time to debate the past," Os interrupts, pointing to the coming storm, which is growing larger by the second. Any minute now it will block out the sun.

And Vane's still not back. . . .

"I've simplified our strategy for a reason," Os says, "Let's not forget that no one here knows Raiden better than me. And I know that his greatest weakness is vanity. He's coming here to prove to his worthless minions that he is no less of a leader because of yesterday's incident. His focus will be on creating a spectacle, and therein lies his folly. The more showy and complicated the attack, the more it disregards basic battle principles. We can already see his vanity run amok by the fact that he's coming from the west—wasting the energy of his forces on unnecessary journeying just for his theatrics. So the best way to take advantage of that kind of thinking is to respond with the very principles he'll be disregarding. If we come at him straight on and tackle each enemy systematically, we'll wipe out half his force before he even notices what we're doing."

I hate to admit that his reasoning makes sense. Though Os is forgetting something key.

"Don't forget that Raiden might be watching. He held back in Death Valley, waiting to see what we'd do, and changed his commands accordingly."

"And it worked so well for him, didn't it?" Os counters. "All three of you got away, and humiliated him in the process. If I know Raiden, and believe me, I do"—he points to his scar—"he'll come at us full force this time, hitting us with everything he has, as many ways as he can, right from the start. He'll be hoping for a quick, decisive victory. Which is why I designed our strategy this way. We need to save our energy, stick with something simple that we know will keep most of us alive so we can hold out long enough to institute the second part of our plan. The part where we use our secret weapon."

He pulls Solana closer, and I can't tell who's more surprised, her or me. Her skin turns paler than her dress.

"Raiden *will* be here," Os explains. "And his primary strategy is always to deprive us of the one thing we need to fight back. He ruins the wind to leave us defenseless, and we're going to let him believe that he's succeeded. We'll use our spikes to take out as much of his force as we can, but at the opportune moment, I'm going to surrender. Let him taste his victory so he'll swoop in to gloat. And that's when Solana will release the winds she's been storing—giving us an entire arsenal we can use to hit Raiden with everything we have."

The rest of the Gales murmur their agreement—and I'm forced to admit that it's a much more clever plan than I'd originally thought. But it worries me that it completely neglects the Westerlies. Unless he has orders for Vane and me that he hasn't explained. Or maybe he just expects us to—

A loud, mournful howl radiates through the valley, followed by another, and another.

Each cry grows louder and more desperate, until my eyes are watering and my jaw is clenched so tightly my teeth start to ache.

"What is that?" Gus shouts, covering his ears.

I do the same, but it barely muffles the next howl, and I feel a tremble ripple through my Westerly shield as it tightens its grip around me.

"It's the sound the wind makes when it's ruined," I tell Gus. "The final cry before the best parts of the draft crumble away."

"Is it always this loud?" he asks, and I shake my head.

These must be bigger winds somehow, or maybe a combination of drafts, like a cyclone or . . .

I suck in a breath as I grab Gus's arm. "I think he's breaking the Living Storms."

Gus's eyes widen. "Can he do that?"

"I have no idea."

But another unearthly howl rages through the valley and I know I'm right. What I don't know is why.

Why ruin his own creation?

What power is he drawing from their pain?

I turn toward Os, watching him as he struggles to keep the other guardians calm.

His agonized expression tells me he recognizes the sound too—though there's something besides pain in his eyes. Something that makes me far colder than the icy air whipping around us.

Hunger.

Os is fighting it—his whole body shaking with the effort. But the craving is still there. Boiling below the surface.

I pull Gus close enough to whisper in his ear—though it's more of a shout with all the noise and chaos. "Keep an eye on Os. This sound is like a drug for him."

Gus follows my gaze and nods. He presses his lips against my ear to shout back, "We need to find Vane."

"No you don't," Vane says behind me, and when I spin around he's appeared almost magically.

For about half a second I'm relieved. Then I notice how pale he is.

"What's wrong?" Gus and I both ask at the same time.

He's shaking so hard I have to hold him steady.

Vane pulls away, wobbling toward the circle of nervous Gales until he finds Os in the center.

"I called the Westerlies from the mountains," he says, his voice hollow. Weak. "I wanted to hear their songs, see if they could tell me what we were up against."

"And?" Os prompts when he doesn't finish.

Vane turns away, staring at the ever-darkening sky. "They said the Storms are too strong this time. There's nothing we can do to stop them."

CHAPTER 37

VANE

nnocent people are going to die because of me.

If I'd moved to some base in the middle of nowhere, maybe I could've kept everyone safe. But I wanted to stay with my family. I wanted to act like my life hadn't changed just because I found out I was a sylph.

And now everyone in this valley is going to pay the price.

The desert grows dim as the clouds finally block the sun, making everything as dark and cold and bleak as I feel.

Raiden's going to win.

"Did the Westerlies say anything else?" Audra asks, shaking my arm and forcing me to stay focused.

"They sang about monsters and a rage that tainted the sky. I begged them to tell me what to do, and that's when their song turned hopeless. It was like that moment in Death Valley when I asked the shield to cover us as we ran. I could feel that the drafts wanted to help. But they just kept repeating 'too strong' and whispering about giants that can't be defeated. There's nothing they can do."

"But it isn't just up to the Westerlies," Gus says after a few seconds of silence. "I thought ultimate power came from the power of *four*."

He holds out his wind spike like it somehow proves everything. But he doesn't understand how it works.

"Every time I've used the power of four, it was always because the Westerlies told me what to do, how to weave them with the other drafts to create the effect I need. And this time they're telling me they can't help."

"So where does that leave us?" Gus asks, turning to Os.

"I could turn myself in," I offer, but even as I say it I know it wouldn't matter. Raiden doesn't want a quiet surrender. He wants to make us an example.

"I'll tell you what you're going to do," Os snaps. "You're going to remember your training and get ready to fight for your life. We'll take care of the Storms."

"But—"

"Did you honestly think we were counting on *you* to save us? Perhaps that had been our hope several weeks ago. But then we saw how seriously inadequate your fighting is—not to mention your crippling aversion to violence. Why do you think we've all pushed so hard to have you share your knowledge? We knew it was use-less in your unskilled hands. So I built today's strategy without any consideration at all for your gifts."

"Is that true?" I ask, glancing between Gus and Audra.

Audra thinks before she nods. "His battle plan doesn't rely on Westerlies. That surprised me, actually. But it seems like that was the right call."

"Of course it was the right call! You forget that I've been fighting Raiden longer than you've been alive. We all have." Os points to the group of Gales, most of whom have gray in their hair.

And they're not looking at me with that desperate *you are our only hope* look I got so used to seeing. If anything they look . . . unimpressed.

I know I should probably be insulted, but it actually feels like: *giant, suffocating weight on my shoulders—gone!*

"Don't misunderstand, I still have high hopes for the power of four," Os adds when the next horrible howl fades. "And I still hope that you will grow to be a great king, despite everything." He glances at Audra and shakes his head. "But for now I won't put the fate of our world in the hands of a stubborn teenager."

I'm so relieved I could kiss him.

Well . . . maybe I would fist bump him instead.

"So what's the plan, then?" I ask, picking up a wind spike and feeling ready for anything.

Os grumbles about my missing his first run-through before he repeats their strategy. It sounds like a smart plan—though the only stuff I know about battles comes from the few times Isaac made me play one of his gory war games. The only question I have is "How do we keep the Storms out of the valley?"

Os doesn't answer. And none of the Gales will look at me.

The taste in my mouth turns sour.

"You're not going to keep them out of the valley, are you?"

"Sometimes we can't protect everyone," Os says quietly. "And I fear today will be one of those days."

"That's not good enough!"

"Excuse me?" Os asks, stepping into my personal space. "You dare to criticize me for something you've already admitted you can't accomplish?"

"I never said I wasn't still going to try."

"And I never said that either."

"You didn't have to. Your plan is for us to move to our base and wait for the Storms to come to us. I get that you want the home court advantage, but we all know they're going to destroy the whole valley before they get there."

"And what would you have us do, charge blindly toward the mountains?"

"It's better than standing back and doing nothing."

"I think it's too late," Gus says, and when I turn and follow his gaze, I feel like I've been stabbed in the heart.

A dark funnel tears over the crest of the mountains in the distance. Followed by another. And a bunch more after that.

From this far away they look like normal tornadoes—though in Southern California tornadoes are hardly *normal*. But even from here I can tell that they're moving like soldiers. Straight lines. Evenly spaced. Marching into the desert on a mission to destroy.

I shout for any nearby Westerlies, relieved when two drafts answer my call.

"Don't," Audra begs, grabbing my arm as I tangle one around me and order the other to form a shield.

I'm tempted to snatch her up and race away to safety—or at least pull her close and kiss her until the world ends.

But this is my fault, and if I don't try to stop it, I'll never be able to live with myself.

I order the Westerly to blast me away before I can change my mind.

The nervous draft can't spin fast enough to completely hide me in the sky—but no one's looking my way anyway. People are jumping out of their cars to stare and snap pictures of the strange storms, and I want to scream at them to get somewhere safe.

But where are they supposed to go? Californians don't have basements or tornado shelters. We have earthquake drills and fire alarms.

"Are you crazy?" Audra shouts as she tackles me in midair.

"Are *you*?" I shout back.

"You can't do this, Vane."

She orders my wind to turn us around.

I order it to hold its course, adding a command for the draft to ignore anything else she says. It works like the Windwalker equivalent of jinx times infinity, and I can't help grinning at Audra as she realizes it.

"This is pointless," she says as she crawls to the front of me, clinging to my chest. "You don't even have a plan."

"Actually I do."

Making it up as I go along *is* a plan. I just never said it was a good one.

"I know this is crazy," I tell her. "But I can't stand here and watch people die."

"But you have to protect yourself, Vane. The Westerly language—"

"Doesn't seem to be as valuable as everyone thought it would be. Or at least *I'm* not as valuable as everyone thought I would be."

Audra pulls me tighter, whispering in my ear—and seriously messing with my concentration—"You're incredibly valuable, Vane, and not just to me."

I sigh. "I have to do this, Audra. But *you* don't. You should go back—"

"I'm not going to let you risk your life without me."

"And I'm not letting either of you risk your lives without *me*," Gus says, swooping up beside us. "Come on, you didn't really think I wouldn't follow you, did you?"

He grins when I glare at him.

"Anyone else back there I should know about?" I ask.

"Nah. Os thinks I'm here to drag you two back to the base. He's moving everyone else into position."

"I'm not turning around, Gus," I warn him.

"Oh, believe me, I know. And I'm in for whatever. What are you thinking?"

"That we have to fly faster."

The Storms have slammed onto the desert floor, tearing into the neighborhoods that sit against the mountain. I try to tell myself that Palm Springs is a snowbird area and that most of the houses are probably empty. But I still feel sick when I hear the crunching chaos of the destruction.

"We should try to get beside them," Gus shouts as he veers right, expecting me to follow.

I order my drafts to race forward instead.

"What are you doing?" Audra yells as Gus loops around to join us.

"The Storms are heading toward highway 111, which will take them right through the heart of the desert, into all the super-populated areas. We need to get them to follow us to the other side of the freeway, where nothing's been built yet. And it's better to do that up here."

This part of the desert is all country clubs and mansions, and none of the rich people bother suffering through the summer heat. I'm sure it's not *empty*—but at this point it's too late to save everyone. All I can do is save as many as possible.

"We need to move faster," Audra tells me, calling for more Westerlies. Only one responds, so she shouts for any nearby Easterlies and two sweep in to help us.

Gus does the same with Northerlies and manages to hail three.

"Does it seem strange to you that there are still healthy winds around?" Audra asks.

"I was just thinking the same thing," I admit. "But maybe the valley is too big to clear completely?"

Audra doesn't look convinced.

"Let's worry about it later," I tell her as the wild, dusty air slams against us, trying to rip us apart.

I let Audra take over flying and she guides us close enough that I can see the Living Storms' shadowy faces. They look like the monsters I remember—but they're *way* bigger this time, and I try not to feel like a tiny bug taking on a giant.

"Now what?" Gus shouts.

"We need to make it notice us."

"I think it already does!" Audra screams, right before the air fills with an earsplitting shriek.

"Dive!" I yell as Gus shouts, "What is that thing?" and a loud crack explodes in the air above us.

The force of the blast knocks me off balance, and Audra barely pulls us out of a free fall.

Another explosion sends a shock wave rippling behind us.

Gus races to our side. "Oh, good, Raiden gave them weapons."

"Wind whips," I grumble. Because evil, mutated Storms weren't bad enough.

"Look out!" Gus shouts as the whip cracks again—and then again—each hit coming so close that we almost miss the more important development.

The Storms have started to chase us.

"Faster!" Audra tells Gus, calling more winds to fuel our weary drafts as we race toward the empty desert in the distance.

"Wait—is that Gavin?" I ask, pointing to a dark shape weaving through the sky.

Audra leans forward, squinting at the horizon. "No. The bird is too big—and its feathers are black."

"But it's coming straight for us."

"Can you take over windwalking for a minute?" she asks, already changing positions.

"Uh, not if you're calling over a giant bird."

"Really? You're *still* afraid of them?"

"You and Gavin scarred me for life."

"Well, it's time to conquer your fears."

The bird swoops closer, circling above us before it dives.

I can hear Gus laugh as I yelp, but I'd like to see him hold steady while some huge bird lands on his shoulder midflight. And bonus: It's a *vulture*, so not only is it huge and heavy with razor-sharp talons, it smells like dead stuff.

Audra wraps her legs tighter around me and reaches up to check the feathers on its stinky black wings.

And then checks them again.

And again.

"It's a message from your mother, isn't it?" I ask, feeling a bit of déjà vu from the last time something like this happened—though that had at least been a small white dove.

Audra nods, her body shaking so hard I feel like I'm going to lose my grip on her.

"What did she say?" I ask, wondering how Arella managed to reach the vulture from her cage.

Audra sighs, staring at the sky. "She wants us to come get her. She says she can help us win."

CHAPTER 38

AUDRA

It's a trick.

It has to be.

Everything with my mother always is.

I shoo the vulture off Vane's shoulder and it hisses at me as it flies away. But it stays circling above us, despite the ravaged winds trying to knock it out of the sky.

My mother probably commanded the poor creature not to leave until it brought me back to her. But I have *innocent* people to protect.

"What are you doing?" I ask as Vane changes our course.

"Heading to the Maelstrom."

"Don't tell me you believe her," I say, changing our course again.

"Look, I know your mother is hard to trust—and I know this feels a bit shady. But we're kinda outnumbered here and your mom is crazy talented. If she says she can help us, I think we should let her."

"How can you—"

I'm so distracted that I don't see the Storm's whip until it's too late.

The stinging cord of air hits us dead-on, cracking so loud my ears ring as the winds carrying us unravel.

I cling to Vane, searching for a draft to stop our fall. But the Living Storm snatches us first, yanking us apart with cold, monstrous hands as it holds us in front of its face like it wants to examine its new toys.

"Hang on," Gus shouts, tossing his wind spike at the Storm's head.

I brace for an explosion of fog and chaos—but the spike bounces off without leaving a scratch.

The Storm's fist tightens around me, squeezing so hard I'm sure it cracks one of my ribs. But I'm better off than Vane. I can hear him coughing and gasping for air as one of the massive fingers wraps around his neck.

Gus's spike slams into the Storm again, aimed for the chest this time.

Again, it rebounds.

"Stay with me," I scream as Vane's desperate choking makes red rim my vision. But his eyes roll back and his body stops struggling.

"Help!" I beg my Westerly shield. I force myself to calm down and concentrate as the loyal draft's song fills my mind.

It's hard to hear over the cracking whips and the raging winds, but I manage to catch a single word that stands out from the rest.

"Inflate!"

Both of our shields swell to three times their size, shoving open the Storm's fists and sending us crashing to the ground.

I scream for a draft to catch us, but none of them respond—and I can see Gus racing toward me, but I know we're falling too fast. All I can do is brace for impact and hope our shields keep us safe.

The ground comes up quick and hard and I wrench my neck as I tumble across the sand. But I'm bruised not broken as I jump to my feet.

Vane wasn't as lucky.

The elbow on his left arm is bent at an angle that makes me wince just looking at it, and I stumble to his side, screaming for him to wake up.

"Come on," Gus shouts, landing beside me and pointing to three Living Storms tearing toward us.

He tells me to wrap my arms around his waist as he throws Vane over his shoulder and blasts us back into the sky only seconds before the first whip cracks.

"What's happening?" he shouts. "Why aren't the spikes working?"

"It must be because Raiden broke the Living Storms."

"That's stronger than the power of four?"

"I don't know. I think it might be."

Aston did warn me about the *power of pain*.

I reach for Vane, hating that he's still unconscious. But when my hand brushes his cheek, his eyes snap open and he coughs so hard Gus nearly drops him.

The coughs turn into a groan as Vane tries to move.

"Careful," Gus tells him. "You jacked up your arm pretty good."

I take a closer look at Vane's elbow and try not to be sick. It's swollen and twisted and obviously out of joint.

"We're going to have to adjust it," I tell Gus as he dips to avoid the crack of another whip. "He'll be in too much pain to fight, otherwise."

"Duck!" Vane shouts as a monstrous fist lunges for us and Gus barely slips us out of its clutches.

I shift my weight so I can let go of Gus with one hand, feeling the air for any usable winds. "We need to make a pipeline. It'll launch us far enough away to treat him without wasting any time."

"And we just abandon the Gales in the meantime?" Gus asks.

"What else can we do?"

"I'm fine," Vane jumps in, but as soon as he tries to move his arm he can't fight back his groan.

"We need to at least warn them about the broken Storms," Gus decides as we dive so close to the ground I'm amazed we don't crash. "Can you send them a message?"

"If I can find a draft."

I stretch my concentration as far as I can and manage to reach a healthy Southerly. It takes three tries to get it to answer my call, and when it finally sweeps in, its song is so scattered I can tell it will only be able to hold a few words.

"Don't trust the spikes," I tell it, hoping the Gales have a backup plan. Then I send the wind away and search for drafts to build the pipeline.

"Any time now," Gus shouts, launching us straight up as a Living Storm jumps in front of us. "It's hard to keep up my speed with two extra bodies to carry."

"I just need one more Northerly."

"What about the one to the east of us?" Vane asks through labored breaths.

I can't feel the draft he means, but he whispers the call anyway, and a weary wind sweeps in and joins with the others I've gathered.

For a second I'm speechless.

Vane's senses are stronger than *mine*?

"Feng had me practice like five hundred times a day," he explains. "He made you seem easygoing."

No.

He did what I was *supposed* to do.

Gus turns to look over his shoulder at the Living Storms right on our tail, and I wonder if he's thinking the same thing I am.

We owe it to Feng—to all the guardians whose lives were lost or destroyed—to stop this.

But first we have to fix Vane.

I shout the command, forming the pipeline right in front of us, and we fly straight into the funnel. The pressure makes my head throb and my eyes water and I'm worried the winds are going to collapse around us. But then we shoot into a gray, cloudy sky, and Gus tangles us in Northerlies and sets us down in the foothills.

I can see the whole valley in the distance. The line of Living Storms towers over the small desert towns, filling the air with a gray-brown haze as they tear their way toward the Gales' base. I hope Os got my message.

"Yep, it's totally dislocated," Gus says, reminding me why we're here. "We need to pop it back into place."

"Sounds like a party," Vane mumbles, forcing a small smile.

"Can you handle the traction?" Gus asks me, and I order myself to nod.

Part of our guardian training includes basic medical procedures. But the idea of doing this to Vane . . .

"Ugh, it's going to be that bad?" Vane asks, grabbing my shaking hand.

"Yeah, this is going to suck," Gus tells him. "But not as much as what's going on down there."

We both follow his gaze and see the Storms curling into a circle, surrounding what has to be the Gales' base. I hold my breath, hoping to see some sign that the Gales can handle them. But all I see are the Storms closing in.

"We'd better hurry," Vane says, and I kneel in the sand, facing him with my knees pressed against his bad arm. His eyes never leave mine as I place both hands on his biceps and pin it to the ground— but he sucks in a sharp breath as Gus bends his elbow up to a right angle.

"Was that it?" he asks, his voice heartbreakingly hopeful.

"Sorry," Gus mumbles. "I'm still trying to get it in the right position." He bends Vane's arm back toward the sand and Vane lets out a strangled cry. "Okay, I think we're set. You guys ready?"

Vane nods as he turns to me. "Kiss me."

"Dude, this is so not the time." Gus groans as my cheeks turn hotter than the desert sun.

"It'll distract me from the pain," Vane insists.

I glance at Gus and he sighs. "He's probably right."

"Of course I am."

The glint in Vane's beautiful eyes makes it impossible not to smile. But I still can't believe I'm doing this as I tighten my grip on his arm and lean close enough to feel his breath on my skin.

"I love you," he whispers.

"I love you too." My insecurities vanish as I press my lips against his.

I try to keep the kiss slow, but the heat between us keeps building until my head feels dizzy from the rush. Somewhere in my blurry thoughts I remember to keep my hands steady when Gus shouts, "Now!"

Vane's lips pull away to let out one muffled scream.

"How does it feel?" I ask as Vane sits up and attempts to bend his elbow. He makes it about halfway before his face contorts with pain.

Gus sighs. "You probably damaged a few ligaments. We need to wrap it to keep pressure on it."

There's barely enough fabric on my dress as it is, but since Gus is still shirtless and Vane can barely move, there aren't a lot of options. I reach for the back hem and tear a thick strand free, trying not to think about how much draftier it feels now.

I tie it around his elbow as tightly as I can. "How's that?"

He takes another deep breath before trying to bend his arm, and this time he doesn't wince. "Better. Though I think it would help even more if you tore off another piece of your dress."

I blush while Gus shakes his head. "Dude, you're hopeless."

"And we need to get back down there." I point to the desert

basin, where the Living Storms are starting to scatter, heading into all the most populated areas.

"Dammit!" Vane shouts. "Why aren't the Gales stopping them?"

He struggles to his feet, but barely lasts a second before he collapses to his knees.

"I'm fine," he promises. "Just dizzy."

But when he tries to get up again, he tumbles forward immediately.

"You're way too weak to fight, man," Gus says as he catches Vane before he lands on his bad arm. "I think we're going to have to leave you here to rest and come get you when this is over."

"I'm not going to hide in a cave while you guys fight," Vane argues, trying to balance on his own. I move behind him as he wobbles, letting him lean against me.

"Just give me five minutes," he begs. "All I need is some air."

"Five minutes," Gus repeats. "We need to come up with a plan, anyway."

We all turn toward the valley, and my chest tightens when I see the Storms spreading even wider. It's impossible to tell if the Gales are still fighting them, but the massive trails of destruction don't look promising.

Vane reaches for my hands, locking our fingers together.

"I don't see any Stormers, do you?" Gus asks, shielding his eyes and squinting at the mountains.

I shake my head as I concentrate on the winds. "I don't feel any trace of them either." Though I'm relieved to feel some of the Gales'.

There's still a chance, even if it's a weak one.

"Would Raiden really not bring them?" Gus asks.

"Maybe he didn't want to risk losing any of them," I suggest.

"Or maybe this is only round one," Vane says quietly. "I'm not picking up any trace of Raiden, either, but there's no way he's not here. He's up to something, I can feel it. I just can't tell what it is."

Gus runs his hands through his hair, pulling it loose from his guardian braid. "So what are we going to do?"

"There's really only one thing we *can* do," Vane says, staring up at the bird slowly circling above us.

The vulture should've lost track of us when we launched through the pipeline. But my mother has a way of always getting what she wants.

I guess that's why I'm not surprised when Vane squeezes my hand tighter and tells me, "We have to go get your mom, Audra. She's the only chance we have left."

CHAPTER 39

VANE

You really think we can trust my mother?" Audra asks, pulling away from me so quickly I lose my balance and have to sink to my knees.

"She told us she could help us, right?"

"That doesn't mean it's true."

Audra calls the creepy vulture and it swoops down and lands on a rock a few feet away, letting out an evil hiss that sounds like a possessed child. Even Gus backs away as it bows its gross red, bumpy head and holds out its massive black wing so Audra can count the notches in the feathers.

"How does she even know we're in trouble?" she asks when she's read the message again. "She's trapped in a Maelstrom. The wind shouldn't be able to reach her."

"I don't know—maybe the birds told her. Or maybe she can feel it. Her gift is pretty powerful, right? Seems like she might be able to pick up on something this huge. I mean, look at that."

I point to the desert, where fires are starting to break out in the rubble. Smoke is mixing with the dust and thunderheads, making it harder to see what's going on—which is probably better. My brain doesn't know how to process that kind of destruction.

Everything I know has just changed.

And the Storms are still raging.

"You don't find it convenient that she's reaching out to us now, offering us vague promises when we're at our weakest?" Audra asks me.

"Of course I do—and it reminds me way too much of the time she used Gavin to give away our location and nearly got us killed. But what other option do we have? Our wind spikes aren't working and the Westerlies told me they can't help us. The Gales look like they're failing pretty epically down there—so what else are we supposed to do?"

I can hear the panic in my voice, but I can't choke down the fear this time—not when people are dying because of me.

"I don't know how to stop this," I whisper. "Do you?"

She hesitates before she mumbles, "No."

Gus looks just as defeated.

"I think we have to let her help us, then," I tell them. "It's the only play we've got left."

Audra looks like she's going to agree with me—but at the last second she turns away.

"I can't trust her, Vane. I *won't*. I made that mistake my entire life. I'm not going to do it again."

Her voice is hard, and I can tell that's her final decision.

But she's wrong.

Unless I'm crazy—but I don't think I am.

"Your mom was different when I saw her," I tell Audra quietly. "Calm, and sometimes almost . . . nice. She didn't tell the Gales about us bonding—and she backed up the lie I'd told to cover for you being gone. She even offered to help me sleep."

Audra laughs, though it's much more high-pitched and squeaky than her normal laugh. "Of course she did—because she wants you to set her free. That's how she works."

"That's what I figured too. But she seemed like she really regretted what she'd done. And she told me she realized that her gift had driven her crazy—like, literally *crazy*. The pain clouded her mind, affected how she thought."

"And that excuses her for murdering two people in cold blood and causing my father's death?"

"Of course not—that's why I left her there in the Maelstrom. But it might mean it's safe to let her out for a little bit. Especially when innocent people are dying and she might be able to help us save them."

Audra wraps her arms around herself, fighting off a shiver. "She's going to escape if you let her out."

"Probably," I agree.

I turn to Gus when she doesn't say anything. "What do you think?"

He runs his hands through his hair before he looks at Audra. "I hate to say it, but I agree with Vane."

Audra nods like she was expecting that. But her jaw is set, and her voice has a definite edge when she tells me, "Then I guess it's a good thing you're the king. I will obey whatever you decide."

"I'd feel better if you'd agree," I tell her.

Her eyes meet mine and her angry mask cracks. Two small tears streak down her cheeks as she whispers, "I can't."

Silence sits between us like a wall.

"I'm sorry," I tell her, wishing there was some magical word I could say to fix this. The best I can come up with is "You don't have to see her. Gus and I will go—"

"No!"

Audra's voice is so loud that the creepy vulture flaps its wings— sending a couple of nasty feathers my way. "She sent her message to *me*. I should be the one to go get her."

She starts to walk away, and I jump to my feet to chase her— instantly regretting it when I fall back down. Especially since I stupidly put out my arms to catch myself.

I'm pretty sure the sound I make is like a dying hyena, and I curl into a ball in the dirt, rocking back and forth. The copper taste of blood tells me I bit my tongue as I fell—but it's good to have something else to concentrate on besides my freaking ruined arm.

"Hey," Audra says, kneeling beside me. "You need to rest."

"I can't—"

"Flying into battle when you're barely functioning is only going to get you killed."

"But—"

She puts a finger on my lips, definitely a good way to shut me up.

Warm tingles ripple through my face, and I close my eyes and hope it's a sign that she doesn't hate me.

"Please, Vane," she whispers, leaning so close I can feel her hair brush my cheeks. "You're not up for a battle. You have to stay here, where it's safe."

"You sure it isn't that you just don't want me around?" It's mostly a joke, but she *was* pretty pissed a few minutes ago.

She reaches up to brush a couple pieces of hair off my forehead, not looking at me as she says, "I don't trust my mother, but I do trust *you*."

"You do?"

She nods.

That makes one of us.

"So I need you to trust *me* on this," she adds quietly. "Stay here while I go release her."

"You're not going there alone—"

"He's right—I'm going with you," Gus interrupts, moving next to Audra. "But she's right too, Vane. You had one of the worst dislocations I've seen. You need some time to recover."

"But what if the guard won't release Arella?" I argue.

I doubt they'd listen to anyone but the king.

"I'm sure her guard is fighting along with the Gales," Gus tells me, which would explain how Arella was able to call the vulture close enough to send a message.

I try one more time to move my elbow, and it feels like someone is sawing it off with a rusty butter knife.

"Fine," I grumble. "But if I start feeling better, I'm heading straight to the Gales to meet up with you."

Audra sighs. "I won't be able to stop you, but *please* promise you'll only do that if you're really up to it."

"Only if you promise to be extra careful. If something happens . . ."

I try to swallow the fear, but it chokes me.

She cradles my face with her hands. "I can take care of myself."

"I know. But I'm still going to worry the entire time. Do you need me to tell you how to find the Maelstrom?"

Audra points to the stupid vulture, which I'm pretty sure is sitting there hoping one of us is about to die. "Her bird will guide me."

"Make sure you walk the last part," I warn them. "Otherwise the winds carrying you will get sucked in."

"Not if we fly with Westerlies," Audra corrects. "I flew right up to Raiden's Maelstrom in Death Valley."

She starts to stand, but I grab her wrist with my good arm. "Promise you'll come back safe."

"I'll try."

I tighten my grip. *"Promise."*

She leans down to kiss me.

It's a fast kiss—more of a tease than anything. But it make the wall I'd felt between us seem to vanish as she pulls her ha free.

I try not to feel like a worthless Vane-blob as Gus carrie to a spot in the shade and props me against a boulder. But I

help sulking as Gus wraps his arms around Audra and she forms a Westerly wind bubble.

I glower at the sky as I watch them float away.

And when they disappear into the clouds, I realize that Audra never promised to come back.

CHAPTER 40

AUDRA

Everything about this feels wrong.

Leaving Vane alone and unprotected in the middle of nowhere.

Setting my mother free.

Even flying with Gus—though at least he seems as uncomfortable as me. He's adjusted his hold twice already, but thanks to this dress, there's nowhere safe to grab.

"What do you think the odds are that Vane will really stay where he is?" Gus asks as he shifts his hands to my waist, holding my bandaged side extra carefully.

"Probably about as good as my mother being a changed woman."

"So I take it you're still pissed about setting her free?"

"I just . . . know my mother."

I know Vane wants to believe she's different now—and maybe she was when he talked to her. But I've learned the hard way that any kindness or concern my mother ever shows lasts only long enough for her to get what she wants.

And now we're about to let her have her way again.

We follow my mother's vulture toward circles of dead palm trees, and as soon as we reach them, the Westerlies carrying us turn jittery. I urge the winds to fly on, but they grow increasingly unsteady, breaking into a panic when a frenzied Easterly swarms around me.

The draft's tone reminds me of my father's voice, but I know there's no way it could be him. Its desperate song begs me to turn away and never come back, and my father would never try to stop me from setting my mother free. He loved her beyond life—beyond reason—beyond air.

He would carry me there faster if he could.

"Wow, the Maelstrom sure does spook the winds," Gus mumbles as the Easterly flies with us, repeating its warning over and over.

I continue to ignore it, and when we reach a series of strange rock formations, the vulture dives and the Easterly finally sweeps away.

We've reached our destination.

The other Westerlies take off the second I unravel them, but my loyal shield doesn't waver, tightening its grip around me like it can feel the evil in the air.

I can feel it too.

The unnatural stillness.

The strange push and pull, dragging me toward the dark opening in the sand up ahead, even though every instinct I have is screaming for me to run away.

"There's something off about this place," Gus mumbles, his hand gripping his wind spike as he searches the air.

"It feels just like the other Maelstrom," I tell him.

Sounds the same too. The horrible screeching that bores into my brain like twisted needles.

Though this one was built by the captain of the Gales.

Gus's eyes scan the valley, but the only signs of life are the vultures. Dozens and dozens of them, lining the rocks, the scrubby plants, even the sand. They watch us with their silent stares as we make our way to the Maelstrom's entrance.

I'm tempted to shoo them away—they won't be getting the meal they've been waiting for. But I know they won't leave. They'll be loyal to *her.*

"So . . . we have to go down there?" Gus asks as I start down the sloped, dark path surrounded by the spinning funnel of sand.

"Unless you want to stay here and cover the entrance," I offer.

For the briefest second he looks tempted. Then he draws his wind spike, holding it in front of him as he pushes past me to take the lead. "Let's get this over with."

I try not to touch the walls—try even harder not to imagine bits of my mother being absorbed by them.

But she's also in the air.

I cover my mouth, breathing as shallowly as I can. Still, every breath makes me want to gag.

I keep my hand to my heart as we walk, wishing I could feel

some small trace of my bond. There's nothing but a cold emptiness.

It makes me want to turn around and run until I find the sky. But I press forward. One foot in front of the other. Each step dragging me away from the light. Into the wasted darkness.

"Okay, I officially hate it down here," Gus says after several more minutes of walking. "I mean . . . it's just *wrong*. There's no other way to describe it."

There isn't.

Maelstroms *feel* as awful as they are.

And once again I can't help thinking that a *Gale* made this.

I almost speak the thought aloud, but stop myself just in time. So I'm surprised when Gus asks me, "What do you think about Os?"

I choose my answer carefully. Now is not the time to cast doubt on our leader. Battles call for trust and loyalty. "I think he's desperate to protect our people."

"Desperate," Gus repeats. He's quiet for several steps, before he asks, "Do you believe the Gales can win?"

My fingers rub the skin on my wrist, finding the remnants of Aston's burn. His haunting warnings still ring in my mind, and I can see now why he was so sure we had no chance. But I have to believe there's still hope.

"No matter how powerful Raiden gets," I tell Gus, "the wind will always be stronger. And I can't believe that the wind will let him keep on destroying it for much longer."

"You talk about the wind like it's alive."

"In some ways it is."

I think of my loyal Westerly shield, journeying with me into this dark place where no other winds dare to go. It stays because it wants to. The same reason it rallied the other Westerlies and came to our rescue in Death Valley.

Yes, some of the winds may be willing to let Raiden dominate and ruin them. But others will *fight*. And if we can enlist their help, get them to join our side, nothing can stop us.

Perhaps that's the secret we've all been missing. It's not about finding the right commands. It's about finding the right *winds*.

Which might actually mean my mother can help us—much as I hate to admit it. She understands the wind in ways none of us ever have. If anyone can find the winds we need, it's her.

A dim light appears ahead and I brace myself for the sight of my mother dangling from a chain, like the victims in Raiden's prison. But when we finally reach the tunnel's end, it's an empty, round cavern with mesh curtains of metal partitioning off two small cells.

Apparently, Os's cruelty has a much finer line.

"Audra?" my mother asks, her voice so weak it's almost unrecognizable.

"Yes," I force myself to say, the single word carrying seventeen years of my pain and regrets.

A pale form approaches the mesh of metal, and when I step closer I can see her face—though I barely recognize her.

I should rejoice at her greasy hair and sweaty skin covering her thin features. But it feels like too much of a waste.

All of it, this whole thing.

My beautiful, powerful mother.

Our small, happy family.

Our quiet, dedicated lives.

It's all been sucked up and torn away. Like my entire existence has been trapped in a Maelstrom of my mother's making.

Tears sting my eyes as she studies me, but I blink them back. I've shed my last tear for this woman.

"You came," she whispers, pressing her hand against the metal.

I take a step back, even though she can't reach me.

"Still my same stubborn girl." She gives me a sad smile and turns to Gus, doing a double take. "You're not Vane."

"Are you sure?" Gus feels his face like he can't believe it.

My mother doesn't smile. "Where's Vane?"

"As far away from here as I could keep him," I tell her.

"But . . . you're his guardian. You're supposed to be with Vane."

"You sure know how to make a guy feel wanted," Gus grumbles, shoving against the mesh curtain, trying to free her from her cage.

It won't budge.

"Didn't think about that," he says, shaking the metal to no avail.

"Try your wind spike," I tell him.

"On what?"

I look closer at the curtain, surprised to find there's no lock. I honestly can't tell how it's held in place.

"I'm so sorry, Audra," my mother whispers, and I glance up to find her looking at me.

She's such a drippy mess, it's hard to tell if she's crying or sweating. But it makes my throat feel thick anyway.

Now I understand why Vane was ready to trust her. I'm feeling the same urge.

But can I?

Should I?

"I had no choice," she tells me, pleading with her eyes for me to forgive her.

My life would be so much easier if I could give her what she wants.

But I can't ignore the rage that's always with me, simmering beneath the surface.

"What are you even sorry for?" I snap. "Killing dad? Blaming me? Murdering two innocent people? Ruining the lives of everyone you've ever met?"

"Yes to all of those things," she says quietly, turning and walking away. Bones poke out of her frail, hunched shoulders as she hangs her head and mumbles, "But mostly . . ."

I can't understand the last words.

It sounded like she said, "But mostly for this."

But that doesn't make any sense.

Or, it doesn't until I hear a loud thump, like metal hitting bone, and Gus collapses. Before I can even scream, the needled edge of a windslicer presses against my throat and a strong arm wraps around me, pinning me against my captor's body.

"You were the one I wanted anyway," a sharp voice whispers in my ear, and it takes a second for my panicked brain to recognize it.

Raiden.

CHAPTER 41

VANE

A frightened cry wakes me from my restless sleep, but when I tear my eyes open I'm still alone.

Still in the middle of the desert.

Still stuck with an elbow that feels like a pack of wild dogs is chewing on it.

But it wasn't a nightmare that woke me.

It was the wind.

I close my eyes as the terrified Westerly surrounds me. Its song is a mess—all jumbled with panic. But one word jumps out.

Traitor.

I start to jump to my feet, but then I remember how not-cool that worked out for me last time and instead use the rock I'd been sleeping against to slowly pull myself up.

The dizziness still hits me, but deep breaths shove it back, and when my head clears I can feel the Westerly coiling around me, trying to drag me where I need to go.

"Hey—easy," I tell it as it almost pulls me over. "What's going on—did something happen to Audra?"

It's a stupid question to ask the wind—and of course it doesn't answer. It just repeats the same panicked song about traitors and tries to pull me into the sky.

I stop fighting and let it.

I hold my wind spike with my good arm, trying to feel ready for wherever this wind is bringing me. But nothing could've prepared me for seeing my valley up close.

I've seen disasters on TV.

I've even lived through a couple.

But this . . .

Mangled houses. Fallen trees. Smashed cars. Police. Ambulances. Firemen. Helicopters.

People are running. Blocking the roads. Screaming and shouting and wailing.

It's chaos.

The kind of thing where reporters will come from miles around and the president will go on TV and try to say something to help people make sense of the destruction. But no one is going to understand this.

I can see the Living Storms still raging, scattered through the different towns—though it looks like there might be fewer of them. It's hard to tell.

It's hard to think.

One Storm is ransacking Indio and Coachella, and I can see two more shredding the mansions in Indian Wells and Rancho Mirage and another whipping through Cathedral City. But the worst of the fighting is in La Quinta, where three of the biggest Storms are tearing through the Cove. My Westerly steers me there.

I fly over my parents' house and it's actually still standing. But Isaac and Shelby weren't so lucky. Shelby's house is okay, but her car is smashed through the wall of her neighbor's garage. And Isaac's street is gone.

Like, *gone* gone.

Not a house. Not a tree. Even the sidewalk's disappeared.

I'm glad I warned them to leave, but what will they come home to? And what about their neighbors?

Fury makes me shake, but I can't decide who I'm mad at.

Raiden may have created the Storms but . . .

They're here because of *me*.

My Westerly picks up speed as we get closer to the Storms, but just as I'm gearing up for the fight of my life, it steers me into the mountains and drops me down on a narrow ledge.

A strong hand yanks me into a small cave.

"Don't let them see you!" Os hisses as he spins me around to face him.

My eyes adjust to the darkness, and I notice he's here with Solana, and they're both crouched in the shadows.

There's a new gash to Os's scar, cutting right through the center, like the mark has been crossed out. But Solana looks a lot worse.

Huge splotches of blood stain her pale dress. I can't tell if it's all hers, but the thick gash on her chin looks pretty gnarly either way.

"What happened?" I ask quietly.

Os points out at the Storms. "What do you think?"

The Storms slam against the mountain next to us, pulverizing the wall of stone until a huge hole forms.

My mouth goes dry and I have to swallow several times before I can ask, "How many Gales are left?"

Os drops his eyes to his hands. "Last count . . . eight—and that's including us."

That's . . . not even half.

"Where are Gus and Audra?" Solana asks after a second.

I was just wondering the same thing.

I'd thought the "traitor" the Westerly was taking me to was Arella. But it brought me *here*.

I scan the tiny cave trying to figure out why. A glint of yellow catches my attention.

"What are those?" I ask, pointing to the strangely colored wind spikes piled at Os's feet.

Traitor, my Westerly whispers again, and I have a horrible feeling I already know.

I pick one up and the winds' pain and misery pulses through my hand like a heartbeat.

"You *broke* the winds inside these?" I ask, dropping the spike and backing away.

"Only the Northerlies," Os corrects as he bends to retrieve it. "And only because there was no other option."

"Yeah, well, clearly the winds disagree, or I wouldn't have been dragged here by a Westerly that kept calling you a traitor."

"A *traitor?*" Os shouts—then covers his mouth and makes us all duck as we wait to see if the Storms heard.

"I'm a traitor?" he whispers after a few seconds. "I'm the one who saved us! I got your pathetic warning only minutes before the Storms arrived, and before I'd had time to blink they'd taken out a third of our force. We tried to run and hide until the three of you came back to help us, but we would've been snuffed out completely if I hadn't realized that Raiden had broken the Storms. The *only* way to fight a ruined wind is with another. So I broke the Northerlies in the spikes and we've been taking down the Storms one by one. We only have a few left."

Traitor, the Westerlies around me whisper.

"There has to be another way—"

"There *isn't!*" Os grabs one of the spikes and hurls it through the cave's opening at a Living Storm that had just discovered our hideout.

The spike tears straight through the Storm's shoulder, making it howl and rage as smoky mist leaks into the sky. Before it even finishes yelping, Os launches another spike straight through its eyes, making the massive Storm explode.

"You see?" Os asks as the ground shakes and the air turns thick and we cough from the dust and debris. "Without these weapons we'd have no fighting chance."

He hands another spike to me as proof, then reaches up to smear the blood off his cheek.

The cut on his face has opened wider from the strain, and I can't decide if it makes him look cruel or strong.

I never thought those two things could be interchangeable, but as I stare at the broken spike, I wonder if maybe they are.

Maybe sometimes the only right choice is the wrong one, and what it really comes down to is being brave enough to make it.

Traitor, the Westerlies snarl, and this time it feels like they're saying it to me. But what else was Os supposed to do? There weren't any other . . .

The thought trails off when I realize that there *is* another option—the one Gus and Audra are already working on.

Releasing Arella wasn't an easy decision either—but it's better than ruining the wind.

But they should be here by now, shouldn't they?

I clutch my heart, trying to feel the pull of our bond. But I feel colder and emptier than I have in a long time.

It could be that Audra's deep in the Maelstrom—but why would she still be there?

What if something's wrong?

I drop the damaged wind spike and reach for a Westerly to carry me—but they all ignore my call, whispering, *Traitor*, and flitting away. I'm searching the air for any other winds that might be willing to help me when a Storm's fist slams into our cave.

Everything crumbles.

I flail to protect my wounded arm as I skid down a rocky slope, not stopping until I'm halfway down the mountain. I'm grateful my Westerly shield didn't abandon me, because I'm pretty sure I'd have no skin left on my chest otherwise.

I'm choking on the dust and sand when I hear Solana scream

and turn my head just in time to see one of the remaining Storms snatch her away.

I shout for Os's help, but his legs are pinned under a giant boulder. Which leaves only me.

Taking on two Living Storms all by myself probably isn't the smartest idea—especially with the winds mad at me and with a superwounded left arm.

But I can still hear Solana screaming.

I've ruined her life a million different ways.

This time I'm going to save it.

CHAPTER 42

AUDRA

I shouldn't be surprised.

My mother's sold me out to Raiden twice before.

But this time I won't be getting away.

Before I could react, Raiden tangled me in a web of sharp red winds, and even with my shield, the cruel drafts shock like lightning every time he steps away from me.

"I'm so sorry," my mother keeps telling me. "I didn't have a choice."

"There's always a choice," I tell her, earning myself a laugh from Raiden.

"When I have control, the only choice is *mine*," he tells me, stepping away and letting the lightning bonds strike so hard, I feel like my skin is melting off my bones.

I crawl to his feet, unable to believe I'm choosing to be close to him. But I have to stop the pain.

He crouches in front of me as I gasp for breath. "If it eases the sting of Mommy's betrayal, you should know that *you* didn't have a choice either. I'm impressed that Os figured out how to build a Maelstrom—but he missed its true brilliance. It's the perfect trap. No way to sense anyone's presence. No winds to call to your aid. All I needed was something to draw you here, and something to keep your army distracted so I could catch my prize unguarded."

"Are you telling me that all the Gales you ruined to make your Living Storms—all the innocent people who died or lost their homes today—were just *a distraction to catch me?*"

Raiden grins. "Makes you feel rather special, doesn't it?"

Actually, it makes me physically ill.

"Why me? I'm not—"

"A Westerly?" Raiden finishes for me. "No, you're even better. *You* were the one who stirred up that haboob in my valley—a brilliant play, by the way. And that, right there, is what makes you so special. You talk like a Westerly. But you think like me."

"I'm *nothing* like you!"

My outburst only makes Raiden smile wider. "Breaking you is going to be fun. Though I had been hoping to catch your little boyfriend as leverage. I guess I can settle for the boy who thought he could kill me."

He stands, and I brace for another jolt, but he only turns to where Gus lies unconscious, tied in the same horrible winds.

Blood streams from a dark gash above Gus's temple, and it's

hard to tell how deep the damage goes. His face looks disturb-
ingly pale.

Raiden kicks him in the chest, filling the cave with the sound
of breaking bone. "Every time you don't cooperate, I'll punish *him*.
Understood?"

When I don't answer, he grabs my fallen wind spike and presses
the sharp end over Gus's heart.

I take particular pleasure in whispering the command to
unravel it.

The Maelstrom devours the drafts as soon as they uncoil. Except
the Westerly, which I wrap around Gus like a shield, relieved when
it obeys.

"You think you're clever, don't you?" Raiden asks, grabbing my
neck and lifting me off the ground.

His grip crushes through my weary shield, cutting off my
breathing. My vision blurs and my lungs scream for air, but I don't
try to fight.

Let it end here—now—when all the secrets are still safe.

But Raiden tosses me backward, letting me cough and heave as
the lightning shoots through my veins.

Spots dance across my vision, and I feel myself start to slip away
when the shocks fade and rough hands pull me to my feet.

"Grab the boy," Raiden orders his Stormer as he shoves me
toward the pathway that brought me here.

"Wait—we had a deal!" my mother shouts behind us.

She shakes the chains in her cage and I almost want to laugh.

Doesn't she realize? Trusting Raiden is like trusting *her*.

It always ends the same.

Raiden hisses something in his wicked language, and the winds in the Maelstrom double their speed.

Then all I hear are her screams.

"I wouldn't get any ideas," Raiden tells me when the exit comes into sight. "Even if you can fight through the pain of your bonds, they'll drag you back to me. And then I'll make you watch as I break your friend apart piece by piece."

He's going to do that anyway.

Just like he did to Aston.

And I . . .

I *have* to be strong.

I have to endure *anything*.

I accepted this responsibility when I let Vane into my heart.

I have no choice but to protect it.

There's always a choice, I can't help thinking, and the weakness makes me sick.

But what makes me far, far sicker is that I'm not nearly as sick as I should be.

Vane could barely function when he thought about sharing his language with *Os*—yet here I am, feeling only slightly queasy at the thought of giving it to *Raiden*?

Clearly, my Westerly instincts aren't as strong as I'm going to need them to be—and if I can't count on them to fuel me, how will I find the strength to resist Raiden's interrogation?

If I'd been holding out any hope that Vane would sense my danger and save us, it's crushed when I set foot on the sand. The desert

It always ends the same.

Raiden hisses something in his wicked language, and the winds in the Maelstrom double their speed.

Then all I hear are her screams.

"I wouldn't get any ideas," Raiden tells me when the exit comes into sight. "Even if you can fight through the pain of your bonds, they'll drag you back to me. And then I'll make you watch as I break your friend apart piece by piece."

He's going to do that anyway.

Just like he did to Aston.

And I . . .

I *have* to be strong.

I have to endure *anything*.

I accepted this responsibility when I let Vane into my heart.

I have no choice but to protect it.

There's always a choice, I can't help thinking, and the weakness makes me sick.

But what makes me far, far sicker is that I'm not nearly as sick as I should be.

ne could barely function when he thought about sharing his langu₄ with *Os*—yet here I am, feeling only slightly queasy at the thoughť giving it to *Raiden*?

Cleᵃ my Westerly instincts aren't as strong as I'm going to need then be—and if I can't count on them to fuel me, how will I find the stᵗᵗ·h to resist Raiden's interrogation?

If I'd be₁lding out any hope that Vane would sense my danger and save ᵥ s crushed when I set foot on the sand. The desert is empty, save for the vultures, and even the Westerlies have all been frightened away.

We're on our own.

There will be no escape.

But I guess it's better this way.

Better that Vane stays safe.

If there were a way to spare Gus, I would give it, but I can at least spare my loyal shield. I whisper the command to release it, begging it to flee far away.

The draft ignores me, clinging like a second skin. And in that simple act of loyalty, I find a hint of strength.

"Feels like your army has done better against my Storms than they should have," Raiden mumbles as he stretches out his palms to test the air.

"Good."

"That's a brave word coming from a hostage."

"Well, I'm braver than you think. You can take me and you can torture me. But I will *never* let you change me."

He barks a laugh, and the sharp sound stirs the vultures. "That's what they all say. Until I find their weakness."

He glances at Gus, then back at me, the threat impossible to miss.

He turns to give orders to his Stormer, and I realize this is it— the last few seconds I'll have before he drags me away to his fortress.

Thousands of regrets race through my mind, but I focus on the breeze that's suddenly tickling my skin.

It's a strong wind.

An Easterly.

And as it braves the treacherous skies of the Maelstrom just to bring comfort to me, I close my eyes and let myself believe it's my father. Come to say goodbye. Come to give me peace.

But when I listen to his song I realize he's brought me a message. The same advice over and over, turning more urgent with each repetition.

Time to let go.

I have no idea what he means, but the next time I inhale, the breeze slips inside with my breath, pressing into the darkest places in my mind.

The melody swirls around my head, and as I focus on the simple verse, something starts to stir.

A pressure.

A gathering.

It's not my essence.

It's not any part of *me*.

And as the mounting rush shocks me with warm tingles, I realize what the wind is telling me to let go of.

Who to let go of.

The Easterly's song turns mournful, echoing my grief as it whispers the command I'll need to give.

It's a familiar word. A word that's defined the last ten years of my life.

But I can't make myself say it.

It's too much.

The wind is asking too much.

I've given everything—suffered anything.

Why must I lose the *one* thing I've taken for myself?

Protection, the Easterly whispers, and the word is like fog, thick and numbing as it clouds my resistance and cools my rage.

This will break my heart—and likely break *me*.

But I know it has to be done.

I give myself one final second to cling to the only thing that's ever brought any joy or hope to my life. Then I close my eyes and whisper the command to rip it all away.

"Sacrifice."

The draft inside me splits into a million blades—slicing and slashing and shredding every part of me until there's nothing but splinters.

The warm, calm shards slip with my ragged breath and vanish like wisps of smoke. The cold, angry pieces cling, hardening into a wall that holds in all the emptiness inside me.

"Stop!" Raiden shouts, snarling something in his wicked language and drowning me in a flood of arctic winds.

They shove and beat and batter my body, trying to force back together what's already lost.

But it's gone.

It's all gone.

Everything that matters is gone.

aiming for the Storm that's carrying Solana. I check my swing twice to steady my nerves, and on the third sweep I let it fly.

The freaking Storm ducks.

I shout commands to adjust the spike's trajectory as it passes, but the angle's too sharp and the spike swishes across the Storm's shoulder, making such a small slice, the wound doesn't even leak any fog.

But it does still piss the Storm off, and I turn to flee as it tosses Solana back to the other Storm and takes off after me.

"Hang on," I shout as I duck the crack of a whip and call the broken wind spike back to my hand.

I race toward Solana, knowing this is probably the stupidest strategy I've ever come up with. But I don't have time to play Keep Away with the evil Storms anymore.

"Take my hand," I shout, stretching out my wounded arm as I duck another blow from the whip. I know it's going to hurt like hell when she grabs on, but I need my good arm for other, even crazier things.

Before she can reach me, the Storm yanks her away, tossing her back to the other Storm and swatting its massive hand at me.

"Get down, Vane!" Os shouts from somewhere behind me, and I decide not to question him, dropping toward the ground as fast as I can.

I glance up just in time to see a spike streak above me, nailing the Storm in the head and making the monster explode.

"Now it's one-on-one," Os tells me, and I steal a quick glance, surprised to see he's still pinned under the rock. I'm not sure how he reached one of the wind spikes, but I'm grateful for the help. I can't afford to waste any more time.

The Storm carrying Solana races away, and I chase after them, cursing every second this is wasting as I go back to my other crazy plan. I sneak up on the Storm's blind side and hold out my bad arm, shouting at Solana to grab on when I pass.

It takes two tries, but she manages to snag my hand. My elbow screams from the pain, but I grit my teeth and bear it, knowing it's only the beginning as Solana tangles our fingers together and I warn her to get ready. When I feel her get a firm hold, I raise my wind spike and slash it through the Storm's wrist, severing its hand and pulling Solana free.

The Storm screams and howls, and I do the same as Solana's weight—light as she is—rips my elbow back out of joint.

"Hold on," Solana shouts as the sickly yellow fog explodes around us, making me want to gag.

She wraps her legs around mine and shimmies up my body until she has a solid hold around my waist. "Are you okay?"

I can't answer.

It takes the last of my energy to order the drafts carrying us to fly as fast as they can toward the Maelstrom.

I hope it's fast enough.

"Got any winds left in you?" I ask when I glance over my shoulder and see the wounded Storm chasing after us. The rage seems to have given it a burst of energy, and I'm guessing we only have about a minute or two before it's right on top of us, unless we get a boost ourselves.

Solana shakes her head. "I ran out in the first few minutes of the fight, after we realized the spikes you gave us wouldn't work. If Os hadn't tried breaking those drafts, we'd all be dead."

I want to shout, *You hear that, Westerlies?*

But I honestly get why they're angry. Just holding the spike, I feel the broken Northerly's pain, and dang, it's *intense*.

"I'm sorry," I whisper, wishing the draft could understand me. *"If there's a way to fix this, I will."*

I didn't expect the wind to actually listen. But three Westerlies wrap around us out of nowhere, boosting our speed just in time to launch us the hell out of the valley and leave the creepy Storms in the dust.

I hope the rest of the Gales will be able to handle them.

And I hope this means the Westerlies have forgiven me—but no matter what, it's time for a change.

No more slacking in my training.

No more fighting to have a normal life.

The only thing that matters is stopping Raiden.

And Audra.

I clutch my chest, realizing our bond is gone.

Not faded.

Gone.

I try to tell myself it's because she's still in the Maelstrom. But everything inside me feels very, very cold.

We pass the crumbling dead palms in Desert Center, and the winds carrying us start to panic. I know they're freaked out by the pull of the Maelstrom, but I beg them to keep flying. They hold out as long as they can, but one by one they pull away until all we have left are the Westerlies.

I guess it's a good thing they forgave me.

The desert is hauntingly empty. Just a few vultures and some footprints in the sand. And when we touch down in front of the rock piles, all my nerves tangle into knots.

Audra's trace is everywhere—but somehow it's nowhere, too. It's like it's her but it's not her, and it can't tell me where she went or what she did. Only that she was here. And that she was in a lot of pain.

Gus's trace makes even less sense, so weak it's like he isn't even alive. And there are other traces in the air too. . . .

A lone Easterly swishes around me, and I focus on its song, searching for some clue to what happened.

It's only singing one word, but it knocks me to my knees.

Sacrifice.

"No!" I scream, stumbling to my feet and tearing into the Maelstrom.

She wouldn't do that.

She wouldn't give up her life that way.

I won't believe it.

There has to be another explanation.

"Hey!" Solana shouts over the screeching, grabbing my good hand as we stumble into the spinning tunnel. "I don't know what's going on, but I'm here if you need me."

I know she is. And it's nice to have something to hold on to.

But it's the wrong girl.

The wrong girl.

Please tell me I didn't save the wrong girl.

Especially since I'm the one who sent Audra here. If I'd listened to her . . .

I stop myself from finishing the thought.

Right now I need to focus on finding her.

A dim glow finally appears ahead, and I take off running, racing straight for Arella's cell.

She doesn't respond to my call, and when I peer through the mesh curtain, I can see her collapsed on the floor. Her skin is a freaky gray-blue and her arms and face are all twisted with pain and when I try to shove the curtain aside it won't move, no matter how hard I try.

"Stop!" Solana tells me as I pound and kick and scream all kinds of things my mom would kill me for saying. "Os told me a word when we were up in the mountains and the Storms were closing in. He didn't tell me what it meant or what it was for but . . ."

She whispers something I can't understand, and the curtain of metal slides to the side.

I scan the small space, desperately searching for Audra or Gus. But no one's here. Not in the other cell either.

"I think I feel a pulse," Solana tells me, her legs shaking as she crouches beside Arella. "But it's really weak. . . ."

"We have to get her back to the winds."

Arella weighs almost nothing, so I could probably carry her even with my bum arm. But I let Solana help me, grabbing Arella's feet while Solana grabs her shoulders and we haul her outside and stretch her out on the sand.

I didn't expect her eyes to pop open with her first breath of air—though that would've been nice. But even when I wrap her up in Westerlies, she's still not getting any better.

"Come on," I whisper, crouching down beside her. "You have to wake up. You have to tell me what happened."

I stare at her cracked gray-blue lips, trying to work up the courage to do CPR. But as I'm leaning down to try it, the Easterly from earlier tangles itself around Arella and starts to spin so quickly that it lifts Arella's limp body off the ground.

Solana and I both back away as the wind spins even faster, turning Arella's form to a blur.

"I think it's helping," Solana says.

I'm trying to figure out what she's seeing when the wind unravels, streaking into the sky as Arella drops back to the sand, coughing and hacking.

"Liam," she screams, flailing her pale arms as she pulls herself up. "Liam, I . . ."

Her voice trails off.

The wind is gone.

"Where are Gus and Audra?" I ask, grabbing her shoulder so she'll look at me.

"It's so much worse than I remember," she groans, hugging herself and rocking back and forth.

I don't have time for her games. "Where's Audra? You called her here and now she's gone—and Gus is too. Tell me what happened."

"I called her here?" Arella asks, staring at the sky. "I don't remember. I don't . . ."

Shadows settle into her features.

"I had no choice," she whispers.

I tighten my grip, feeling my fingers sink into her skin. "What does that mean?"

"Raiden."

"What?" I scream, lunging for Arella's throat. "I trusted you! I—"

Solana blocks me, and I'm shaking too hard to resist.

Audra was right.

I never should've asked her to come here. And now she's . . .

"Where is she?" I whisper, afraid I already know the answer.

Arella stares at the sky. "Raiden took her—*but I didn't have a choice!* He told me to call Audra or he'd . . ."

"Or he'd what? Kill you?" I ask, wishing Solana would step aside so I could strangle Arella myself. For once I think I'd be able to. "Looks like he tried to do that anyway."

"There are some things worse than death, Vane. And I knew Audra had the power of four. I thought she'd be strong enough to fight Raiden. I didn't think he'd be able to take her."

"Take her where?" I yell as she closes her eyes, shivering again.

"I'm not sure. It feels like he built a pipeline right there"—she points to a dent in the sand about a hundred yards away—"and launched her and Gus somewhere very far away. I'm guessing his fortress in the mountains. That's where he always took the others."

I want to cry, scream, punch something really hard. But I don't have time for a meltdown. If Gus and Audra are in Raiden's prison, I have to go—now. "Where is his fortress?"

"You can't go after her, Vane."

"Tell me where it is!" My scream echoes off the foothills, but Arella doesn't even blink.

"I can take you," Solana offers quietly. "I know the way to that city better than anyone. We can leave as soon as you're ready."

"I'm ready."

She touches my wounded arm—her fingers barely brushing the skin—and a sharp pain ripples through my body. "You're hurt, Vane. You need to get treated."

"I need to get to *Audra*."

"She might not be in as much danger as you think," Arella interrupts, and I swear if I had the energy I would drag her back down to her cell.

"She's with *Raiden*!"

"Yes, but . . . I don't think she has what he wants anymore." She closes her eyes, waving her hands through the air. "Don't you feel it?"

"Feel what?"

It almost looks like she's smiling as she tells me, "She broke your bond."

I clutch my chest, trying not to believe her.

But I don't feel any sort of pull.

Is that why her trace feels so weird in the air?

Tears stream down my cheeks before I can blink them away, and I realize I'm leaning on Solana way more than I want to. "Why would she do that? Why would she . . ."

But I know the answer.

"To protect the Westerlies," I whisper.

Audra would never let the fourth language fall into Raiden's hands. So if she was afraid she couldn't protect it, she would just get rid of it.

"Does it even work that way? Can she forget it completely?" I whisper, not sure what answer I'm hoping for.

"I don't know," Arella admits, closing her eyes. "I didn't know bonds could share languages. But it feels like it."

Everything is spinning too fast and I . . .

"So, we're not bonded anymore?" I ask as Solana helps me sit on the sand.

"*She* isn't."

"What does that mean?"

God—for once could she just answer a question *completely*?

"It means that *you're* no longer a part of her. But *she's* still a part of you. Unless you decide to let go. . . ."

She rubs the skin on her wrist, where her bracelet used to be.

Her *link*.

I always thought it was sad the way Arella clung to her connection to her husband, despite the fact that he was gone.

Now it gives me hope.

I'll be holding on to Audra with every ounce of strength I have left.

I close my eyes, taking slow breaths.

I *will* get Audra back. And I'm going to bring Gus back too.

But to do that we have to move fast.

Every second counts.

CHAPTER 44

AUDRA

I t's cold in the tower.

Chilled air seeping through the bars of my narrow window.

Thick frost coating everything I touch.

Raiden offered me a blanket when he tossed me onto the rough stone floor and barred the heavy iron door. But the only thing I want is my freedom, and since he's not willing to give that, I'll find a way to take it.

I've combed the walls for the guide Aston mentioned, but he must've carved it into a different cell. Maybe the one Gus is locked in. Wherever it is, I'll find it.

In the meantime I keep my back to the wall, never sleeping— barely breathing. Listening to the mournful wails of the broken

Northerlies and promising myself that when Raiden comes for me, I'll be ready.

He doesn't believe the secret is lost.

It's why he's kept me alive.

Why he's kept Gus alive.

Waiting for the right time to break me.

But it's gone.

Everything is gone.

Everything except the gentle breeze I can still feel brushing my skin. Wrapping around me. Still determined to shield me.

I don't deserve its loyalty.

But in this dark, frozen place, far away from the warmth and peace and things that hurt too much to think about, it helps to have something to hold on to.

And even though I can't understand the words it sings, I have a feeling I know the theme of its melody.

Hope.

CHAPTER 45

VANE

The Gales are declaring a victory, but it feels like a defeat.

The rescue workers are still pulling people from the rubble, and the entire valley is in a state of emergency.

Only seven guardians remained after Os eliminated the last Living Storm, and three had serious injuries. But it's enough to hold down the base while they call for reinforcements.

I told them I don't have time to wait.

Arella and Solana popped my elbow back into place—which sucked a whole lot more without Audra there to distract me.

But thinking about her hurts more. *Way* more.

Gus too.

I have no way of knowing if they're okay, but I have to believe Raiden won't do anything to them.

They don't have the power he wants.

All he can use them for is bait to try to trap me.

And I'm heading out tonight.

I wanted to go alone, but with my arm down for the count, that probably wouldn't be a good idea. So I'm bringing Solana and Arella.

Arella, because of her gift—and because every time I let her out of my sight, she manages to betray us.

And Solana to guide us to Raiden's city—and because I need *someone* I can trust.

Os wanted to come too, but someone needs to stay here and figure out what to do about all the destruction in the valley. The people in the desert deserve our help and protection. We can't make up for what they've lost, but we can make sure it never happens again.

It was the first real order I've given. The first time Os obeyed without question. First time it made sense to be called Your Highness.

It still felt *weird.*

But I think I'm ready.

I've bandaged my arm.

Texted my parents a quick update, followed by about fifty more texts answering all my mom's questions—she wonders why I never text her.

All I have left to do is change.

The uniform the Gales gave me has gathered dust for too many weeks. It's time to step into my role.

The pants aren't so bad—but the jacket is just as itchy as I thought it would be, and it hurt like hell slipping it over my arm.

And I'm *not* growing out my hair so it can be in some ugly braid.

But I'm a Gale.

A *guardian.*

And I'm getting Audra back.

ACKNOWLEDGMENTS

I wish I could thank every single person who's supported me as I've worked to bring this series into the world. But since I don't have the space for that, I want to start by thanking you—yes, *you*. The *reader*. If you've made it this far you've obviously read the story, and *that* is the greatest gift anyone could give me. I'm truly grateful that you've shared this piece of your time, and I hope you'll continue on for the rest of Vane and Audra's journey.

pauses for a group hug

My acknowledgments also wouldn't be complete if I didn't call out a few people who really go above and beyond to inspire me and guide me every day. I'm sure I'm probably forgetting some of you (and if I am, blame deadline brain!), but for now I'll say:

To Miles (a.k.a. The Most Patient Guy in the Universe), thank you for bearing with me through all the long drafting days (and even longer drafting nights), for pretending not to notice how many times I wore the same frumpy sweatpants, and for never complaining about being left alone with the cats. I truly have the best husband *ever*.

To my parents (a.k.a. The Dream Team), thank you for loving these books as much as I do, for the plethora of rides to and from the airport, and—most important—for understanding when I disappear down the drafting rabbit hole. I'm so glad you're always there when I resurface.

To Laura Rennert (a.k.a. Super Agent Extraordinaire), thank you for helping make this dream come true, and for guiding me through the many complicated realities that come with it. I am so grateful you're only an e-mail away. Thank you for always replying.

I also must thank Taryn Fagerness (a.k.a. Co-Conspirator in My Plan to Take Over the World) for bringing this series to so many amazing countries, Lara Perkins (a.k.a. The One Who Helped Me Discover Haboobs) for inspiring me in surprising and hilarious ways, and the rest of the Andrea Brown Literary team for being an awesome support group.

To Liesa Abrams Mignogna (a.k.a. the *real* Batgirl), thank you for the constant support, the lightning-fast reads, and for being Vane and Audra's number one advocate. I don't know how I would ever survive these deadlines without you. Thank you for making this job fun.

I also want to thank the amazing people at Simon & Schuster (a.k.a. Team Awesome) who work so hard to prepare and promote my books, especially Katherine Devendorf, Regina Flath, Bethany Buck, Mara Anastas, Paul Crichton, Siena Koncsol, Carolyn Swerdloff, Emma Sector, Julie Christopher, Mike Rosamilia, Michelle Fadlalla, Venessa Carson, Anthony Parisi, Ebony LaDelle, Matt Pantoliano, Michael Strother, Lucille Rettino, Mary Marotta, and the entire sales team. Massive thanks also go to Angela Goddard for designing my breathtakingly beautiful cover and to Brian Oldham for his gorgeous photography.

To Kari Olson (a.k.a. Number One Drafting Cheerleader), thank you for giving me the confidence to keep going and the guidance to keep me on course. I also greatly appreciate how very many inappropriate jokes you resisted making. I'm sure it wasn't easy for you. ;)

To Sara McClung and Sarah Wylie (a.k.a. The Sara[h]s), and to C.J. Redwine (a.k.a. Queen of Wisdom *and* Absurdity), thank you for being you. Life gets busy and sometimes months slip by, but somehow you're always there when I need you most. I will do my best to return the favor.

To Faith Hochhalter (a.k.a. The BookBabe—because there really is no better title), thank you for the apparently unlimited supply of knowledge, encouragement, and general brilliance. I'm grateful for every second of Faith-time I get.

To Heather Brewer (a.k.a. The Rock Star), thank you for coming through with a hilarious interview when I needed it, and for all the ways you prove your overall awesomeness. To Kiersten White (a.k.a. The Voice of Reason), thank you for always pointing out the many ways I make things so much harder than they should be—and for all the awesome lunches. To Debra Driza, Kasie West, and Amy Tintera (a.k.a. Two Blondes and an Introvert), thank you for going on an adventure with me in Texas, and for restoring my faith in events and promotion. To Lisa Mantchev (a.k.a. Agent Sister #1), thank you for regularly checking on me and always finding a way to make me smile. To the brilliant and inspiring ladies of Friday the Thirteeners (a.k.a. My Safe Place), thank you for being a constant sounding board and steady support group to lean on. To Lisa Cannon,

Kirsten Hubbard, Nikki Katz, Andrea Ortega, and Cindy Pon (a.k.a. Brunch Buddies!), thank you for the fun times and the unfailing encouragement. And to Katie Bartow (a.k.a. Goddess of Blogging), thank you for the countless ways you've given your time, energy, and platform to champion my books.

I also want to give a special thank-you to all the amazing booksellers, teachers, and librarians (a.k.a. The Best People Anyone Will Ever Meet) who've helped me get my books in the hands of readers. The longer I'm around this business, the more I realize just how much your support and enthusiasm truly means. You are the heart and soul of this industry, and I am eternally grateful to have you on my side. And to all the bloggers, BookTubers, and any other people who go online and talk about books they love (a.k.a. The Cool People), thank you for helping me spread the word about this series.

And last, but definitely not least, I have to thank everyone who takes the time to follow or subscribe to any of the places I cause shenanigans on the Internet. Thank you for putting up with my randomness, for giving me an excuse to procrastinate, and for patiently wading through all my haboob jokes. Now you finally know what they mean!